Alex had the strange sensation that he could see—almost feel—two avenues open to him.

One, the easy one, where he walked away from this situation. These things were not unheard of in society, and usually the young lady—the victim—in question wasn't lucky enough to have a savior to hand. Had he not been here, Miss Bolton would now be affianced to Sir Peter, and that would effectively be that.

Unfortunately, Alex *had* been here, and it seemed that he was going to take the second avenue, which he was pretty sure would be hell. He had the strangest sensation that he was observing the scene from a distance and could see catastrophe unfurling and could do nothing to avert it.

"We will be married by the end of the week," Sir Peter said.

"No." Alex stepped forward, now holding his jacket. "The young lady is my fiancée. Unhand her immediately." For God's sake. He was speaking like an actor in a cheap melodrama. And, a lot more importantly, he'd just announced that Miss Bolton was his *fiancée*.

Author Note

I hope you enjoy reading *How the Duke Met His Match* as much as I enjoyed writing it!

We know that women in England had far fewer rights and career options in the Regency era than they do today, but that didn't mean that there weren't a lot of strong, independently minded women who did their best to live their lives the way they wanted to. I wanted to write about one of those women, someone who would do her best to maintain her independence no matter what life and the laws and customs of her time threw at her. And that was Emma!

She was of course more than a match for Alex, the duke—a still-grieving widower with a sometimes-cold exterior covering a heart of gold. But I think that she also met her match in him in that he was perfect for her: open-minded and caring enough to respect women more than a lot of men at that time did, and also of course very good company and devastatingly attractive...

I also enjoyed setting the story mainly in England's beautiful Somerset, a southern county with rolling countryside and many picturesque villages.

Thank you so much for reading!

SOPHIA WILLIAMS

How the Duke
Met His Match

HARLEQUIN
HISTORICAL

HARLEQUIN®
HISTORICAL™

Recycling programs
for this product may
not exist in your area.

ISBN-13: 978-1-335-59563-8

How the Duke Met His Match

Copyright © 2023 by Jo Lovett-Turner

For questions and comments about the quality of this book, please contact us at CustomerService@Harlequin.com.

Harlequin Enterprises ULC
22 Adelaide St. West, 41st Floor
Toronto, Ontario M5H 4E3, Canada
www.Harlequin.com

Printed in U.S.A.

Sophia Williams lives in London with her family. She has loved reading Regency romances for as long as she can remember and is delighted now to be writing them for Harlequin. When she isn't chasing her children around or writing (or pretending to write but actually googling for hero inspiration and pictures of gorgeous Regency dresses), she enjoys reading, tennis and wine.

Books by Sophia Williams

How the Duke Met His Match
is Sophia Williams's debut for
Harlequin Historical.

Look out for more books from Sophia Williams
coming soon.

Visit the Author Profile page
at Harlequin.com.

To George

Chapter One

London, 1817

Alexander, Duke of Harwell, froze for a second as Lady Cowbridge, smiling broadly, ushered her daughter towards him. She couldn't have indicated her intent more clearly had she produced a bishop and had their wedding banns read.

This had to be about the tenth such approach made to him in the past hour. Enough was enough. Alex unfroze, inclined his head very slightly in the direction of the two ladies, and turned to march himself straight out of the ballroom's nearest doors.

Before he'd managed to cover the ten feet or so to the end of the room, yet another dowager placed herself in his path. This one was resplendent in a jade-green dress and was holding a bejewelled hand outstretched towards him. She gave the lavender-clad young lady she was accompanying a little push with her other hand, so that she stumbled almost right into Alex.

As he executed a swift sidestep to avoid a collision, Alex caught a glimpse of the younger lady's expression.

Her eyes were downcast, long dark lashes against her cheeks, and her brow was furrowed in a slight frown. By contrast, the older woman was looking straight at him with her wide smile increasing, as though she was about to address him.

Alex muttered, 'Excuse me,' and almost leaped out of the long, glass-panelled doors ahead of him into the garden.

He should have resisted his friends' entreaties to attend this ball. He didn't remember the season being quite as awful as this, though. Had the mothers and guardians of marriageable young ladies been as determined in their pursuit of him—like vultures circling their prey—the last time he was single? He didn't think so. But perhaps the full decade that had passed since then had dulled his memory. Or perhaps his elevation from viscount to duke had increased their determination.

Safely through the French doors, he was hit first by intense heat from the remarkable profusion of lanterns clustered around the door-frame, and then, as he moved a little to his left along a terrace that seemed to run all the way beside the house, by the freshness of the clear February night. And, God, that was good.

He closed his eyes and leaned his head back against the wall of the house, allowing himself a long moment to appreciate the peace, the coolness of the air on his cheeks after the claustrophobic warmth of the ballroom and the faint scent of the autumn leaves from the trees in the mansion's small garden, infinitely more agreeable than the cloying perfume inside.

Amazing to think that he'd actually loved London life ten years ago.

Right now, all he wanted to do was to go home to

Somerset. In fact, maybe he'd bring forward his return to the country. He missed his land, the open space, the opportunity for long walks and hard riding. And his local friends and tenants. And, of course, he missed the boys, his sons. It didn't feel right to be away from them for any extended period since they'd lost their mother. Yes, maybe he'd return home tomorrow. Ask his man of business and his lawyers to attend him there.

His thoughts were interrupted within a couple of minutes by a couple crashing out through the doors and coming to a halt only a few feet from him. Instinctively, he moved further along the terrace into the shadows. He had no desire to stand right next to a lovemaking couple, and he wasn't ready to re-enter the ballroom. So shadows it was.

He hadn't moved far enough. The couple's voices carried very clearly to him across the still night.

'Let go of me,' the woman hissed.

Not a lovemaking couple, apparently.

Alex turned reluctantly to look at them, illuminated by the lanterns, as the woman seemed to struggle in her partner's hold. The man pulled her close to him with one arm and with his other hand gripped her face far more tightly than a lover would. The woman continued to struggle, and then suddenly went quite limp.

Alex took a couple of steps closer. He had no desire to get involved in any lovers' tiff, but what he'd seen so far indicated that this was something more sinister than that. He should check that the woman was all right. If he was sure then that all was well, he would apologise for interrupting them and leave them to it.

He opened his mouth to speak just as the woman, as suddenly as she'd gone limp, dipped her head and bit the man's arm, and simultaneously seemed to kick him on the shin from beneath her dress. The dress was a pale lavender, like the one that the green-clad lady's younger companion had been wearing. Perhaps the same woman.

The man jerked and let go of her, spitting the words, 'You vixen,' as she picked up her skirts and began to run towards the ballroom.

Alex was contemplating landing a punch to the man's face, to teach him a lesson in addition to the kick and the bite, when the man lunged forward and caught the young woman around the waist, pulling her back against him.

'You'll pay for that,' he growled as she tried to resist his pull, her arms flailing.

Alex sighed internally—he'd so much rather just go home and go to bed than get involved with this, but clearly he had no choice—and stepped forward.

'It appears that the lady doesn't wish to be mauled by you,' he said.

'Mind your own business.' The man's voice was slightly familiar, maybe someone Alex had known in town in his younger days.

Alex shook his head. 'Let go of her now,' he said, injecting as much steel into his voice as he could.

He could see the man properly now in the flickering light. Sir Peter Something. Always with a group of men scrabbling at the edge of polite society. He could see the woman's heart-shaped face too. She had clear, light brown skin and deep brown eyes, which were glistening right now. Definitely the young lady who'd been with the woman in green just inside the ballroom.

Sir Peter looked up at him and shrank away, as though scared, but pulled the lady with him. She did something with her leg and Sir Peter gave an unattractively high-pitched little howl and then shook her a little.

'Enough.' Alex took a step towards them and clamped his hand round Sir Peter's—puny—forearm, until he let go of the lady with another little mewl of pain. Truly pathetic. Alex moved between the two of them and held his arm out to the lady.

She looked at Sir Peter, and then at Alex, and then took the proffered arm. 'Thank you, sir.' Her voice was remarkably steady, given the situation.

They began to move together towards the steps, away from Sir Peter, the young lady gripping Alex's arm very tightly. Thank God he had been here. She'd done a good job of fighting Sir Peter off, but she'd have been no match for him in the end.

Alex was going to take her inside, return her to her chaperone, make sure that she was safe with her, and then leave.

'Do you—?' he began.

He was interrupted by a sudden commotion at the ballroom door above them and a man shouting, 'Miss Bolton, Sir Peter.'

As Alex looked towards the door Sir Peter launched himself at the lady—presumably Miss Bolton—and attempted to kiss her. Miss Bolton got one arm free and dealt him a forceful blow to the ear, which made Alex smile and Sir Peter howl yet again.

'You will not treat me so when we're married,' Sir Peter panted.

Really? Alex shook his head. Everyone was aware that rogues attempted to compromise young women into marriage fairly often, but Alex hadn't personally witnessed such an attempt before. The commotion at the door was increasing now, and the man who'd just spoken was shouting inside the room about what he'd just seen. Presumably a co-conspirator.

Alex felt his lip curl. He held his hand up and addressed the gathering crowd. 'I have been here the entire time and this man has in no way compromised this lady. Nothing untoward has happened between them.'

'Incorrect,' Sir Peter shouted, apparently a lot braver with a crowd supporting him. 'This young lady has given me her virtue. She is my fiancée.'

The woman in green who'd been with Miss Bolton inside the ballroom pushed her way through the throng and planted herself in front of them. 'Emma, is this true?'

'No, Aunt, of course not.' Miss Bolton's voice was shaking a little now.

'Look at her gown.' Sir Peter's voice was triumphant.

Alex's eyes followed where the man's spindly finger was pointing. The bodice of Miss Bolton's gown was torn, exposing most of her full breasts. It must have been ripped during their tussle. Miss Bolton looked down too, and pulled ineffectually at the fabric, while Alex began to work his arms out of his tightly fitting jacket.

'Miss Bolton and I will be married tomorrow,' Sir Peter announced. 'I have a special licence.'

'Emma, how could you?' her aunt moaned.

'I couldn't and I won't,' Miss Bolton stated.

'Yes, you will.' Her aunt spoke out of the corner of her mouth, as though that would prevent anyone from hearing her. 'You are ruined.' She indicated with her arm towards the crowd at the doors.

'No.' Miss Bolton visibly shuddered.

'Yes.' Sir Peter put his arm around her waist.

She tried to move away and he gripped her more tightly, pulling her further from Alex.

Oh, God. Alex had the strange sensation that he could see, almost feel, two avenues open to him. One, the easy one, where he walked away from this situation. These things were not unheard of in Society, and usually the young lady—the victim—in question wasn't lucky enough to have a saviour to hand. Had he not been here, Miss Bolton would now be affianced to Sir Peter and that would effectively be that.

Unfortunately, Alex *had* been here, and it seemed that he was going to take a second avenue, which he was pretty sure would be hell. It was as though he was observing the scene from a distance and could see catastrophe unfurling but could do nothing to avert it.

'We will be married by the end of the week,' Sir Peter said.

'No.' Alex stepped forward, holding his jacket. 'The young lady is *my* fiancée. Unhand her immediately.'

For God's sake. He was speaking like an actor in a cheap melodrama. And, a lot more importantly, he'd just announced that Miss Bolton was his *fiancée*.

Sir Peter didn't let go of Miss Bolton. Alex took another step closer and glared at him, and the man's grip on her slackened. Alex moved right next to them, clenching his fists, and Sir Peter shrank backwards. Nothing more pathetic than a cowardly bully.

Alex moved in front of Sir Peter and placed his jacket around Miss Bolton's shoulders, his hand brushing the bare skin of her upper arm briefly as he held the jacket so that she could put her arms into the sleeves. He fancied that he felt her shiver as he touched her, and thought he understood why; it felt oddly...what, intimate perhaps? When it absolutely shouldn't.

He shook his head slightly. His mind was going in all manner of strange directions.

She looked up at him, her eyes huge in her small face, and whispered, 'Thank you.'

'My pleasure.'

Which was about as far from the truth as you could get. He was struggling to process what had just happened, but he did know that it was bad, very bad. He'd just announced that they were *engaged*. He had just committed himself very publicly to *marrying* this lady. Marriage. He didn't want to remarry. For his sons' sake, for his own sake, for Diana's memory's sake. But he clearly wasn't likely to have any choice now. He couldn't honourably let Miss Bolton down.

God. He wanted to put his head in his hands and swear and swear.

He couldn't do that, of course. It would be rude to Miss Bolton; and many dozens of people were watching them, chattering about them. He wanted to shout about the hypocrisy of the *ton*: the way in which they regarded themselves as above ordinary people and yet fed almost feverishly on others' misery, mob-like.

The hum of the crowd's chatter began to increase, the air practically throbbing with it now. He and Miss Bolton both needed to leave.

He cleared his throat and held an arm out to her.

She stared at his arm for a long moment, and then took it with another whispered 'Thank you.'

He could feel her almost trembling, and reached his other hand over to press hers briefly for comfort. And strangely, for a moment, it felt as though the two of them were banded together against the rest of the world. Which was ridiculously fanciful and entirely untrue. They were complete strangers to each other, and, while it seemed unbelievable that they might indeed soon be banded together in name, they wouldn't be in practice. He would not be having any kind of real marriage with Miss Bolton—Emma—or any other woman. He just couldn't.

He closed his eyes briefly and then began to move towards the house.

And then the woman in green, Emma's aunt, trilled, 'Your Grace,' and sank into a deep curtsey before them.

It cost Alex a big effort not to roll his eyes above her head or snap at her. Now did not feel like the time for social niceties.

As Emma's aunt rose from her curtsey, a thought struck him and he looked down at Emma again, suspicious. Had this entire scene been enacted by her and her aunt to entrap him? Were they in cahoots with Sir Peter? He went very still for a moment, replaying the events of the last few minutes in his mind. No, highly unlikely.

He felt Emma shudder slightly again. No. Unless she was an outstanding actress, this absolutely couldn't be a scene of her making.

'Allow me to escort you home now?' he said to her.

'Thank you. I think that would be for the best. I must apologise. I am not normally so pathetic. I will recover my spirits directly. I must apologise also for your having been dragged into this situation.'

'Not at all,' Alex said with great insincerity.

God, he wished he'd left the house by the front doors after speaking to Lady Cowbridge. Or even just danced with Lady Cowbridge's daughter. Although, looking down at Emma's slim shoulders, dwarfed by his jacket, and her elegant neck beneath her dark brown, nearly black curls, he hated to imagine what might be happening to her at this moment if he hadn't been here. Nearly as much as he hated to imagine what was about to happen to both of them.

Barely credible, but he really had just announced to half the *ton* that they were betrothed. As in he really was going to have to marry her, because her aunt was right: she would be completely ruined if they didn't marry.

He shook his head for about the tenth time this evening. After his wife's death in childbirth he'd decided never to remarry. Even just the idea of allowing himself to love again and therefore lay himself open to the possibility of further loss was too painful to bear. And yet here he was.

Although, of course, this wouldn't be a love match. It would be one person helping out another, a marriage in name only. So he wouldn't, in fact, be betraying Diana's memory. He'd have to explain as soon as possible to Emma that this would not be a real marriage. He hoped very much that she wouldn't be too upset by that. If she was, it couldn't be helped, unfortunately.

Oh, God. What if she wanted children?

Why the *hell* had this had to happen?

He nearly groaned out loud, and then realised that Emma was speaking again.

'I wonder if I could possibly impose on you for a further few minutes of your time?'

It was an odd question to ask when they were about to be tethered for a lifetime, in name at least.

He was prevented from replying by Emma's aunt, wreathed in smiles, grasping their hands.

'Your Grace, Emma, I must congratulate you. Such wonderful news.' She half turned and waved to the hordes jostling behind her, almost as though she was seeking witnesses, just as Sir Peter had; and her rather odd turban—green, like her dress—slid to one side of her head.

She pushed the turban back into place, turned again to Alex and Emma, and said, 'I was well acquainted with your mother. I am Lady Morton.'

'How do you do?' Alex said, not bothering to try to smile.

Lady Morton really wasn't going to care whether or not he was happy; her ecstasy would do for all of them. He thought for a moment of his first betrothal—his and Diana's happiness, the sheer bubbling joy that had kept him permanently smiling and laughing for weeks afterwards—and wondered briefly if his head might explode.

Lady Morton began to talk volubly about weddings.

Alex just wanted to leave, get away from this nightmare.

Lady Morton's conversation turned to the miracle it was that her darling Emma had melted the heart of the Ice Duke. Really? The Ice Duke? That was what people called him? For God's sake.

He sensed Emma stiffen beside him and felt instant remorse. This situation was, of course, much worse for her than for him.

Her whole body seemed to heave and he looked at the top of her head more closely. Was she crying? He should get her out of here immediately, give them both a chance to begin to come to terms with what had happened.

'I'd like to escort my fiancée home now,' he told her

aunt, impressed that he'd managed not to choke on the word *fiancée*.

He'd walked the short distance here from his house, so he hoped Emma and her aunt had come in a carriage; it would be much better if they didn't have to walk back now. He should agree on a time to call on Emma tomorrow, so that he could explain that he could be married in name only.

'Of course.' The turban slipped again. 'Do you have a carriage? If not, please take ours. Dear Lady Cowbridge will take me home, I'm sure.'

Lady Cowbridge, who had beaten her way to the front of the scandal-drawn crowd swirling around them, looked as though she'd sucked a lemon. She gave one of the most insincere smiles Alex had ever seen and nodded her acquiescence.

Despite everything, Alex almost laughed out loud. From the looks of her, it would be some time before Lady Cowbridge would be forgiving Lady Morton for her ducal wedding triumph.

Emma squeezed the underside of his forearm surprisingly hard, and he looked down at her again. She must be desperate to leave.

'Good evening.' He nodded around the crowd and then began to walk forward with Emma through the hundreds of ball-goers, all of whom seemed to be attempting to get a close look at the two of them. They were obviously going to be the subject of much gossip for the next few days or weeks. Since there was going to be no way of avoiding the wedding, they should get it out of the way as soon as possible and escape to the country for a long time.

Being taller than most people, he had a very good

view of the fashionables swirling around them. Literally hundreds of people pushing. He caught a couple of snatches of waspish comments and felt Emma's shoulders tense. Glaring at anyone who dared to look directly at him, he tightened his hold on her and they picked up speed across the long room. Eventually, they reached a series of footmen and a butler in the large, marbled entrance hall.

The butler opened the front door to them as their hostess, Mrs Chardaine, pushed her way towards them and dropped into a deep curtsey, tittering as she did so.

'I shall be proud forever that you announced your love affair to the world at my house,' she said, fluttering her eyelashes at him. 'Such a great pleasure.'

'The pleasure is all ours.' Alex didn't smile.

'Thank you so much for a most delightful evening,' Emma said, not looking as if she was smiling very much either.

They finally made it out of the house, down the steps and into Lady Morton's carriage about five minutes later.

Emma sank onto the upholstered bench to the right of the carriage door and Alex seated himself opposite her. This was the first time he'd been able to take a good look at her. She was beautiful, but in a very different way from the current fashion for pale skin and blonde hair. Her skin was the warm light brown he'd noticed before, and her eyes and hair were very dark. She was perhaps a little older than he'd assumed she was, definitely in her twenties rather than in her late teens as most debutantes were. Maybe slightly older than he had been when he'd met and married Diana.

She started speaking almost before the footman had

finished closing the door behind them and Alex had sat down.

'Thank you so much for rescuing me. Obviously I won't hold you to your promise.' She was holding her shoulders square inside his jacket, which swamped her slender frame, and looking him straight in the eye, as though she meant what she said. 'I'll tell my aunt in the morning that it was all a ridiculous mistake.'

Alex felt his own shoulders actually physically relax for a moment at the relief of it, until a voice of reason from somewhere deep inside him shouted that telling everyone it was a mistake wasn't an option.

'You can't possibly do that,' he said. 'You'll be ruined.'

'No.' Her dark curls swung round her face as she shook her head with force. 'To speak distastefully frankly about money, I'm an heiress with a significant fortune. There will be men who are prepared to overlook what happened this evening. There is no need for you to marry me.'

'Yes, there is. You will be ruined otherwise,' he repeated.

'No, I won't. There are any number of impecunious aristocratic men who would be delighted to marry my dowry.' She cocked her head to one side and narrowed her eyes slightly. 'From the little I've seen of you, I would say that you have need of neither a wife nor a fortune?'

He looked at her for a long moment. He felt as though he should actually pretend that he did need one or the other or both.

He wasn't going to pretend.

'Correct,' he said.

'Then I cannot allow you to make this ridiculous sacrifice on my behalf.'

Alex raised his eyebrows. It was unusual for a young

lady to state that she would or would not allow a gentleman to behave in a certain way. Although nothing about this situation was usual.

'It isn't a sacrifice,' he said, the words sounding hollow. 'It would be my very great pleasure.' Oh, God, no. He didn't want to sound as though he wanted their marriage to be anything other than in name. 'That is, I...'

Emma snorted. In a small, very ladylike way, but it was definitely still a snort. 'Absolutely everything about your demeanour tells me that it would be a huge sacrifice and certainly not a pleasure. Clearly neither of us loves the other. I agree that some men, particularly those who have no need to marry for money, might be deterred by the events of this evening from wooing me, but I'm very sure that men like Sir Peter will still be happy to marry me.'

'Exactly. Sir Peter. A middle-aged roué, who would almost certainly treat you badly.' Alex thought for a moment with disgust of when Sir Peter had held Emma in his arms.

Emma opened her mouth and then closed it again, and then visibly drew a breath and said, 'Obviously, Sir Peter would not be my ideal husband. Indeed, I would rather work for my living than marry him, and will do so if necessary. However, I have it on great authority, that of my own aunt amongst others, that I "smell of the shop"—delightful phrase—and that that will already have deterred a number of suitors, but nonetheless my fortune has continued to attract a great deal of attention.'

'I'm sure that the attention is due to your beauty and your conversation,' Alex said with reflexive politeness.

Emma snorted again. 'Much like all the attention you received this evening was entirely due to your broad shoulders and wit rather than to the fact that you are a very rich widowed duke.'

Alex found himself giving a snort of his own—of laughter. 'Fair enough,' he said. 'Yes, I'm sure that you have received a lot of attention, for both good and bad reasons, but I'm not sure that any man with whom you might be able to live happily will now offer for you. You might not, in fact, have the opportunity to meet any more respectable and eligible men because if you don't marry me all fashionable doors might be closed to you. I think that you perhaps underestimate the snobbery of the *ton* and their delighted horror of scandal.'

'I think that you perhaps underestimate my father's fortune.'

Alex shook his head. 'I cannot see that you have any alternative but to marry me.'

'I'm grateful for your concern—indeed I'm very grateful to you for having rescued me from Sir Peter— but I do not feel that my future is any concern of yours.' She picked up her reticule as the coach slowed. 'Thank you again. If I might impose on you just a little longer, I'd be very grateful if I could keep your jacket until I reach my bedchamber. I will ask one of my aunt's footmen to return it to you tomorrow.' She bestowed a brittle little smile on him and moved forward as the carriage door began to open.

Alex frowned. Something was niggling in the back of his mind, something in addition to the big issue, which was that she was clearly doing the wrong thing.

He leaned forward himself and spoke to the coachman. 'My fiancée and I have not yet finished our conversation. Please drive on for another few minutes.'

'Actually, we *have* finished our conversation.' Emma's eyes were flashing as the coach drove off again. 'I would like to go inside now.'

She thumped on the silk-upholstered wall of the carriage with her fist.

'I'm sorry.' Alex banged on the wall with his cane and the coach came to a halt. 'That was very rude of me. I shouldn't have overridden your wishes like that. Could I ask one further question before you go inside?'

He'd worked out what had been niggling him.

Emma pressed her lips together for a moment, as though she was trying not to sigh, and then after a pause said, 'Yes, of course.'

'What did you mean when you said that you'd rather work for your living than marry me, and might do so?'

Chapter Two

Emma wanted to glare at the duke, get out of the carriage, go inside her aunt's house and up to her bedchamber, crawl under her covers to digest the fact that her prospects had changed so dramatically in such a short space of time, and then come up with a plan. But she owed the duke a huge debt. She was still shuddering every time she recalled that without his intervention she might now be betrothed to Sir Peter and she was truly grateful to him.

She widened her lips into the best approximation of a smile she could manage, and said, 'I meant that I don't *need* to marry because I am very well able to work instead.'

The duke's eyes were narrowed. 'But why should you need to work? What of your great fortune?'

Emma *really* didn't want to talk about this. But, again, she owed the duke a lot, so the very least she could do was be polite.

'My father left me his fortune as dowry on condition that I marry a man from an aristocratic family within two years of his death. If I don't, I inherit nothing. Ironically, I don't even know whether Sir Peter's birth would be acceptable under the terms of the will.'

The duke raised his eyebrows but said nothing.

For some reason, it suddenly mattered to her what he thought of her father.

'It sounds worse than it is,' she told him. 'I'm sure my father truly only wanted the best for me. It's often difficult to know what the best for someone is.'

That was what she'd told herself, anyway, when she'd been *incandescent* with fury when their family lawyer had explained the terms of her father's will to her.

'He was a textiles manufacturer from Lancashire and my mother was the daughter of an earl, whose father cut her off when she met and married my father. Being excluded from her own family's social circle made my mother miserable. My father hired governesses for me and sent me to an exclusive seminary in Bath, because he wanted me to be able to take what he thought of as my rightful place in society. He didn't want me to be as miserable as my mother.'

No need to mention that her mother had been *so* miserable that she'd left Emma's father and gone to live in Paris.

'Except he was very comfortable living with me, so he didn't actually want me to leave until he died.' *So* annoying that her voice *still* wobbled when she talked about losing him. 'So I'm a lot longer in the tooth than the average debutante. In fact, I really shouldn't be called a debutante. Anyway, thanks to his obsession with educating me like a lady, I'm *extremely* well-educated—much better than most ladies, in fact—and so I flatter myself that I would make an *excellent* governess.'

The duke looked at her for a long moment, his eyes

grave. 'I'm sorry to hear about the loss of your father. And to hear about the situation in which you find yourself with regard to marriage.' He paused and then continued. 'But, being brutally frank, I'm not convinced that many families would happily engage a governess who had just been ruined in front of half the *ton*.'

'I would very happily be a governess to a family living in the country.'

He shook his head. 'News travels.'

Hmm. Maybe he was right. Emma swallowed hard. She was *not* going to cry. This wasn't the worst thing that could happen to anyone. She was only twenty-five, which was still quite young if you weren't a debutante. She was healthy; she was resourceful. She would manage.

'In that case, I will approach the headmistress of my old seminary.'

'I imagine that news travels just as quickly to seminaries and the parents of prospective pupils.'

Yes, he was right. She hadn't been thinking clearly. It must be the shock of the events of the evening.

'Fine. There are other options. I could be a housekeeper.'

'Really?'

Honestly. So sceptical. Of *course* she could be a housekeeper.

'Yes.'

'I haven't been involved in hiring a housekeeper myself, but I wonder whether you would be expected to have some experience.'

'I do have experience. I looked after my father and our house for several years.'

'I'm not sure that would be sufficient.'

Emma pressed her fingers to her temples for a moment. 'I'm sure I could find *something*.'

'And I am genuinely not sure you could. Not something palatable, anyway.' He sat back and looked at her for a long moment, his brow slightly furrowed, while Emma fought tears again.

Why had she become separated from her aunt for that moment, so that Sir Peter had been able to get hold of her arm and pull her towards the garden? Things had been going perfectly well before this evening. She'd received several depressing proposals from men whom she'd been sure would be difficult husbands, but at least three pleasant, impecunious younger sons of two earls and a viscount to whom she thought she might be able to be reasonably happily married had looked as though they were on the brink of proposing to her.

She'd had high hopes that at least one of them would be so grateful to get his hands on her fortune that he'd agree to her retaining some independence and travelling after their marriage. And if none of them had proposed, she'd been prepared to walk away from her father's fortune and this world, to which she didn't really belong anyway, and work as a governess and hope to save enough to be able to travel when she was older.

It was difficult to comprehend that both options seemed to have been removed from her grasp in one fell swoop.

The duke smiled at her, and Emma suddenly wondered what it would be like to lean, both physically and metaphorically, against his broad shoulders.

'I really believe that your best option now is to marry me,' he said.

The kindness in his green eyes was almost too much

to bear. For a moment, she wavered. Of course, of the options available to her right now, marrying him would be by far the best one, if only she could allow herself to treat another person so shabbily. She couldn't, though, because he clearly had no actual desire to marry her. It was one thing accepting the loan of his jacket and his offer of temporary escape from the predicament in which she had landed; it would be another accepting his offer to spend the rest of his life married to a complete stranger just because he'd been in the wrong place at the wrong time.

A thought struck her. His affections might well be already engaged. 'Are you…?' How to word it? 'Is there not someone with whom you are already acquainted that you would rather marry?'

'No.' He spoke the word so baldly that Emma gasped.

'No,' he repeated in a milder tone, and shook his head. 'No one else.'

She closed her eyes for a second and then said, 'I'm truly grateful to you for all your help this evening, but I cannot accept your very kind offer.'

Ridiculous that it felt more difficult to turn down the clearly extremely reluctant duke than it had to turn down the eleven sincere offers of marriage she'd already refused.

Her aunt had been beside herself about some of those refusals. She might actually expire with anger when she discovered that Emma had refused the duke, and was very likely to refuse to have her to reside with her any longer. She really hoped that her aunt wouldn't ask her to leave immediately. She would need some time to organise employment, and it would be a lot more enjoyable doing that while living in a mansion in Berkeley

Square than in whatever cheap lodgings she would be able to find herself.

Things were going to be dreadful for a while. She'd better end the conversation immediately, or she might actually finish by accepting the duke's offer.

'Thank you. I should now bid you goodnight,' she said.

The duke made no move to open the door. Well, she would open it for herself.

She untwisted her fingers—she now realised she'd been clutching her reticule ridiculously tightly—and reached out for the door handle. It was utterly ludicrous that she actually felt a momentary twinge of sadness at the thought that she would never see the duke again. Maybe it was because he was one of the few people she'd met in London who'd been genuinely kind to her, with no apparent ulterior motive.

As she began to turn the handle, the rumble of his deep voice cut through her thoughts.

'I have a proposal for you. You're right that I have no desire to get married. But I do need a governess for my three young sons. We lost their mother four years ago.' He paused for a moment, as though collecting himself, and then continued, 'Marry me, in name only, and act as governess to my boys. I will settle your entire dowry on you. I think this is a bargain we could both benefit from. You won't be forced to marry a man who might treat you badly, and you'd be financially independent, while I will no longer have to fight off matchmaking ladies who'd like their daughter to be a duchess, and, more importantly, I'll have found a governess for my sons. I've interviewed an extraordinarily large number of unsuitable candidates and was beginning to despair.

Had I had the good fortune to interview you, I would have offered you the job.'

'Really?' Emma hesitated, and then released the door handle and perched back on her seat. 'In that case, could I not just be your governess?'

The duke shook his head. 'I had already thought of that. There would obviously be gossip if the woman who had been announced as my fiancée became my sons' unmarried governess. I do not wish there to be any gossip surrounding my household, for the boys' sake.'

Emma nodded slowly. He was probably right. Wasn't his offer madness, though? Surely he couldn't really be so desperate for a governess that he'd happily marry someone to whom he didn't wish to be married?

The duke cleared his throat and shifted his eyes away from hers before looking back. 'I should point out that in accepting this bargain you would be relinquishing the opportunity to achieve a love union or have children. I would not like any scandal to attach to us.'

Emma nearly gasped out loud again. He *really* didn't want to get married. Unless he just found her particularly unattractive, of course. What he was suggesting sounded like a remarkably unusual bargain. Unbelievable, in fact.

'I don't want a wife, but I really do want a governess,' he said, as though reading her mind.

He smiled at her, a slow, lopsided smile that got to her somewhere deep inside as it grew.

'And I think you'd be wonderful with my children. I have a beautiful dower house on my estate, which is in Somerset. You would be welcome to live in it if you'd prefer your own household.'

Emma shook her head. This was all too much to take in.

'I... Being honest, I really don't know,' she said.

Before her father's death, she hadn't really thought about marriage beyond an infatuation at the age of eighteen with one of the factory managers that had come to nothing after her father had heard of it. He had banned them from seeing each other, and the manager, to Emma's extreme disillusionment, had fallen in with her father's wishes, telling her that he had no option because he couldn't support a wife if he had no employment.

She'd then assumed that, as the possessor of a significant fortune, she would, unlike the vast majority of women, be able to live however she liked after the far distant event of her father's death. By then she'd reflected on how her parents' incompatibility had destroyed their relationship, despite or even because of their mutual love, and had come to the conclusion that the only reason for her to marry would be to have children. And that if she did decide she wanted to marry, it would be to someone whom she liked and with whom she felt she could live happily, rather than to someone with whom she was deeply in love, because, from what she'd seen, passionate love could easily turn to hatred.

Her decision had been made for her by the terms of her father's will, of course. Once she'd recovered from her fury, she'd decided that she would make the best of it; she would hope to find someone pleasant with whom she could rub along quite happily, and hopefully they would have children. Indeed, the majority of her fury had been because it was just so *rude* and overbearing of her father to have dictated to her in such a way.

She suspected that she'd already come to the conclusion before his death that she wanted to have children and therefore wanted to marry. And now, she realised, she really did very much want to have children of her own. Could she give up that opportunity? Or had it already been taken from her because the only proposals of marriage she might receive beyond this cold-blooded, marriage-in-name-only one from the duke would be from men like Sir Peter, and she couldn't bear to marry someone like that?

She'd have the duke's children to care for, of course. Although only as their governess, and if their marriage ended in separation she might not continue to see much of them.

'Perhaps I could call on you tomorrow and you could let me know then, if that will allow you sufficient time to come to a decision?' he suggested after a couple of moments.

'Yes, please.' She really did need some thinking time.

'Excellent.' And there was that smile again.

As he moved in front of her to open the door and descend the carriage steps, her eyes were drawn to the bunched muscles across his shoulders, clearly visible through his shirt.

It was unusual for an aristocrat to have such a developed physique. Perhaps he boxed. His arms looked very strong too. Very...solid.

'Miss Bolton?'

Oh. He was waiting to hand her down.

She clutched the jacket tightly as she stood up, to avoid giving him another view of her chest, and moved to tread down the steps. And, goodness, it was difficult balancing when your hands were full of jacket. Her foot missed the second step and she began to sail through the air, one hand still holding the jacket and the other scrabbling against the side of the carriage to save herself.

Within a very short space of time the duke had her,

his firm and also very muscly forearm barely moving as he supported almost her full weight, before righting her with ease and helping her down the remainder of the steps.

She took a final step onto the ground and said, 'I must thank you again.'

She was annoyed to hear a tremor in her voice. It must be all to do with shock and nothing to do with how embarrassingly aware she suddenly felt of the strength in his arm, of how the fabric of his shirt stretched deliciously across his chest, just in line with her eyes.

'Not at all,' he said.

'Mmm.' She looked up at him and saw him swallow. Which made her swallow too. He had a very firm neck, and his hair was just longer than was strictly fashionable, curling a little over his collar. And…she was staring. She was staring at him. He'd saved her from Sir Peter, he'd saved her from falling out of the carriage, and she was staring. And his forearm really was very strong. And she *really* had to stop staring.

And, goodness, she was still holding his arm.

She let go very suddenly, as though it were very hot.

'So, thank you. And goodnight.' Her fake breezy tone sounded utterly ridiculous. 'So, I'll go inside now. Thank you.'

Good heavens, what was happening to her? This was insane.

She took a deep breath and, still clutching the jacket across her chest, moved towards her aunt's house.

'Of course.' The duke moved with her. And now she had nothing to say to him. Nothing. She could comment on how beautiful the still night was. But it wasn't really, nights were usually much more beautiful in the countryside, and also it just felt too mundane and inane a topic following the magnitude of the conversation they'd had inside the carriage. Maybe she could comment on how wonderful the ball had been. No. It hadn't been wonderful; it had been awful.

She glanced up at the duke's face. He was staring straight ahead at the house, his profile stern, apparently not at all tempted to speak either.

They trod side by side across the pavement and up the wide steps to the imposing front door of her aunt's house in continued silence, and it was one of the most excruciating short walks of Emma's life.

When her aunt's butler, Finch, punctuated the awkward silence by opening the door wide for her and bowing her inside, she could have kissed him.

'Thank you so much, Finch,' she said, almost jumping over the threshold in her relief.

Then she stopped and turned round. Obviously, she ought to bid the duke a formal goodnight.

She held her hand out to him. 'Good evening, Your Grace.'

The duke remained motionless for a moment, and then took her hand in his much larger one. And, of course, his hand was firm and strong, like the rest of him. And, *really*, she was almost blushing now. For no good reason whatsoever.

'Good evening.' He inclined his head over her hand, and, finally more in control of herself, she wiggled her fingers. He let her hand go and turned and went back down the steps. And insanely—truly *insanely*—she felt almost bereft, as though she was suddenly adrift in a boat on a choppy lake, with her only oar gone.

She shook her head. Her thoughts were utterly nonsensical. She did feel, however, as though she could do worse than putting herself under the duke's protection. As long as he would truly allow her a high degree of independence.

Three minutes later, she'd exchanged a couple of words with Finch before whisking herself upstairs and into her bedchamber. She was desperate to get rid of Jenny, her maid, so that she could plonk herself down on her bed and just sob for a few minutes at the enormity of everything that had happened this evening. And then she would have to begin to work out whether she should—could—accept the duke's offer.

'You're wearing a gentleman's jacket, miss.' Jenny, who had been with her since they were both very young, more of a companion and close friend than a maid, sounded both scandalised and delighted, clearly expecting a comfortable gossip about the ball.

'My dress tore, and, um, one of the gentlemen there was kind enough to give me his jacket.'

'Indeed!' Jenny raised her eyebrows and waited.

Emma said nothing.

'Did you have a lovely evening, miss?' Jenny picked up Emma's hairbrush.

'I did, thank you.' Emma swallowed a big lump in her throat. 'But I have the headache now. Thank you so much for your help, but I think I'll prepare myself for bed this evening.'

'Lady Morton won't be pleased if you do that.' Jenny wasn't budging. 'She'll think it doesn't befit your station. She already thinks it doesn't befit your station to have *me* to help you.'

'Well, luckily Lady Morton isn't here to witness my

appallingly unladylike wish to nurse my headache alone. So we don't need to worry about her. Thank you again.' Emma held her hand out for the brush.

Jenny looked at her for a while and then gave it to her. 'Call me if you need anything. Shall I take the jacket?'

'Thank you, lovely Jenny, but I'll keep the jacket here until I'm in my nightclothes.'

Emma pulled it a little more tightly round herself. She really didn't want Jenny to see her dress torn as it was. And, to her shame, she *liked* the feel of the jacket about her shoulders and body. It felt...maybe comforting? And it smelled deliciously masculine.

Emma suddenly realised that Jenny would hear all about her engagement from the other servants and be hurt that her mistress, her *friend*, hadn't told her herself.

'I had a very stressful evening. I promise I'll tell you all about it tomorrow morning. Promise. But I just need to sleep now.'

Sleep. Ha. She was more likely to be awake all night, wondering what she should say to the duke tomorrow.

'Goodnight, then, miss. If you're sure.'

'I am. Thank you.'

Descending for breakfast had been a mistake, Emma thought six hours later, eating toast and fruit while her aunt talked at both high volume and high speed, with no apparent need for breath, about Emma's forthcoming wedding, wedding dress, wedding trousseau, wedding reception, wedding everything. And it seemed that she was very much looking forward to visiting 'my niece, the Duchess of Harwell'.

When Lady Morton began to talk, with an affected dab at her eye with a napkin, about how delightful it would be to be great-aunt to the duke and duchess's children, Emma felt genuine tears forming behind her own eyelids and decided that enough was enough.

She popped the rest of the apricot she'd been eating into her mouth and pushed her chair back. 'I might perhaps take a walk in the garden square,' she told her aunt.

'Make sure you take a parasol. The February sun can be surprisingly strong,' her aunt said. 'And do, of course, take Jenny or a footman. The future Duchess of Harwell must not be seen walking unaccompanied.'

Emma very much wanted to be alone with her thoughts. 'On reflection, I might instead retire to my chamber and write some letters.'

'As you wish, my dear. What time did you say the duke would be calling this morning?'

'Eleven o'clock.'

'Unfashionably early, but one must make allowances for a man deeply in love.'

Emma managed to smile, and to refrain from rolling her eyes, and left the room to return to her chamber.

Half an hour later, she was thoroughly sick of her circular thoughts.

The whole idea was preposterous. Although in many ways ideal.

She didn't want to marry for love and, if the duke was true to his word—which she sensed he would be—this arrangement would allow her as much independence as she could hope to gain so that she could travel. And being governess to the duke's boys would allow her many of the benefits of motherhood.

But was he just being chivalrous? He clearly didn't need or want a wife. Did he really need and want a governess? And would he really have chosen her for the post? Would she be taking advantage of his kind nature in accepting his offer?

Enough. She should go for a walk. Fresh air was a commodity sadly lacking in London upper-class life, and the stuffiness of the house was making her headache even worse.

If she took Jenny with her, she could take the opportunity to tell her that she was—for the moment—engaged. And if she went now, she'd have time to come back and spend half an hour adjusting her hair and her dress before receiving the duke.

An hour and a half later, Emma allowed Jenny to give a final twitch to the dress they'd decided she would wear to take the duke's call—a primrose-yellow sprig muslin that Jenny said showed Emma's lovely skin and dark curls off very well—and said, 'Thank you. I might just spend two or three minutes alone to compose myself.'

'Of course, miss.' Jenny blinked hard, sniffed loudly, and waved her hand in front of her eyes. 'I'm that pleased for you I'm going to cry.'

Jenny had charged headlong down the 'it's so exciting' path, and Emma just hadn't been able to find the words to say out loud that the duke only actually wanted her as a governess. She *had* told Jenny that she was sure that, should the marriage indeed take place, she and the duke would maintain quite independent lives, and that she hoped to travel to India in due course to visit her grandmother's birthplace, but that had just had the effect of increasing Jenny's enthusiasm rather than dampening it.

'We don't even know that the marriage will go ahead.' Emma didn't want Jenny or anyone else to get excited about something that might not happen. She'd realised that she herself *did* want it to go ahead, because of *course* it was her best alternative, but she just couldn't agree to the duke's proposition if he didn't seem sincere in wanting her as his governess.

'Of course it will, miss. Why wouldn't it? Oh, *miss*. You're going to be a *duchess*.'

Emma did her best to blink back her own tears and to smile through the immense headache that was now throbbing at her temples.

'Indeed,' she said.

Ten minutes later, Emma had regained her composure and was walking in her best seminary-learned stately and composed manner into her aunt's blue saloon.

And there was the duke, directly opposite the door, standing with his back to the marble fireplace, looking straight at her without even the hint of a smile on his very handsome face.

Emma checked over her shoulder and, yes, she really was the person at whom he was looking in such a forbidding manner. It was difficult to believe he was the same person who'd rescued her last night. Now she could understand why people called him the Ice Duke; it wasn't just because he appeared frozen to all the ladies who set their caps at him, it was because he was capable of looking like *this*.

Like a man who was very unhappy at the prospect of going through with the offer he'd made last night.

She was going to have to tell him that, on reflection, she didn't want to accept the offer. She couldn't ruin a stranger's life.

He shifted his position slightly and his broad shoulders seemed to expand even further, filling a good half of the gilded mirror above the mantelpiece. He really was very big. And almost raw in his stern masculinity. It seemed quite ridiculous that he was wearing such tailored clothing; it was like seeing a lion in a dress.

'Emma, my dear?'

Oh, her aunt had been speaking.

'I believe you have not heard a word I said. I will leave you and the duke alone for a few minutes. There can be no need for me to leave the door ajar, I believe, when I understand that you are to be married within the next few days.'

Few days! And the door not ajar! Was her aunt actively trying to ensure that they were even more compromised into marriage?

Well, yes, she probably was.

'Good morning.' The duke's voice was so deep. Emma rubbed her arms to try to dispel sudden goosebumps.

'Good morning.' She took a long breath, feeling suddenly distinctly light-headed and wobbly on her legs. And tearful. But she must *not* cry. It was entirely understandable and to be expected that the duke didn't want to go through with marriage to her, and she should accept it with good grace.

She gestured to the sofas behind her. 'Shall we sit down?' She walked towards the nearest sofa and arranged herself in the middle of it, so that the duke couldn't possibly imagine that she was inviting him to sit next to her.

'Thank you.' The duke sat himself stiffly down on a sofa at right angles to the one she was on.

He gave her a half-smile and cleared his throat.

Emma waited.

He didn't say anything.

And she couldn't find any words.

She should speak immediately. Release him from his obvious agony. It was the only honourable course of action open to her; she couldn't effectively force him to marry her. Maybe it would be better if she stood up again, to signal to him that he should leave.

She rose to her feet and said, 'Your Grace. I'm certain that you are regretting your very generous offer last night. I fully understand, and indeed have no wish to go through with the charade myself. I thank you again for your kindness and bid you goodbye.'

Chapter Three

She was all huge dark eyes and riotously curling hair and heaving chest. She was… She was beautiful.

And Alex did not wish to think about that. He'd come here this morning hating the fact that he'd found her attractive nearly as much as he hated the idea of marrying her. He'd been desperately hoping that she'd have decided overnight that she didn't want to go through with it. He'd been planning that, if she *did* repeat that she didn't want to marry him, he'd thank her and suggest that he settle a sum of money on her, to ensure her financial independence, and then walk away hugely relieved.

But now he was with her, and she was saying exactly what he'd wanted to hear, and he knew both that she wouldn't accept any financial settlement from him and that he couldn't stand by and watch the ruination of her life.

It beggared belief that she would genuinely choose near-certain poverty or marriage with someone like Sir Peter over the proposition he'd outlined last night. She was clearly just being stupidly kind in not wishing to hold him to a promise that she'd thought he hadn't wished to make. So he was going to have to persuade her that he genuinely wanted to marry her. Difficult, because he really didn't.

Ignoring convention, he remained seated.

'I do not regret my offer, and I don't regard it as generous,' he said slowly, searching for words that would convince her. 'I would very much like you to be governess to my children. Their names are Freddie, John and Harry, and they are nine, seven and four years old. They're lively, but never malicious. I should warn you that Freddie and John do like to play jokes involving planting large insects in the way of people they think will scream on sight of them, so you should make sure that you don't scream the first couple of times they do it and then they'll stop.'

He was rewarded with a small smile from Emma.

'Have you had other governesses?'

'Six. Or seven. I forget exactly. The boys got rid of all of them, about which I am now delighted, because I know you would be so much better than they were.'

She narrowed her eyes. 'Hmm. Why is that?'

'You fought Sir Peter. You didn't indulge in any kind of vapours. You're clearly very kind. You state your case clearly and succinctly.' Good Lord. If he carried on like this he'd be a fair way to convincing himself that he genuinely wanted her instructing his boys. 'I think you would be an excellent governess.'

He was fairly certain from the way she was half frowning that he'd given her food for thought.

'Also, it would be of great benefit to me to be married, so that matchmaking chaperones no longer hound me. I really would be deeply grateful if you would marry me.'

She looked at him and swallowed, but didn't speak.

'I feel as though I am fortunate that fate threw us together yesterday evening,' he said. 'Our marriage could be the perfect solution for both of us.'

He was pretty sure that it would be a reasonable solution to *her* problems, anyway, as long as she didn't mind too much not having children. He was also pretty sure that he was doing a good job of sounding sincere.

'Really?'

'Absolutely. Please marry me? According to what we agreed last night?'

'*Definitely* really?'

'Definitely really.' Alex dug deep inside himself and produced a smile.

'I...' She drew a deep breath and then said, 'Thank you, Your Grace. If you're certain that you will benefit from our arrangement, then I in my turn am deeply grateful to you and I accept your offer.'

Good. But also terrible.

Alex shoved away the many negative thoughts jostling for prominence in his mind and focused hard on the fact that he was doing the right thing.

'Thank you.' He stood up to join her; he felt as if he ought to, now that they'd come to an agreement.

'No, thank *you*.' She had her hands clasped together, fingers locked so hard that her knuckles were whitening. Alex stood a couple of feet away from her, wishing that he'd remained seated and very conscious of his own hands hanging loosely by his sides as he watched hers clasping even harder.

'So.' He cleared his throat yet again. 'Would you be happy for me to make all the arrangements for the wedding? And would you be happy to travel immediately afterwards to my estate in Somerset?'

Emma nodded. 'Yes.'

'That's wonderful.' He choked slightly on the word *wonderful*. 'Perhaps in a week from now?'

He was going to have to journey back to Somerset for a night or two, to explain to his sons that they'd be having a new governess and that she would be called the Duchess of Harwell. Thank God they were too young to understand about things like marriage and stepmothers.

'Perfect.' She smiled a tight little smile that didn't reach her eyes. The miserable smile pierced his own misery and on impulse he reached forward and took her clasped hands in his.

'We can make this work to both our advantages,' he said. 'We really can.'

'I hope so.' Her hands relaxed slightly, and she allowed him to hold them separately in his. Looking down at the top of her dark head, he felt a surge of sympathy for her.

'I'm so sorry this has happened to you,' he said.

She looked up at him, tilted her head slightly to one side, raised her eyebrows and said, 'Although to hear you speak it couldn't have worked out better for you, because you need me as a governess.'

Honestly. So cynical.

'I do need you as a governess.' He smiled blandly at her. He'd suddenly wanted to make that clear, because there was something about her dark liquid eyes, the way she was looking at him, that had him feeling things he hadn't felt for a long time. Physical things, though, not emotional. And, rationally, that didn't matter. Physical attraction he could deal with. What he couldn't deal with ever again, and wasn't going to, was falling in love with someone.

Images of Diana struggling and then fading after giving birth to Harry, her coffin at her funeral days later and his three motherless sons flashed into his mind. The loss of Diana… He never wanted to experience pain of that magnitude again.

The saloon door rattled and began to open and the darkness cleared from his head. Good Lord, he and Emma were still holding hands.

Emma snatched her hands from his, as though they'd been doing something they shouldn't, and took a couple of steps away from him, turning to face the door and smoothing her skirts with her hands as she did so.

'Your Grace, Emma.' Lady Morton swept into the room, beaming. 'Do forgive my interrupting you. I come bearing wonderful news. The Bishop of Locke is able to marry you on Wednesday.'

'But today is Saturday,' Emma said. 'That's only four days away.'

'Fortunately, Madame Gabillard is able to fit you in this afternoon, and will work tirelessly on Monday and Tuesday to prepare dresses for your honeymoon. I had thought of a wedding dress similar to Princess Charlotte's silver one last year, but we don't have time for that, so I think the cream gown with silver overlay—the one that you were planning to wear to the Castlereaghs' ball, dear. The wedding breakfast is easily arranged. My own household will be able to prepare it with only a little additional help, and we can host it either in our ballroom here or in the duke's. I've already spoken to Tubbs about flowers. We will send invitations directly. The Duke and Duchess of Harwell will be forgiven for inviting their guests at such short notice. The breakfast will be very well attended.'

Alex drew breath, not sure which of the woman's false assumptions to tackle first. 'That's very kind, but I am able to make my own wedding arrangements,' he told her. 'I have business to undertake before the wedding. We are planning to marry next week. And—'

'Your Grace.' Lady Morton sank into a deep curtsey. Too deep. She wobbled alarmingly and panted, 'Emma.'

Emma and Alex both hurried over to her and hauled her up with an arm each. Lady Morton righted herself, but didn't let go of their arms, so that the three of them were standing in an uncomfortably tight circle.

'Thank you. I do not wish there to be any scandal attached to my niece, Your Grace. As her guardian, I must request that you marry as soon as possible.'

'One week is hardly a long engagement, Aunt,' Emma said.

'I must insist.' Lady Morton's voice was suddenly steely, and so was her grip on their arms. Alex looked down. Red marks were actually appearing on Emma's skin.

'Your Grace? I presume that, like most young men who have just got engaged, you are eager to enter into marriage as soon as possible. Wednesday.'

'I… Yes, of course. However, I have important business to undertake first.'

'I'm sure that as your wife, Emma will not prevent you from undertaking any important business. Although I trust that it is not of a delicate nature.' She screwed up her face and waggled her eyebrows.

'Aunt!' gasped Emma.

'No,' Alex almost snapped. 'It is not of a delicate nature.'

Not the kind of 'delicate nature' Lady Morton was

obviously implying. He hoped that marriage to Emma wouldn't mean that he had to spend much time with her aunt. He looked at Emma, who was clearly trying not to laugh, and to his surprise found his own lips twitching a little.

Lady Morton was squaring her shoulders, blatantly prepared to fight for Wednesday. He supposed he could explain to his sons after the marriage that they had a new governess. And…stepmother. He felt his entire face tighten. The word 'stepmother' was all wrong. As though he was being disloyal to Diana.

'Wednesday?' Lady Morton still hadn't released her grip on their arms.

'I'd be delighted,' Alex said after a long pause.

'Wonderful.' Lady Morton let go of their arms and reached up to pat his cheek, while Emma, half laughing and half grimacing behind her, mouthed, *Are you sure?* at Alex.

He nodded at Emma and took a step backwards, away from the cheek patting.

'Thank you for making the arrangements with the bishop and the church. I will visit the bishop myself to finalise preparations. And thank you for the offer of planning a wedding breakfast. Emma and I have, however, decided to leave for Somerset immediately after the ceremony finishes, and will not therefore be holding a breakfast.'

He wasn't going to refer to her mention of a honeymoon.

'No.' Lady Morton shook her head decisively. 'There must be a breakfast. Many of my friends are extremely desirous of attending and wishing you well.'

'I'm so sorry, Aunt.' Emma looked as desperate as he

felt to avoid a breakfast. 'The duke and I have to leave immediately once our nuptials are completed. He has urgent business in Somerset.'

'Sounds like a complete faradiddle to me.' Lady Morton plumped down onto the sofa on which Emma had just been sitting. 'However, if I can't persuade you, I can't. We shall have the wedding breakfast without you. Should I have the bill sent directly to you?'

Good Lord. Outrageous. Alex couldn't help smiling again at her effrontery, though.

He glanced over at Emma, whose eyes were dancing.

'Absolutely,' he said. 'And now I must take my leave of you. I have much business to attend to before Wednesday.'

'Outmanoeuvred. I'm sorry,' Emma whispered as he bent his head to kiss her hand.

He smiled at her and bowed at her aunt.

As he left, he heard Lady Morton say, 'You need to marry him as soon as possible, Emma, so that he can't escape.'

'Aunt.'

Almost exactly four days later, Alex was standing at the front of St George's Church in Hanover Square with his younger brother, Max, and the Bishop of Locke, waiting for Emma and trying very hard not to remember that the last time he'd stood waiting in this exact spot in a church he'd been waiting for Diana.

'Nervous?' Max nudged him, grinning.

Alex summoned a smile from somewhere, and said, 'Ha, yes.'

He really wasn't enjoying deceiving Max, but he'd been so happy for him, and Alex had been so pressed for time, that in the end he'd just gone along with Max's pleasure that he'd finally met someone new. Max was bound to hear a fuller version of the gossip surrounding the betrothal soon, and then Alex would explain. When he'd come to terms with it himself.

Max nudged him again as the door at the back of the church opened and Emma entered on the arm of a thin, older man. Perhaps an uncle.

'She's beautiful,' Max said in Alex's ear.

Alex nodded. Objectively speaking, yes, she was. The simple pale blue dress that she was wearing set off her slim figure and dark beauty perfectly. Although hadn't her aunt mentioned silver? Maybe Emma had put her foot down. Her hair was done in ringlets, falling down her neck, and she had a hint of colour in her cheeks.

It wasn't her beauty that caused Alex's heart to clench, though, it was the fact that, in contrast to when he'd last seen her in her aunt's drawing room, trying not to laugh about her aunt's outrageous behaviour, now she could barely meet his eye.

And the fact that when you'd been through a *real* marriage once, one like this felt all wrong.

He turned to face the front, suddenly almost overcome with misery.

Max squeezed his arm and whispered, 'Diana would have wanted this, you know.'

No. She really wouldn't have wanted him to enter a loveless union.

'Thank you,' Alex croaked.

Damn Max for being at least partially intuitive, knowing he was thinking about his first marriage. And damn this whole hellish situation.

Emma took her place at his side and he painted a

smile on his face before looking down at her. She was staring straight ahead, almost unnaturally motionless. God, he was self-centred. This was no worse for him than it was for her. In fact, it might be a lot worse for her than it was for him. From what he'd seen of her, she didn't strike him as a woman who was particularly desperate to be a duchess, and that was essentially all he had to offer her.

'This won't take long,' he whispered.

'I know.' Her voice was a lot steadier than his. She still wasn't succeeding in meeting his eye, though.

The bishop hurried through the service at a remarkable pace. Alex couldn't work out whether he was just bored with repeating the same lines yet again, or whether Lady Morton had warned him that she thought there was a danger of the groom absconding.

And soon they were at the main part of the ceremony. The part from which there was no going back.

'With this ring, I thee wed.'

For the second time since he'd met Emma, Alex had the sensation that he was watching this experience from afar, as though it wasn't really him doing the actual getting married. Emma's hand was very cold, so cold that it was easy to slide the ring onto her finger, despite the fact that her hand was shaking somewhat.

They offered each other lips-pressed-together smiles and a few minutes later the service was over and it was time to walk down the aisle towards the outside world as man and wife. They looked at each other, and then Alex held his arm out because for the moment they clearly had to behave like a normal couple. After a moment's hesitation, Emma took his arm lightly and they began to process down the aisle.

Alex was acutely aware as they walked that Emma was holding herself stiffly away from him, nearly as stiffly as he in his turn was holding himself away from her.

And finally, after what had felt like an extraordinarily long walk—that aisle must be a lot longer than the average—they were outside the church.

'I shall miss you so much, my darling Emma.' Lady Morton hugged her niece, before almost shoving her into Alex's chaise.

'I'll miss you too, Aunt. Thank you for everything,' Emma said as Alex handed her up into his curricle.

Alex winced as Lady Morton squeezed his cheek and said, 'Enjoy yourselves tonight,' before he jumped up next to Emma. He would have laughed under any other circumstances.

The door closed behind them and here they were, together, alone, the two of them, complete strangers, newly married in name only, trapped together on a lengthy journey.

Thank the Lord Alex had his horse excuse ready.

'Beautiful weather today,' Emma said as she arranged herself in the corner of one of the seats.

Alex sat down on the other seat in the opposite corner.

'A lovely day for a journey,' she added.

'Indeed. But somewhat chilly. There are blankets here, and I've asked my housekeeper to prepare a foot warmer for you for the journey. She should have it ready when we get to the house.'

'Thank you. The current fashion for wedding garb is sadly lacking in consideration for a lady's comfort. But I'd assumed we were leaving London immediately?' Emma's luggage had already been collected by one of Alex's grooms from Lady Morton's house.

'We are.' Alex cleared his throat, suddenly feeling a little…not rude, maybe awkward. 'But I'm going to ride alongside the chaise. The only way to get my horse home.' Not precisely true. If he'd really wanted to travel inside the chaise he'd have trusted his head groom to ride Star, his horse. 'We're going back to the house so that I can ride from there.'

'Oh, I see. That makes great sense. And I'll be able to read my novel without having to make polite conversation with you.' She twinkled at Alex and surprised a laugh out of him.

A few seconds later, they drew up outside his house.

'We'll stop for luncheon and a break for the horses at around one o'clock,' he told her. 'If you can drag yourself away from your book, of course.'

She smiled at him and he nodded—a little awkwardly—and then opened the chaise door. Maybe he should travel inside the carriage with her. It would be more polite and his riding separately might give rise to gossip. No. He didn't want to spend too much time with her. He really didn't want to get close to a woman again.

Chapter Four

Emma found herself staring at the door that the duke had just closed behind him. It might be a metaphor for his clear signal that he planned to keep her closed out of his life as far as possible. That was completely understandable, of course, but, if she was honest, her spirits, which had not been high when she'd woken up this morning—her wedding day for goodness' sake—were now dragging even lower.

A journey spent in splendid isolation in this luxurious, velvet-upholstered carriage was going to feel very long, and a life spent in splendid isolation in the no doubt luxurious ducal castle would also feel very long.

Well, she would just have to make the best of it. She would have the duke's sons to care for, and he might accept her help in visiting tenants, and hopefully she would be able to make some local friends. And maybe, in time, despite his obvious reluctance, she and the duke might become good friends.

And now, at least she had time to read her book. She'd told the duke that she would be pleased to have some time to read—she'd even managed a little joke, of which she was very proud. She felt as though it was good to maintain one's dignity when one's husband had effectively told one that he didn't wish to share one's company at all. And she *was* pleased, actually, to have some peaceful reading time after the past few days packed morning to night with wedding preparations for a wedding neither of the two participants had wanted.

A few minutes later, she slapped the book closed, narrowly avoiding slamming her finger in it. It really was impossible to concentrate when out of the corner of her eye through the window she could see grooms, maids, all sorts of people bustling about, getting Alex's horses ready and finalising the packing of other carriages containing valises, trunks and servants.

It felt quite ridiculous, being incarcerated here by herself, so she was delighted when there was a knock on the door.

It was Jenny.

'The duke suggested that I travel with you, miss, oh, my goodness, *no*, Your *Grace*.' Jenny was practically bouncing on the spot, looking as though she was going to burst from excitement.

'Oh, *miss*.' Her eyes were saucer-like. 'Look at all the velvet. This is going to be *wonderful*. I'm so glad you're a duchess now.'

Hmm. It was kind of the duke to have thought of Emma's comfort, but maybe there was something to be said for isolation after all. Perhaps a journey alone would have been a good time for her to have begun to digest the fact that this morning she'd got married, when a week ago she hadn't even met the duke.

Jenny stopped bouncing and said, 'Would you *like* me to travel with you?'

Emma looked at her. She really didn't want to hurt

her feelings, and solitude *was* boring, and she could always pretend to bury herself in her book if she didn't want to talk. She was also likely to have a fair amount of time by herself over the coming weeks and months if the duke was intent on avoiding her, so she should probably take any company she could get.

'That would be lovely, Jenny.'

Jenny bounced herself into the chaise and took up residence on the opposite bench, while Emma tried not to find it annoying that so many people were pleased about her marriage.

'I've never been to Somerset before, miss.'

'Nor have I.'

'How long do you think it will take to get there?'

'I don't know.' Emma frowned, not pleased that she was so much at the mercy of the duke's whims. He had, of course, shown her nothing but kindness, but she would have liked to have had an idea of exactly where they were going and how long the journey would take.

She caught a glimpse of him out of the window, moving in their direction. He'd changed into riding wear, which showed off his strong physique marvellously well. Emma felt herself begin to smile in anticipation of him coming to speak to her again. She looked at the door, expecting him to knock, or open it. And…nothing.

And then the chaise jolted and began to move. Without another word from the duke.

Jenny actually clapped. 'Oh, miss, *Your Grace*, this is so exciting, isn't it?'

No, it really was not. More…profoundly depressing.

'Yes,' Emma said. 'I think I might read my book, if you don't mind.' She pulled it out of her reticule.

'Of course, *Your Grace*.'

This *Your Grace* thing was going to become annoying very quickly.

'You may continue to call me "miss" if you wish, Jenny.'

'Oh, no, miss, Your Grace, I couldn't do that.'

Emma smiled at her and shrugged internally. It probably wasn't going to be the worst thing about her new life.

The morning was long. Emma divided her time between trying to read but failing to turn more than a handful of pages—normally she was a voracious reader—and trying to look at the scenery and possibly catch a glimpse of Alex out of the window without catching Jenny's eye and having to talk. And, of course, just *sitting* the entire time. Frankly, doing absolutely nothing while feeling quite passionately irritable about life in general was exhausting.

When the chaise drew smoothly to a halt in a yard in front of an inn, Emma found herself almost beaming in delight. Luncheon. Something to *do*.

There was a knock at the door and it was pulled open.

'I hope you don't mind my intruding.' The duke's head and shoulders appeared inside the carriage and suddenly it felt significantly smaller. 'We stop here for luncheon.'

Emma regarded him, her head slightly on one side. Her husband. Her *husband*. How…odd.

As she had observed, his broad shoulders and sheer solidity showed off his riding wear to perfection, and the austere simplicity of his clothing was also perfect. It made one think very disparagingly of the frivolous frock coats worn by more foppish men.

Objectively speaking, he did look good.

Subjectively speaking, though, he was annoying.

He seemed to have literally no concept that she might not want to stop here, and that he should have asked her whether she would *like* to stop. Why should men make every single decision, from whether or not they should travel together, to when they should stop on the journey? Obviously she should be grateful to Alex—and she *was* grateful to him—but literally everything other than the fact that they'd got married in the first place seemed to be on his terms. Of course, it was the way of the world that men made all the decisions, but why should it be that way?

'Is this the only inn on our route? I'm not particularly hungry yet.' Emma realised immediately that she was starving. She also sensed Jenny twitching on the opposite side of the chaise; she was probably hungry too.

The duke looked at her. She really wished she could read the expression on his face.

'We need to change the horses here,' he said. 'The next good inn is twenty miles distant. If you'd prefer to wait until then to eat, we can, of course, do that.'

'Thank you.' Emma smiled at him while her stomach growled. Apparently she'd just bitten off her nose to spite her face.

The duke hesitated briefly and then said, 'Jenny, I wonder if I could have a moment alone with Her Grace?'

'Of course, my lord, Your Grace.' Jenny almost fell out of the chaise in her haste to comply, and was only saved from falling flat on her face by the duke catching her arm.

Emma's mind immediately went to when he'd caught *her*, the evening they'd met, and a shiver ran through her entire body.

Once he had Jenny solidly on her feet outside the chaise, the duke put his head through the door again and asked, 'Would you mind if I joined you inside the chaise for a moment?'

'Of course not.' Emma moved her skirts out of his way, taking her time to allow her suddenly uneven breathing to settle.

Being alone in here together seemed very…intimate. Especially since Jenny would probably be watching them from a discreet distance—or possibly not so discreet. It felt much more intimate than it had the evening after the ball, because she'd been far too stressed then to think about the intimacy. Since they were now man and wife, they might be expected to be in any number of intimate situations, of course.

A lot of women would be sad in her position— desperately sad—about the fact that they wouldn't be engaging with their husband in the most intimate situation of all. But, other than the fact that it meant that she wouldn't be having children of her own, Emma was fortunate in being perfectly happy about that. *Perfectly* happy. Really. She had no particular desire to engage with the duke in that kind of thing at all. Really.

The duke pulled the door closed behind him and took the seat opposite her, where Jenny had been sitting. Emma swallowed. Each time she'd seen him, she'd been struck by how *large* he was. Right now, it seemed as though he was filling the entire chaise, which previously had seemed extremely roomy for two people.

He cleared his throat. 'I've been thinking. Obviously, for our own reasons, neither of us wishes there to be any gossip about our relationship.'

Emma inclined her head, her throat suddenly tight with an emotion she couldn't name.

'During our journey, therefore, I think that we should eat our meals together—in a private room, if possible, as that will be expected of us—and sleep in adjoining bedchambers.'

He was clearly right. And frankly, after the boredom of the journey so far, Emma realised she would welcome conversation with him over their meals. And they ought to get to know each other a little better, given that they were, effectively, co-conspirators.

There was no reason whatsoever for her to feel a little hot at the thought that they would have adjoining bedchambers for a night. Or two nights?

She really wanted to know how long the journey was going to be. During luncheon would be an ideal time to question him. There were a lot of things she'd like to know about her future life.

'I agree,' she said.

'Still not hungry?' he asked.

Emma wondered if he'd actually heard her stomach rumble.

'I have just this moment become a little hungry. Perhaps it would make sense to luncheon here after all.'

Enough was enough when it came to her asserting her right to eat when she wanted to.

The duke bowed his head.

Emma was fairly sure he was hiding a smile as he did so, which should have been annoying, but made her smile too.

The ducal crest and servants had worked a lot more magic than the mere greasing of palms that Emma's father had been able to do when he had travelled as a plain mister, however rich. The landlord of the inn and his staff were all bowing so low Emma was surprised they didn't lose their balance.

'Our best private dining room is at your disposal, Your Grace.' Had the landlord bowed any more deeply his ample stomach would have been dusting the ground, and had his smile been any broader his face might have split.

'Thank you very much.' Emma and the duke spoke as one, and then glanced at each other as one, which shouldn't have pleased Emma as much as it did. Given that her life had just taken a huge turn for the unknown, though, there was something nice about feeling that the two of them might occasionally be... She didn't know quite what. Maybe a team?

The two of them made *very* small talk—exclaiming over the delightful cottage garden they could see from the window of the dining room and commenting on the carved panelling in the room—until the table had been laden with more food than two adults with even gargantuan appetites could possibly eat and the landlord had bowed himself out of the room a final time.

'Can I help you to some of these sweetmeats?' The duke looked as though he was going to continue with the small talk.

'Yes, please,' said Emma, not even looking at the dish. While she had him with her, she had questions for him that were a lot more important than sweetmeats. She passed him her plate and said, 'Could I possibly ask you a few questions?'

'Of course.' He inclined his head.

'Firstly, could I ask what my duties as governess will be?'

'Duties?' The duke spooned three choice sweetmeats onto her plate and looked around the table at the other food, as though she hadn't just asked a very important question. 'No duties. As I said before, I'd be extremely grateful for your help with the boys, but I can't possibly ask you to take on formal duties. If you're happy to be involved in their care, or indeed take charge of it, I'd be delighted, but, equally, if you don't feel that you wish to be involved, I will look for another governess. If you do wish to be involved, then of course we can discuss matters of import, for example the hiring of tutors and a broad timetable. Buttered cauliflower?'

'No cauliflower, thank you.' Emma was fast losing her appetite, not something that happened to her very often. 'Was your professed need for a governess perhaps an invention?'

He placed three cauliflower florets very carefully on his own plate before looking up at her. 'It wasn't an invention. I do need a governess for my boys. I find, however, that I cannot possibly instruct *you*. You're—' he waved a fork at her '—you. *You*. The Duchess of Harwell. *You*.'

'I'm only the Duchess of Harwell because you were forced to marry me, and the only reason I agreed to your sacrifice was that you told me that you needed my help.'

Emma cut one of the sweetmeats in two, hard, her cutlery clattering against the plate, and sniffed as quietly as she could. Tears and anger were battling inside her, and she didn't wish to give in to either of them.

'I would like to help with the boys. If you would like me to.'

She'd believed they'd had a bargain, but it seemed that he'd completely hoodwinked her. He'd clearly just told her that he needed her help to prevail upon her to accept his offer. Out of kindness, of course. And she'd allowed herself to believe he needed her help because she'd *wanted* to believe it, because it was her best option. Really, she'd hoodwinked her*self*. Also, she couldn't *make* him allow her to help with his children—and indeed she didn't want to press her services where they weren't wished for—but if she couldn't help with them, what was she going to do with herself all day, every day?

'Yes, of course, and thank you. But not as an employee or a servant or social inferior of mine in any way. I didn't mean that I can't instruct you because you're a duchess now; I meant I can't instruct you because you're *you*, Emma, the person you are. I plan to settle your dowry on you so that you can live in any manner or style you like. As I mentioned before, there's a dower house on the estate to which you may wish to remove in due course. You would be very welcome to have it refurbished to your own specification.' He smiled at her, apparently unaware that she was now... Well, she didn't know what she was, but it wasn't good. She was either furious, or desperately miserable, or both.

'We had a bargain and I intend to stick to my side of it,' she told him. 'I would very much like to help with the children. Perhaps I could also help you in visiting tenants who might be in need?'

'Certainly. Thank you.' The duke busied himself with the food on his plate while Emma blinked back another few tears. She was, of course, being ridiculous. There was no reason for her to feel tearful; this was hardly the worst thing that had ever happened to anyone. Many of the debutantes she'd met in London would be ecstatic to be in her position now, setting aside the fact that they wouldn't be having children of their own. Really, she was very lucky.

She loaded a second mouthful onto her fork.

'These sweetmeats are quite delicious,' Emma said eventually, into the fairly long silence during which they'd both…chewed their food.

Oh, the romance of this wedding day. She didn't want a passionate love match, but this… This wasn't how she would ever have imagined her marriage to be.

'Yes, they are.' The duke's conversation was as scintillating as hers.

There was more chewing from both of them, and then he said, 'You said you had more than one question for me?'

Oh, yes. *Would you mind if I travelled to India to explore my grandmother's birthplace if I'm not going to have anything else productive to do with my time?*

No. Maybe not a conversation to have until she'd gauged how conservative he was.

'Yes. I wondered how long our journey to Somerset will be?'

'Assuming that no unforeseen incidents occur, I hope to arrive tomorrow evening. One night at an inn, therefore.'

'Wonderful.'

And then they lapsed into near silence for the remainder of the meal, any conversation revolving entirely around the food—which was nice, but not outstandingly so, although any deficiencies in quality were made up for in extreme quantity.

After what felt like a long silence-filled time later, which turned out to have been perhaps twenty minutes, the duke said, 'If you don't mind, I feel that it might be better for us to be on our way sooner rather than later,

so that we arrive at our staging inn this evening well before nightfall.'

Emma gave him a big smile in relief that the meal
was at an end and in response to the fact that he'd asked,
rather than told, her about their departure.

'Of course.'

An extraordinary number of people seemed to have
gathered in the inn's entrance hall to witness their departure. During the extreme bowing and curtseying that
ensued, a woman stepped forward and introduced herself as the landlord's wife.

'I'm so sorry that I wasn't here before, Your Grace,'
she addressed Emma. 'I was shopping in the town. Praise
be that I got home in time to see you.' Goodness. The al-
lure of a duchess.

'Indeed.' Emma smiled at her.

'I wondered—' the woman must have thighs of steel;
her curtsey was remarkably low and yet still steady
'—whether Your Grace would like to see my kittens?'

'Kittens?' Was that a euphemism for something? Or
a country word?

'Baby cats, Your Grace.'

Emma laughed. 'I'm so sorry. You must think me quite
odd. I hadn't realised what you meant. I'd love to see
your kittens.'

'And then we must be on our way,' the duke said.

Emma turned to look at him, one eyebrow raised. He
might be reneging on the governess part of their bargain;
he was *not*, if she could help it, going to renege on giving her autonomy.

'If you don't mind,' he clarified after a pause.

Emma smiled. 'I'm sure we can spare a few minutes,' she said, 'and then I think we'll need to leave.'

'Oh, my goodness. They're adorable,' she breathed a couple of minutes later as the landlady opened a stable door for her. 'How old are they?'

'Two months, Your Grace.' The landlady dropped into yet another curtsey. Emma really wished she could ask her to stop curtseying, but she was fairly sure the woman would be offended. It seemed as though she was going to have to get used to being curtseyed to.

She bent down and then knelt on the straw next to where the kittens were lapping from a bowl.

'Your dress, Your Grace. If I might be so bold.'

'I'm sure it won't be damaged. This straw looks very clean.'

And it was her wedding dress, but her wedding had been a complete fake and she knew that she would never wear the dress again, because today was not a day that she was going to want to remember.

'May I?' She indicated one of the kittens, which had finished drinking.

'Please do.'

Emma reached forward and picked the kitten up, stroking its silky fur. The tiny creature mewled and arched into her.

'It's beautiful,' she said.

Today was a very lonely day, and it seemed that her life might be quite isolated from now on. Her new husband clearly had no interest in any kind of friendship with her, and she could already see that the vast majority of people she met were going to be very interested in her, but not actually in *her*, just in her persona as a duchess. Even Jenny, whom she'd known for over a decade now, was trying to treat her differently now she was a duchess.

It felt wonderful for another living creature to wish to cuddle into her, as the kitten was doing, for no reason other than that they were fellow creatures.

She picked up a piece of straw and tickled the kitten with it, and soon they were playing together. For a few moments she forgot that she'd got married and just enjoyed the kitten.

And then a large shadow appeared above her and she heard the duke say, 'I'd like to leave now, if you're ready.'

No, she wasn't ready, but she might never be ready, and of course it would be better to arrive at the next inn before nightfall.

'Of course.' She carefully picked up the kitten and with great reluctance placed it back with its mother. Now she needed to stand up. She looked around. There was nothing to hold on to. She was going to have to scramble to her feet by pushing herself up from the ground, which she wouldn't mind at all without an audience, but as it was…

The duke stepped forward and held his hand out to her. Yes, that was clearly her best option. A bit of an analogy for her marriage to him, really.

'Thank you.' She took his hand and found herself almost flying to her feet.

The duke loosened his fingers on her hand, as though he was going to let go, and then re-tightened his grip and drew her arm through his. Of course: he'd done it to avoid gossip, which they'd agreed they both wanted to do, so she smiled up at him in her best wifely manner, actually a very easy thing to do, because he did

have a lovely face when he wasn't doing his stern Ice
Duke thing.

He was looking at her, and smiling back at her, and
Emma felt her entire body bask in the smile even though
she knew it was fake.

'Your Grace?' The landlady was scrape-the-ground
curtseying again. 'If I might make so bold? Would Your
Grace like to take the kitten? It will be very difficult for
us to find homes for them all.'

Emma realised immediately that she'd *love* to take
the kitten. She looked back up at the duke, who rolled
his eyes slightly.

'Is it practical to transport a kitten from here to Somerset in the chaise?' he asked.

'Oh, yes, Your Grace. We can provide a box and bed-
ding and food and milk.' The landlady was nodding em-
phatically.

'I'd love to,' Emma said, ignoring her new husband's
raised eyebrows. 'I wonder… Would it be lonely without a sibling?'

'Probably,' the duke said, rolling his eyes more, but
smiling. He turned to the landlady. 'You must allow me
to pay you for the kittens.'

'Oh, Your Grace. I couldn't.' She already had her hand
held firmly out. 'Thank you.'

In the end they took three kittens, and Emma's mood
had lightened considerably at the prospect of something
to do and the company the cats would provide.

'People are certainly very interested in the movements of the Duke and Duchess of Harwell,' Emma murmured as she and the duke stood in the courtyard while
the landlady gathered together necessities for the kittens.

More people than she'd imagined the inn even held had assembled to see them off.

'They are.' He didn't smile. 'I appreciate the many advantages of my station, but it would take a better man than I to enjoy that side of my life.'

Emma felt strangely comforted from knowing that he didn't love this weird adulation either.

'It's better at home in the country, though. People get used to your title and possessions, and to some extent start treating you as the person you are, especially the household retainers who've been with our family for many years, and some of my tenants, not to mention friends.' He looked down at her. 'Are you sure you're happy to travel in the chaise with the kittens? It could be very difficult. And possibly smelly.'

Emma laughed. 'I'm very happy to,' she told him.

'Have you spent much time with cats?' he asked.

'No.' She could see his lips twitching. 'What?'

'Nothing,' he said, smiling blandly.

A few minutes later, as she sat in the chaise and watched him ride off, she realised that she was almost looking forward to seeing him later, when they stopped for the evening.

Chapter Five

As Alex strode away from the chaise in the direction of his horse, he could have sworn he heard a little squeak, possibly of pain, from Miss Bolton—Emma, the new duchess, how to think of her?—in the interior of the chaise. Maybe one of the kittens had scratched her.

He wondered how long it would be before she'd be seriously regretting her impulse purchase. He was fairly sure that unless the cats were lulled to sleep by the movement of the vehicle they'd play merry hell with her. So much so that he was almost tempted to travel in there with her, just to enjoy the spectacle.

Not that tempted, though. He really didn't want to get too close to her, and he always enjoyed riding.

Mid-afternoon, he saw ahead of him, on a long, straight stretch of road, a broken-down stagecoach, half tilted into a ditch, with passengers struggling to disembark and trunks and bags strewn across the road. Reining in his horse, he stopped and dismounted, looping the reins around a tree and securing them before heading over towards the coach to help passengers out.

A few minutes later, working in his shirtsleeves, he heard another carriage come to a halt and realised that it was his own. Shortly after that, Emma was standing next to him on the dusty road, asking what she could do to help.

'You would be best placed by returning to the chaise and continuing your journey,' he told her. 'This is no place for a gentlewoman.'

There were some extremely angry people using some extremely fruity language not far from them, and Alex had already had to wade in to prevent an argument coming to serious blows.

'I am an adult, not a baby, nor a Bath miss. Some of these people are clearly in distress. Why would I not help?'

Alex tried very hard not to sigh out loud, and was pretty sure that he'd succeeded.

'Obviously you *can* help,' he said, 'but a duchess is always a target for thieves and vagabonds, and the stagecoach is not a particularly—' he sought for a polite word '—*exclusive* mode of travel. It is entirely possible that one of the passengers might seek to relieve you of some of your jewellery, for example.'

'Then I will shoot them.' She said it so calmly that he really couldn't tell whether or not she was joking. It *sounded* like a joke. Because obviously she *wasn't* going to shoot anyone. Except... He'd already noticed that when she was joking there was a little quirk to her lips. And the quirk was not there.

'Just through the fleshy part of their arm or leg, obviously. I wouldn't want to kill them.' She patted her reticule. She really didn't seem to be joking. Did she have a pistol in there?

'My father, while not a duke, was an extremely wealthy man, and he wished to ensure that his only daughter was protected.'

This time Alex did not succeed in not sighing out loud. 'I'm not sure that a shooting, even just through the fleshy part of someone's limb, would help any of us. And there would, of course, be the risk that your aim faltered and greater injury occurred.'

'It would not falter. I was taught very well and I have an excellent aim.'

'Real-life situations are not the same as practice ones, though,' he pointed out.

Why was he even engaging with her?

'True,' she said. From over her shoulder.

Because, totally ignoring Alex's wishes, she was on her way to speak to some female passengers, who were sitting by the side of the road.

He'd already noticed during their stop at the staging inn, when she'd blatantly pretended that she wasn't hungry just to make a point, that she was clearly not planning to allow him to tell her what to do in any way. Which, of course, was completely understandable, and he didn't *want* to tell her what to do. Most of the time, anyway. Right now, he would very much have appreciated her doing what he'd asked.

He nodded at two of his grooms, both of whom immediately moved towards Emma. Their mere presence would protect her, and he, of course, would be constantly looking over his shoulder to check that she was all right.

To give her her due, she really did help very enthusiastically, and her presence did, to some extent, quieten people down, partly because so many of them were watching her open-mouthed. His grooms did a very good job of intimidating the livelier of the little crowd, and it was not long before Emma had managed to calm a woman who'd been having full-blown hysterics.

Soon Emma was sitting in a little group of other women, talking away about their children, from what Alex could hear, and very quickly it was as though they were fast friends. He'd better just hope they didn't have any kittens or other animals to sell her.

When the stagecoach was eventually righted, and its broken wheel shaft mended—Alex hadn't felt he could leave before that—he joined Emma in bidding farewell to all her new friends.

'I'll try that new recipe, Your Grace,' said an older woman dressed in a voluminous grey dress and wearing a large, bright yellow hat.

'You'll be delighted with the results, I'm sure,' Emma told her.

Alex nodded at all the women and then said, 'I believe that the stagecoach is ready to depart, and we should be on our way too.'

'She's a lovely duchess,' the lady in the yellow hat told him.

Alex nodded. It did look as though she was going to be. And, to be fair to Emma, she *had* helped, and there had been no unpleasantness nor any problems. Perhaps she genuinely would be able to look after herself with a pistol as well. It certainly seemed as though she was a woman who should not be underestimated.

He nodded and smiled at the woman. 'I agree.' He held his arm out to Emma and she took it, and they made their way back to the chaise, where her maid had been patiently waiting with the kittens.

'You should take a short walk to stretch your legs, Jenny, before we set off again,' Emma told her.

'Thank you, Your Grace, if you're sure.' Her maid smiled broadly at her, and Alex reflected that there was a fighting chance that even his famously prickly house-keeper might like Emma.

Once Jenny was out of earshot, Alex leaned in so that no one else could possibly hear, and said, 'You should keep that pistol very much out of sight. And be careful.'

As he leaned, he caught Emma's scent, which re-minded him of summer, and something sweet, and made him just want to keep on standing close to her.

That didn't feel right, so he took a step backwards, which gave him an excellent view of the little flash of anger in her eyes as she said, 'Should I *really*? Thank you so much for your sage advice. I was planning to wave it around and, indeed, hand it to any aspiring high-wayman on a platter to help him with his job.'

Alex laughed. 'Fair enough. I'm sorry. Perhaps I sounded a little patronising there?'

Emma raised an eyebrow.

'*Very* patronising,' he said. 'My apologies.'

'Thank you.' She nodded at him and entered the chaise, immediately bending down to speak to the kit-tens, sounding a lot happier to be talking to them than to him.

'I'd planned to stop near Andover, at a good staging inn that I know. Would you be happy to spend the night there?' he called into the chaise in the interests of har-mony; in an ideal world he and Emma would be on good although distant terms.

She turned to look at him, cuddling a kitten, and be-stowed a wide smile upon him, which transformed her face from very pretty to…extremely beautiful. Objectively speaking.

'I'd be happy to, thank you.' And then she turned back to the kitten.

'Excellent, then. So…have a good journey,' he said to her back.

'Thank you. And you,' she said over her shoulder, one eye still on the kittens.

Excellent, then.

Alex arrived at the inn at which they were spending the night a little before Emma. He took his horse round to the stables, and then returned to the yard in front of the inn to wait for her, so that they could enter the building together.

When the chaise drew up, he moved forward to open the door, interested to see how Emma and Jenny had fared with the kittens.

'Pleasant journey, I trust?' He held out his arm to Emma so that she could descend the steps.

'Delightful,' she said, smoothing her somewhat dishevelled hair as she reached the ground.

'Did you get a lot of reading done?'

'We were both somewhat occupied with the kittens,' she said, with as much dignity a woman with straw in her bodice and scratches on her arms could produce. Alex laughed out loud as Emma continued, 'I shall enjoy reading my book this evening instead.'

'Not planning to share your bedchamber with the kittens, then?'

'Jenny has very kindly volunteered to find a place for the kittens to stay overnight, perhaps in the stables. They are *truly* delightful.'

'But?'

'Very lively and not yet trained. Although *certainly* delightful.'

As Alex laughed again, he was interrupted by his head groom, who had a question about one of the horses.

'Forgive me,' he said to Emma, handing her over the threshold into the inn. 'I'll return to you very soon.'

When he got back, Emma had her back to the main door into the inn's reception area and was engaged in conversation with a little group of other travellers, who all appeared from their attire to be members of the *ton*. He could see from the way she was holding herself that she wasn't enjoying the conversation.

When she'd been chatting to the stagecoach travellers, he couldn't have said precisely how, but she'd looked relaxed. Now, her shoulders were just a little frozen, and her head was angled to one side in a slightly unnatural-looking manner.

'Indeed, you played your hand remarkably well,' one of the other ladies in the little group said, accompanying her words with a titter.

Alex thought he recognised her as one of the many women who'd been thrown, or had thrown herself, in his direction during the course of the last few weeks.

'Did you have any accomplice beyond your aunt?' she continued.

'Perhaps Sir Peter was the accomplice,' mused another of the ladies in the group.

This one bore a strong resemblance to the first one—in both looks and apparent nastiness—and accompanied her words with a gloved finger to her chin and an artful tilt of her head, as though she was thinking.

Emma visibly stood a little taller, as though she was

bracing herself, and her voice was a little higher than usual when she said, 'I'm afraid—'

Alex strode forward before she could continue—because really there was nothing she could conceivably say in response that would improve the situation—and slid his arm around her waist, sure that the only effective way of shutting down this gossipy cattiness was to demonstrate, if he could, that their union was at least some way towards a love match.

As he pulled her in, tight against his side, she gasped and looked up at him. From nowhere, he was struck by the thought that she fitted very well against him, as though their two bodies might have been made for each other. As might many people's, though, actually. That was just human biology.

The two women and their companions—an older woman whom he recognised as Lady Castledene, presumably their mother, and two men, perhaps brothers—were all looking at him and Emma appraisingly.

Alex really did not appreciate the way they were doing so. If they wanted something to appraise, he was going to *give* them something to appraise.

He dropped a kiss on Emma's forehead, catching that delicious scent again, and squeezed her waist a little more tightly. Her curves really did mould very well against his side.

'Your Grace.' Lady Castledene had produced a sycophantic smile and was curtseying very deeply. 'I do hope that you find yourself…well.'

She rolled her eyes, just very slightly, in Emma's direction as she spoke. Emma stiffened and Alex glared. How *dare* this woman imply…well, the truth. Yes, obviously it was the truth, of course he wouldn't have married Emma or anyone by choice. But how *dare* she be so rude to Emma? And in front of him. Emma was a good person, and Alex was going to do everything he could to prevent her becoming a social pariah.

He wanted to be extremely rude to Lady Castledene and her party, but that probably wouldn't be the right approach, given that they probably didn't realise he'd overheard the last part of their conversation before he'd joined them.

'Yes, very well, thank you,' he said, continuing to grip Emma's waist very tightly. 'I count myself a very fortunate man and am greatly looking forward to taking my wife home to begin our honeymoon.'

He pressed his lips again to Emma's hair, which felt odd, given that they really were not man and wife in the conventional sense, but was no great hardship, because that scent was just...*tantalising*. It drew you in.

He looked Lady Castledene in her narrowed eye and smiled. It really shouldn't be too hard to convince people that he was happy to be married to Emma. By anyone's standards she was a beautiful woman, and she was known to be an heiress, and the *ton* was a hugely shallow environment. They—*he*—just needed to brazen things out.

'Indeed.' Lady Castledene produced a smile of her own, very tight-lipped, and added, 'We must wish you well, Your Grace.'

She'd actually managed to turn her body so that it was as though she was speaking only to Alex and not to Emma.

'Thank you.' Alex bowed his head, shifted himself and Emma a little, so that they were both facing the group, and said, 'We're both very grateful for your good wishes.'

'We enjoyed your wedding breakfast, but were concerned that something might be amiss when we saw that you weren't able to attend yourselves.' Lady Castledene gave him a smug *How will you trump that?* smile.

'We wished to return home to the children as soon as possible. The only thing that's amiss is that the journey is long, so we haven't yet been able to be alone to begin our honeymoon,' Alex said.

Thank God they wouldn't know that he'd chosen to travel separately from Emma today. In hindsight, that had been a mistake from a gossip perspective.

'If you'll excuse us?' He removed his arm from Emma's waist and took her hand, linking his fingers through hers, and tugged her gently towards a doorway through which he could see his man, Graham, indicating, presumably, the private dining room that had been arranged for them.

He kissed the top of her head again as they went through the door, as Graham made a discreet exit.

Alex waited until the door was firmly closed before releasing Emma's hand and walking round to the other side of the table that had been laid for them to pull her chair out for her.

'Thank you,' she said as she sat down. 'And I must thank you also for rescuing me. Again.'

Alex shook his head. 'I'm only sorry that you had to experience that.'

'It wasn't a great surprise,' Emma said, taking a small bread roll from the basket he was holding out for her. 'I've met those women before on several occasions, and they had a lot to say about my father's origins.'

'I'm sorry.'

'Really, there's nothing to be sorry about. There are nice people and not-so-nice people everywhere, and I don't think I'm the only woman not to have loved her Season. There might be a particularly large amount of venom amongst the *ton*, but I always feel that one of the reasons so many of them engage in such awfulness is that they just don't have enough to *do*. I can't imagine a lot of people thriving in that environment.'

'I think you're right.' Alex broke off a piece of his own bread roll. 'Although, in fairness, I did have a lot of fun during the Season when I was young.' He paused for a moment as he was hit by a memory of meeting Diana, then collected himself and continued. 'But men have boxing and horses and financial affairs with which to busy themselves, in addition to all the social events.'

'Indeed. Whereas for women there's only gossip, shopping and visits to the dressmakers. And perhaps it isn't so enjoyable for slightly older men?'

'I certainly didn't enjoy *this* Season,' Alex agreed.

'Partly because you were being hounded by fortune-hunters such as myself?' Emma said.

'Exactly.' He smiled at her. 'That plan you hatched with Sir Peter and your aunt was *fiendish* in its ingenuity.'

'I know. We are geniuses.' Emma paused. 'Joking aside, I'm going to apologise and thank you one more time.'

Alex shook his head. 'Don't. We both know that neither of us would have chosen this, but I'd like to think we can make things work adequately for both of us.'

He was beginning to think that he was going to be able to cope reasonably happily with Emma being in his life. It was a positive sign that they could already laugh together about how they'd been compromised into this situation. He wasn't sure it was going to be so good for her, though. She obviously didn't have a single friend in Somerset and, going by the way she kept chatting to people, she was sociable and would be lonely if she was ostracised by the neighbours.

'I wonder whether, with your permission, it might be sensible to demonstrate our mutual affection a little more in front of those people.' Good Lord. He'd just had the thought that it might be a good idea to *kiss* her in front of them.

'They are some of the most gossipy of all the gossips,' Emma said. 'Maybe we ought to. If you think it wise?'

'Probably.'

Good Lord again. He didn't even *mind* the thought of kissing her, since there was going to be a good reason for it. If it happened. It might not happen. They might not see them again.

Maybe they should change the subject.

'What do you know of Somerset?' he asked.

Dinner was pleasant. Emma was very interested in the history and geography of the south-west of the country, and had interesting knowledge to impart on Lancashire and the rest of the north-west, an area that Alex had never visited.

They whiled away the time with amiable conversation, which at times even led to proper laughter on both sides.

'So, the pistol?' he found himself asking some time later. 'Your father deemed it important to educate you at a seminary for young ladies…and also to teach you to shoot?'

'Yes, indeed, and to fence. And to assist him in the

running of the factories. I learned about the machinery, the different fabrics, and the economics behind the business. My father taught me as he would have taught a son. He was very forward-thinking.'

'Indeed.'

Not so forward-thinking that he hadn't tried to force his daughter into marriage with an aristocrat, whether she wanted it or not.

'Other than in regard to his ideas on marriage, of course,' she said, as though reading his thoughts. She paused, and then asked a little hesitantly, 'And you…? Were you very young when you got married?'

'Yes,' he said. 'Twenty-three.'

Emma smiled at him and tilted her head a little to the side, as though expecting or hoping for elaboration. He wasn't going to elaborate. He couldn't talk about Diana this evening. He might become uncomfortably emotional.

He reached for the pitcher between them and said, 'Would you like more wine? I find this a very tolerable red. If you enjoy wine, you will be pleased to hear that we maintain a large cellar at the castle.'

He began an anecdote about smugglers on the Somerset coast, and before long had Emma laughing and the conversation moved far away from any further questions about his late wife.

'Would you like another drink?' he asked Emma some time later, when they'd agreed that the inn's cook was very good but that they could neither of them eat any more.

'No, thank you. I think…' She looked at him, as though trying to gauge what he'd like her to say. 'I think

I might perhaps go to bed now. Unless you'd like to stay downstairs a little longer?'

'Now is perfect for me.'

But he was thinking of the oddness of their going upstairs together, and from her suddenly more reserved demeanour it looked as though Emma was too.

They moved towards the door together—very politely, barely speaking—and Alex opened it for Emma to pass through.

As luck would have it—as though the woman had been listening out for them—the door opposite them opened precisely as they were leaving the room, and one of Lady Castledene's daughters came out.

'Good evening,' she said.

'Shall we?' Alex said into Emma's ear.

'Yes,' she whispered.

He reached his arms around her waist from behind and turned her towards him in what he hoped was a convincing show of husbandly ardour. Then he leaned down to kiss her on the lips, one eye on the woman opposite, whom he was pleased to see was now outright staring at them.

He lingered in the kiss for a moment, wanting to ensure that he looked suitably enthusiastic, and moved his hands to cup Emma's face, because that was what you did when you were kissing someone passionately.

The kiss was as chaste as a kiss on the lips could be, and purely for show. And then...

And then he became aware of the softness of Emma's lips, smelled that frankly almost intoxicating scent again, and felt his entire body begin to respond to her nearness, to the sensation of her lips under his, his hands on her face. He found himself moving his hands into her

thick hair, holding her tight against him, enjoying—
really enjoying—the way she was beginning to open
her mouth to him.

Their tongues met, and explored, and almost danced
together, and then he lost awareness of their surroundings, deepening the kiss ever more, conscious only now
of Emma, and the way it felt as though his entire body
were aflame.

She tasted wonderful. Sweet, tempting, in a different
way from Diana.

Diana.

He didn't want to enjoy kissing a woman he *knew*.
And he didn't just *know* Emma, she was his *wife*. He
didn't want to become close to her and then lose her.
One terrible grief in a lifetime was enough.

He could feel himself freezing, his hands, body,
mouth now unnaturally still. Emma was clearly sens-
ing his stillness too; she herself had stilled and with-
drawn slightly.

He opened his eyes, which he must have closed somewhere along the way, and, yes, that damned woman was
still standing opposite them, still staring.

Well, they'd been at it long enough now, he judged,
for it not to look odd if they stopped.

He drew back slowly, keeping an arm around Emma,
and coughed.

'Good evening,' he said to the lady.

She might still gossip about Emma having compromised him, but she would be less able to describe him
as an unwilling participant in their marriage now.

She flushed a deep red and whisked herself back inside the room out of which she'd come. Which was ideal,
because it made Emma look up at him with pure glee

on her face, which made him laugh, which made what could have been a very awkward post-fake kiss moment much less awkward.

He held out his arm to her again and they headed over to the inn's staircase.

'Your Graces.' The landlord had emerged from nowhere—he must have been waiting for them so perhaps he'd witnessed their kiss too—and was bowing. 'Allow me to escort you to your chambers.'

And up the stairs the three of them went.

Alex's man was waiting outside his room and Jenny was outside Emma's, a little further along the corridor.

'Thank you so much,' Emma said to Jenny. 'But I think I can prepare myself for bed this evening.'

'Oh, no, Your Grace, I need to help you.' Jenny swivelled her eyes in the direction of Emma's door, clearly keen to be involved in her wedding night preparations.

Alex had to try hard not to wince.

'Really, Jenny, there is no need. Thank you, and I'll see you in the morning.' Emma's voice was impressively steely; if she used that voice on Alex's sons they might even do as they were told.

As Jenny left them, followed by Alex's man and the landlord, Alex opened the door to his chamber and held it so that Emma could go in ahead of him.

She walked straight into the middle of the room and then turned to face him as he closed and locked the door.

'I think we should lock your door too,' he said, very quietly, in case any of the apparently many interested parties were listening on the other side of the door.

He looked at the bed. He was going to have to remember to make it look as though they'd both been in it for at least a portion of the night.

Emma was looking at the bed too. 'I'll take great care to make my bed in the morning so that no one can tell that I slept in it,' she said. 'Fortunately I don't toss and turn at night.'

Alex really didn't want to think about Emma in bed, in her nightdress. Perhaps her maid had put a wedding night gown out for her. Well, of course she would have done.

He swallowed. This was not going the way he'd planned; he didn't want to be having thoughts of this nature about Emma. Time to bid her goodnight and force his thoughts in a more sensible direction.

Chapter Six

'Excellent,' the duke said.

'So, goodnight, then,' said Emma, trying hard not to stare at his face, his chest, his…everything.

For the last few minutes, since their amazing kiss downstairs, she'd been struggling not to think all manner of things she shouldn't.

Why had he seemed so lost in the kiss and then suddenly frozen?

What might have happened next if they'd been alone in a room together?

How would she have felt if it had continued?

Would it ever happen again?

She hoped not, obviously. Really, she did. Although it *had* been very nice.

The duke swallowed again and Emma realised that she was staring at his strong neck, the movement of his Adam's apple, his jawline, those firm lips that had only a few minutes ago been against hers…

'Goodnight,' he said. 'Sleep well.'

His eyes slid to the wide bed to the side of them as he spoke, and Emma's followed his, and now she was swallowing, too, as her mind went in all sorts of direc-

tions about what a normal wedding night with him might
have entailed.

'Thank you. And you too,' she said, and stepped forward, fast, to get herself into her own bedroom and stop
having these ridiculous thoughts.

She put her hand on the door handle and turned. Nothing. She jiggled a bit. It was locked.

'Um. Your Grace. Alexander.' How should she address him? She turned to face the duke, to discover that
he was already searching for a key, along the mantelpiece and then on the shelves in the corner of the room
at the end of the wall the door was in.

'Call me Alex.' He opened two drawers in a little
table in the córner and closed them again. 'It must be
here somewhere,' he said.

Emma squared her shoulders; it was hard not to feel
put out that he sounded *quite* so desperate to get rid of
her. Although he was probably tired after his long ride
today. And perhaps he wanted to be alone—as she did,
she reminded herself—to digest the fact that for better
or worse they, two complete strangers, were now legally
bound together.

As the duke—Alex—reached for a high shelf, she
saw the muscles in his shoulders flex, and shivered, remembering how he'd looked earlier today when, in his
shirtsleeves, he'd been working with the coachman and
coach hands to right the stagecoach.

And she'd been pressed right up against all that muscle and hardness earlier, when they kissed.

For the first and last time, obviously.

'I can't find a key anywhere.' Alex turned round, put
his hands on his lean hips and scoured the room with
his eyes. 'This is ridiculous. It must be an oversight.'

'Perhaps we should go and ask for it.'

'I doubt people would expect us to have noticed yet.'

Emma nodded. It was true. They would be expected to be otherwise engaged. Kissing and…more. You couldn't grow up in the country, even with a father as protective as hers had been, without gaining a certain amount of knowledge of the way intimacies worked. And you really couldn't spend several hours in a chaise with Jenny on your wedding day without gaining further knowledge on the subject.

Five minutes' more fruitless searching convinced them both that there was no key to be found.

'Right,' said Alex, hands on hips again, 'we need a plan. You can sleep on the bed and I'll sleep in this chair.'

Emma slightly wanted to cry at the ridiculousness of their supposed wedding night and she *really* wanted to use the chamber pot, and she didn't want to do either of those things in front of Alex.

'I know what we could do,' she said, finally summoning up some clear thought. 'If you went round to my chamber via the corridor, perhaps with your boots off, that would look, um, intimate, husbandly, and you could perhaps, if you don't encounter anyone, just stay in there while I stay here?'

'You're right. Panic was clearly addling our brains.' Alex took his boots off, and then also his jacket, while Emma focused on a picture on the wall, again not wishing to look as though she was staring at him, particularly because she actually *did* want to stare.

'Yes, I think the best thing would be if I stay in there and then return in the morning. Perhaps we can swap then, to get dressed. Right. I'm off.' He did an exaggerated tiptoe towards the door, which made her laugh through the misery that had suddenly threatened to engulf her.

'You look as though you're an actor in a farce,' she hissed as he poked his head out of the door and looked left and right.

'This *is* a farce,' he whispered, and then made a dash for it, closing the door behind him, while Emma tried not to reflect on the fact that many a true word was spoken in jest.

Alex had just referred to their situation as a farce and...that did not feel good. Even though it was true.

She looked at the closed door for a moment and then shook her head. There was no point standing here feeling maudlin about her new life situation. Things could be worse.

She looked over at the bed. Things could be better, actually. Practically speaking, she didn't have a nightgown, or her hairbrushes, or *anything*. She'd very much like her book, at the very least, because she didn't feel as though she was going to sleep easily tonight.

She walked over to the bed and thumped down in the middle of it, then sniffed and wiped under her eyes with her forefingers as a couple of tears trickled out. She shouldn't be feeling this miserable. Tonight wasn't going to be wonderful, but once they arrived in Somerset things would be much better.

She flung herself backwards and wriggled herself into the very comfortable bed. She needed to cheer up immediately. This really wasn't the worst it could have been; it was in fact far better than it might have been. Of *course* she could be happy in a marriage with Alex without intimacy. It would just be like living with a friend. She might, for example, have been dealing with Sir Peter's husbandly advances right now. Or already on her way to living in penury. And this bed was *so* comfortable.

Hearing a clatter at the connecting door, she raised herself on one elbow. And then Alex walked through the door, saying, 'Surprise. The key was in the other side.'

'Oh. *Oh.* I can't believe we didn't think of that.'

'That's panic for you.'

'Well, thank goodness.' Emma gave up on trying to sit up from where she was—the bed was so soft that she'd sunk too far down to be able to get herself straight up—and turned onto her side, trying to ignore the fact that this was remarkably undignified.

As she turned, Alex's legs and—she gulped—more appeared in front of her, and he put his hand out.

'Thank you,' she said.

He hauled a little too hard and she almost flew off the bed, landing against his hard chest. He let go of her immediately and took a step backwards, clearly extremely eager not to touch her at all if he didn't have to.

'I think I misjudged your weight.' He smiled the slightly twisted smile she was already coming to recognise as very particular to him.

'Yes.' And suddenly she was so tired of this day. 'Goodnight, then.'

'Goodnight.'

Once she was in her own room, she locked both the door to the corridor and the connecting door and then lay down on the bed, the events of the day jostling in her brain.

The 'I now pronounce thee man and wife' moment featured heavily, and so did the acquisition of the kittens, of course, as did the true nastiness of Lady Castledene and her party. But the thing that she couldn't stop thinking about the most was the kiss. Or The Kiss, as she was fairly sure she'd think of it in her mind for evermore.

She'd kissed a few men before, including a couple of the men who'd proposed to her—while she'd decided that she didn't need or indeed *want* to be in love with the person she married, she'd thought it would be better to *like* them, both emotionally and physically, so she hadn't been averse to a little experimentation—and none of those kisses had been anything compared to the one she'd shared with Alex.

And it hadn't even been a proper one; it had only been for show.

It might be the last time she ever kissed a man.

After several hours tossing and turning—she was going to have a *lot* of work to do before she left the room in the morning to make her bed look un-slept-in—Emma was finally in a very deep sleep when she was woken by what she realised was a persistent tapping on the connecting door.

She dragged herself out of bed and walked over and opened it, putting only her head round the edge, so that Alex wouldn't see her in the embarrassing wedding-night nightgown her aunt had had made for her and Jenny had put out for her to wear last night.

She'd worried a lot during the night that she'd been too enthusiastic when Alex had kissed her, and she really didn't want to look as though she was throwing herself at him when he clearly had no interest in her.

'I'd very much like to leave as soon as possible,' Alex told her. 'If that's all right?'

'Of course. I'll be ready as soon as I can.'

Maybe she should make the bed very carefully and

then call for Jenny, she thought as she closed the door. Or maybe that would be too risky. Maybe Jenny would be able to tell, somehow, that they hadn't…

Yes, she should probably dress herself.

Living a life of deception was going to be ridiculously complicated. She and Alex should probably find a way of her removing to his dower house as soon as possible.

Fifteen minutes later, she was extremely hot from trying to do up all her buttons. She was never going to manage to look suitably duchess-like without help from *someone*. The question was: should that someone be Jenny…or Alex?

She walked back to the bed that she'd spent ages smoothing down earlier, and then looked around the room. Going by what Jenny frequently had to say, about all sorts of people from all walks of life, she had a very strong nose for lying and also for anything to do with marital or extramarital relations. She'd probably have a strong nose for a lack of marital relations too.

Sighing, Emma walked over to the connecting door and knocked, before opening it slightly. Alex was sitting on the chair in the room, putting his boots on.

'Good morning. I wonder if you could help me finish dressing? I thought that might be best, just for today.'

'Of course.' Alex stood up, one boot on and one boot off. 'As you will see from my footwear, I also decided that today it would be best to dress myself, and am also struggling.'

Emma laughed. 'I imagine that your man and Jenny would both be delighted to know that they're genuinely indispensable. I'm sure you'll be able to do my buttons up, but I wouldn't let you loose on my hair, and I have literally no idea how anyone gets someone's foot inside boots that fit as tightly as those.'

'I know. Graham is a true genius.' Alex moved towards her. 'Where are these buttons?'

Emma felt suddenly breathless, as though her dress was too tight, which was ridiculous, given that it wasn't even fully done up yet.

'Just at the top, at the back.'

She turned round for him and lifted her hair out of the way. How was it that she was fully dressed and was indeed asking him to dress her *more*, and yet felt almost naked at this moment?

She sensed Alex move closer to her and lift his hands towards her neck. She could barely breathe. He took the fabric very gently and tugged at it a little. The room was completely silent other than the sounds of their breathing—such as it was in Emma's case—and the very faint rustle of the silk as Alex tried to do up the buttons.

'This is a lot more difficult than you would think.' Alex's breath skimmed across her skin as he spoke. Clearly, he had his head bent close to her so that he could see what he was doing, and Emma was sure that the tiny hairs on the back of her neck had risen.

'Jenny's obviously a genius too.' Emma cleared her throat to get rid of the croak that her voice suddenly contained.

'Would you mind if I…?' Alex's voice was croaky too now. 'If I moved your hair a little further?'

'Of course not.'

Emma was braced for the contact, but she still almost jumped a mile when Alex's fingers brushed the skin at the base of her neck as he carefully lifted her hair. She was remembering now how he'd thrust his fingers into her hair during their kiss last night.

'Nearly done,' he grunted.

Emma was struggling not to close her eyes and just melt into the feeling of his fingers against her when suddenly she felt actual pain. *'Ow,'* she squeaked.

'Don't move.'

He tugged some strands of hair very gently, and, *oh*, his fingers against her scalp and her neck felt good.

'You have some hair caught in a button. I am *really* not good at this.'

'Mmm,' Emma said.

He was wrong. He *was* good. *So* good. His fingers were gently moving more of her hair now, and she just wanted to lean into his hand. If she just took a step she'd be leaning against his very solid chest, too, and…

And… What was she *thinking*? He was literally doing her buttons up for her, very incompetently; and this wasn't a matter of *intimacy*, it was just a matter of expediency.

His fingers were still working at her neck and it was utter torture. In a very blissful way.

'This time I really have finished.' His voice sounded heavier than usual. He stepped backwards and Emma turned round, suddenly incredibly self-conscious for no good reason at all.

'Thank you so much.'

The hairs at the nape of her neck were going to be standing on end for hours to come at the memory of how he'd touched her there, she was sure. She was struggling to remember what time of day it was, even. *Breakfast*. It was breakfast time.

'Should we perhaps go below stairs for breakfast now?' she suggested.

'We should. As soon as I've wrestled myself into my other boot.'

'I'd like to offer to help, but I've no idea what I could do.'

'I'll be fine.' Alex sat down again and inserted his foot into the boot. 'I'm a grown man. Of course I can dress myself. How hard can it be?'

Very hard, it seemed.

Emma gave up on politeness quite quickly and laughed and laughed, which was an excellent way of recovering from his doing up her buttons.

Finally properly booted, Alex stood up and shook his head at her. 'I'm not sure people are going to expect the Duchess of Harwell to behave with such a lack of decorum.'

'I'm not sure people would expect the Duke of Harwell to be so incredibly incompetent at putting his own foot into a boot.'

They smiled at each other and then Alex said, 'Right. Breakfast.'

'Your Graces.' The landlord was bowing almost as low as had the man at the inn where they'd stopped yesterday at midday. 'I must apologise. I didn't realise you would be descending so early in the day for breakfast. Allow me just a minute or two to make a private room available.'

'Do you mean that you're going to ask someone to leave a private room?' Emma asked.

'Yes, Your Grace. I'll make sure that they're quick.'

'No, please don't.' Emma was horrified: this felt awful. It was a good reminder that she was going to have to be on her guard constantly to ensure that other people weren't frequently inconvenienced just because she was a duchess. 'We can very well eat in the public room.'

'But Your *Grace*. You're...' The landlord gave a hand wave in her direction that clearly meant *You're a duchess*. 'You're newly married.'

'Even so, we cannot be the cause of the ruination of others' breakfasts.'

'And we will have many other breakfasts together, just the two of us, once we reach our own home,' Alex said, so soulfully that Emma nearly laughed. 'My wife and I are indeed very well able to sit in the public room. I see that there is a table free there.'

He held out his arm to Emma and turned towards the table.

'Very good, Your Grace, if you're sure.'

Settled at the table in the public room, Alex broke his fast with ale and steak, while Emma chose a selection of fruits and some toast. They filled the first few minutes of their meal with low-voiced small-talk, about the journey to come and the Somerset climate, until very suddenly Alex leaned in and said, 'The Castledene party—and they are staring.'

Emma's hands were empty, and he reached across and took them in his and drew them towards him.

Emma said, *'Oh,'* and then tried to change it into something that sounded more amorous than surprised. *'Ooh.'* No, that just sounded odd.

'Ooh?' Alex whispered, still holding on to her hands.

'I was trying to sound amorous.'

When he was looking at her in that half-laughing way, it wasn't actually very difficult to imagine feeling amorous. In a purely physical way, obviously.

Alex squeezed her hands, then let go of them and picked up his cutlery again. 'They definitely noticed.'

'You look very smug.'

'We're excellent actors.'

'Oh, yes, we are.' Emma batted her eyelids at him and pouted, and he grinned at her. This acting thing really wasn't that difficult with someone who was as easy to be with as Alex. She'd found it a lot more difficult to pretend that she enjoyed the company of most of the men her aunt had been so desperate for her to get to know earlier in the Season.

She heard a loud throat-clearing behind her, and glanced over her shoulder as one of the Miss Castledenes stared at her for just a second too long—clearly on purpose—and then dropped her eyes without smiling.

She turned back to Alex and almost gasped at the way his eyes had become like flints and his lips had tightened to a thin line. His Ice Duke demeanour again. She hoped that he'd never look at *her* like that.

'Bordering on the cut direct,' he said. 'I will *not* have you treated like that.' He put his cutlery down, took her hands in his again, and said in a low voice, 'We should have thought of this before, but I suppose we've been caught up in too much of a whirlwind. We should concoct a story about how we first met.' He smiled at her. 'We were, of course, secretly courting before the ball at the beginning of the week.'

'Oh, yes. And we kept our mutual affection secret because we sensed that it was something perfect and we didn't want to risk it being spoilt by too much attention.'

'Yes, our love was pure and strong, but also delicate and fragile.'

'Alex, you should try your hand at poetry. I think you would be competition for Byron himself.'

Alex laughed and then, making his eyes very wide, said, 'I'm not a natural poet. It is you and you alone who brings this out in me. It has been so since the first moment we laid eyes on each other.'

'Across a crowded ballroom?'

'Certainly not. Nothing so mundane. We were…' He stopped and frowned, and then said, 'Um, what *were* we doing? We didn't meet at a ball or any other kind of party, did we? Because people would have seen us. And obviously talked.'

'Don't you remember?' Emma said, struck by a brainwave. 'You were my knight in shining armour. I was riding early one morning with my maid when my horse ran away with me and I was saved by you on your horse. As we were riding alone, neither of us knew who the other was, and neither of us wanted to reveal our true identities, but we both knew that Cupid's arrow had immediately struck and that we should keep our pure, strong but delicate and fragile love to ourselves for the time being, especially as neither of us was sure that Society would approve the other as an appropriate match for us. We then met surreptitiously in a variety of secret locations. We were on the brink of announcing our love to the world when Sir Peter forced our hand by attempting to compromise me. We are now, of course, deeply grateful to him, as we might otherwise have ended up waiting longer to marry.'

'I like that,' said Alex, nodding approvingly. 'Have you perhaps invented a big lie before? You're very good at it.'

'Never.' Emma shook her head. 'But I agree that I do seem to have a great talent for it. I'm pleased to have discovered it.'

'Yes, I'm sure it will stand you in excellent stead on any number of future occasions.' Alex squeezed her hands again and then let go. 'I'm still hungry. I can't keep holding your hands because then I can't eat.'

'Is not love alone enough to sustain you?'

'Love and just a little more of this steak, purely because it really is delicious and I don't want to offend the landlord. And I have a long way to ride today.' He took a mouthful, and then said, 'Actually, I ought to ride in the carriage, I think, if you don't mind. Just for the first part of the journey.'

'Yes, you're probably right.' Emma eyed Miss Castledene, who was now staring at them from across the room. 'I almost want to *slap* that woman.'

Alex nodded. 'Indeed. So, we're agreed about me coming in the chaise with you for the start of the journey? I wonder if it might be better for Jenny to travel in one of the other carriages at that point.'

'Definitely.' If Jenny was with them they'd have to play-act all morning. 'But we can still have the kittens with us.'

'Really?'

'Really. They're adorable.'

And they would also be something to concentrate on instead of Alex, because this was suddenly feeling too much again. It was confusing. Currently, they were trying to demonstrate to everyone that they were a normal married couple to avoid gossip. How and when were they going to stop that?

She wanted to ask Alex, but she wasn't sure how to

broach it. Maybe it would be easier once they were in Somerset. They would settle down, the staff would learn that they weren't a particularly amorous couple, and everything would become easier. *Hopefully.*

A few minutes later, Alex had finished demolishing his steak and was sailing past the Castledene group with Emma on his arm.

'I shall look forward to calling on you in London, Your Grace,' said the younger Miss Castledene to Emma, who nearly gasped out loud at her effrontery.

How could anyone go from that level of rudeness to pretending to be friends with someone mere minutes later? Lady Castledene and her older daughter were both nodding vigorously.

'I shall look forward to receiving you,' Emma said, and almost achieved a real smile. Really, her acting skills were superb, if she said so herself.

'I think it worked,' Alex said as they got into the chaise.

'Really?' Emma wasn't so sure.

'Well, of course. People will hate you for a while, because you snaffled a duke, and there are never that many of us available on the marriage mart at any given time. But once they've come to terms with the fact that you are the new duchess, and as long as no gossip attaches to you and you are seen to be regarded highly by me, they will all endeavour to be your friend and invite you to everything.'

'How delightful,' Emma said. 'I look forward to a lifetime of fake friendships.'

'Indeed.' Alex smiled at her and Emma smiled back—

a real smile—and then they both fell silent, and she remembered that they were near strangers, bound together only by their farcical marriage.

Chapter Seven

Alex would never under normal circumstances choose to travel in an enclosed space with three cats, but it was actually a relief when his groom deposited Emma's kittens with them.

His plan to remain aloof from her had very much not gone to plan during their stay at the inn, and he was keen to withdraw a little, but he didn't want to be rude, and it wouldn't be particularly pleasant for either of them to travel entirely in silence—unless Emma was actually engrossed in her book for hours on end—so the kittens would be a welcome diversion.

He settled back into his corner of the chaise, unable to help smiling as Emma immediately started cooing over the kittens and tickling and playing with them.

He really did need to remember to maintain a distance between the two of them. He'd enjoyed their kiss far too much—indeed, he might easily have gone a lot further had they been alone—and during breakfast he'd found himself furious on Emma's behalf that the Castledenes were being so insolent to her.

Apparently, he'd already started to care a little for her.

As a friend, he supposed. You didn't enjoy kissing your friends, though. Well, maybe you did when the friend was such an attractive woman. It had probably been just a natural physical reaction.

It was fortunate that they'd be arriving in Somerset by the end of the day. He'd switch to his horse again well before that, too.

He'd better remember to agree with Emma in advance of the horse change where they were going to stop for their luncheon; there was no point annoying her in that regard again.

'You're beautiful,' Emma told the kittens, for about the twentieth time.

Alex laughed. 'You're spoiling them.'

'I'm not. I'm just stating facts.' She kissed one of the kittens on the nose and it purred contentedly. She and the kittens did make a lovely picture together as she played with them, her thick, silky, dark brown hair falling over her face and their tiny black bodies.

'Are you enjoying travelling with them?' he asked as she got one of the kittens into the box they'd brought for it in the nick of time.

'Of course,' she said.

When the kitten had finished its business, she picked it up and deposited it with its siblings in their bed, shut the basket, then leaned back against the bench and closed her eyes for a moment, the picture of exhaustion.

'You know, I would never have guessed that you hadn't been familiar with cats before.'

Emma ignored him. 'We might need to stop and change their straw.'

Alex sniffed. 'Sooner rather than later, do you think?'

'Probably.'

'I knew you'd soon think better of having them as travel companions.'

'No, they're delightful. I think they could do with a sleep, though. They're very young.'

'Of course.'

She narrowed her eyes at him. 'Are you laughing at me?'

'Yes, I think I am.'

'Hmm. Well, if you don't mind, I think I'm going to read my book now.' She made a great show of pulling it out of her reticule, before shooting him a cheeky little grin, at which Alex could do nothing other than smile.

He couldn't help noticing that she didn't turn a lot of pages while she was supposedly reading. But he shouldn't talk to her. He was supposed to be remaining aloof. It really was very boring, though, just sitting doing nothing. This was why he'd always rather ride.

'What are you reading?' he asked eventually.

'A book called *Emma* by the author of *Pride and Prejudice*.'

'Oh, yes.'

Diana had read and enjoyed that. He took a deep, slow breath to dispel the unwelcome dark thoughts that often still washed over him when he was reminded of his loss, and then raised his head to find that Emma was looking at him.

'Are you all right?' she asked.

No. Not really.

It was odd when your new wife—Emma *was* actually his wife—reminded you of your late one. Especially when you'd had no wish to marry the new wife.

'Just a…difficult memory. My late wife enjoyed those books.'

He frowned. He hardly ever mentioned Diana, and certainly not to near strangers, but, oddly, he could almost imagine talking more to Emma about Diana, telling her what an avid reader she had been, and even how much he missed her. It was as though over breakfast they'd breached the barrier between mere acquaintance and the beginnings of a friendship, which was not what he'd been planning.

'I'm so sorry; it must be very difficult. You must miss her hugely.'

Alex swallowed hard and nodded. 'Yes. Thank you.'

They both lapsed into silence, and it was a relief when they arrived at the next inn. Firstly, because the cats' straw really did need to be changed, for the comfort of their travelling companions, and secondly, because it gave Alex the opportunity to switch to horseback. It was unsettling, talking so much to Emma.

'So we'll meet in about an hour and a half for luncheon,' he confirmed with her before they set off again.

The inn at which they'd agreed to stop was a small one, which Alex hadn't used before, his favoured one being closed for refurbishment following water damage, and it didn't contain a private room. It also didn't contain any guests whom either of them knew personally, so they were able to sit down in the public room without incident.

'May I ask a few more questions about life in Somerset?' Emma said.

'Of course.'

'I presume that your household is a large one?' she asked, once the landlady had placed a steaming rabbit stew in front of them and apologised for a second time that she didn't have any more elegant fare for them, and Emma had reassured her for a second time that there was nothing that she wanted more at this moment than rabbit stew.

'Yes, I suppose so. Yes, it is.' Alex hoped Emma wasn't going to try to work the conversation round to Diana again. He took her plate and picked up a ladle. 'Are you hungry?'

Emma looked into the tureen, where there were a few lumps of something that was presumably rabbit in a thin broth with blobs of grease floating on the top.

'Just a little,' she said. 'It looks delicious, but I ate very well at breakfast.'

Alex nodded, also strongly tempted to rely on his breakfast to see him through until dinnertime.

'So, your household?' Emma prompted, staring at the three twisted pieces of meat and the oily liquid he'd placed in her bowl.

'You'll meet my—*our*—housekeeper, Mrs Drabble, when we arrive.' Alex was surprised to note that he didn't particularly mind the thought of sharing his staff with Emma. 'She's a wonderful housekeeper, but notoriously difficult. If you ask…' His words petered out as he thought that the best person for Emma to have asked about Mrs Drabble would have been Diana.

'Your late wife?' Emma supplied after a pause. 'I'm so sorry.'

'Thank you.' Alex turned his attention to his stew to hide his emotion, and unwisely took a large mouthful.

He was still chewing some time later, grateful that Emma hadn't said anything further about Diana, when she leaned forward and said in a low voice, 'Will I also meet your chef?'

'Emma. What are you implying…?' That this food was the most inedible he could remember tasting in years? There were many advantages to being a duke, and one of those was that he was nearly always served well-cooked meals made from high quality ingredients.

She twinkled at him, and he laughed around the piece of gristle he was *still* chewing.

When he'd eventually swallowed it, he pointed his knife at her plate accusingly. 'Have you had any?'

'Yes.' Emma nodded. 'You gave me a large portion, which I've very much enjoyed, but having had an equally large breakfast, I find myself unable to finish these last three morsels.'

'You're already utilising your newfound talent for invention,' Alex said. 'I'm impressed.'

'Thank you.' She beamed at him and he laughed again.

They passed the rest of the mealtime in inconsequential chatter, before setting off in good time to arrive in Somerset before dark, Emma in the chaise and Alex riding at a safe distance from her far too beguiling presence, but close enough to keep an eye on her entourage.

Once they were within striking distance of the castle, and Alex was sure that he was no longer required for Emma's protection, he rode ahead in order to arrive well before the carriages. He wanted both to welcome Emma—while this situation hadn't been his choice, it hadn't been hers either, and it was clearly the least he could do—and, more importantly, greet his sons and explain to them that there was a new member of the household.

'Papa,' hollered Freddie, the oldest, tearing across

the great hall towards him, followed by his two younger siblings.

Alex swept the three of them into a huge bear hug and just stood there, holding them tightly for a while. He hated the fact that he'd had to be away from them, and he hated the fact that he was about to foist upon them a new— God, *what*? Stepmother? Governess? Temporary house guest before she moved to the dower house?

He couldn't believe that only a few hours ago he'd been sitting merrily eating with her and laughing about rabbit stew. He should have been thinking about the impact her arrival might have on his sons. And last night… he'd only been thinking about Emma.

All wrong.

'Did you bring us presents?' asked Harry, the youngest.

Alex laughed. 'Excuse me, young man. You should be pleased to see me, not wondering if I have presents for you.'

'I am pleased to see you, but did you bring me a present?' Harry said.

'I might have a little something in one of the coaches when they arrive.' *Oh, yes, and also a new duchess.* 'Boys, there's something I need to tell you.'

'Is it a bad present?'

'No. The presents are *splendid*.'

They were. He didn't like the idea of spoiling them any more than the sons of dukes were by the very nature of their birth going to be spoilt, but on this occasion he'd taken some time the day before his and Emma's departure from London to buy a life-sized rocking horse, which he had to acknowledge was entirely a guilty purchase.

'I need to let you know that I have…'

He looked at them. Freddie and Harry favoured him, but John, his middle son, was completely Diana. Their mother. Whom he could not and did not want ever to replace. He couldn't describe Emma as their stepmother, or his wife. He just couldn't. He had to, though, because she *was* his new wife. Legally.

'I have married someone. Her name is Emma and she's very nice. I think you're going to like her. She's going to spend a lot of time with you, a bit like a governess would. So you won't need another governess. For now, anyway.'

John and Harry both nodded, but Freddie said, 'That's strange. Will she be called the Duchess of Harwell? Like Mama and Grandmama?'

'Er, yes, she will. She is…' Alex cast around in his mind for some words—good words—to make this sound better. 'It's just a name,' he said eventually. 'The Duchess of Harwell. Like there are three grooms called Mikey.' The boys had always loved that coincidence. 'Now there's another Duchess of Harwell. Because I, er, married her. So I'm the duke and she is the duchess.'

Excellent avoidance of the words *wife* and *stepmother*.

John and Harry nodded again, but Freddie shook his head. 'That does *not* make sense,' he said.

Correct. It did not.

They were interrupted by the sound of carriages outside.

'And here's the carriage with your present in it,' Alex said.

And here was Emma too. God, he was a coward.

In his defence, this was not an easy situation, and it was not one he'd wanted or planned *and* he'd only had a few days' preparation for it. However, Freddie's furrowed brow and look of suspicion were causing his stomach to twist uncomfortably.

He'd had the whole journey to prepare for this. He should have practised how he was going to tell them.

He realised as he went outside with the boys that, despite the advanced hour of the day, Mrs Drabble had what looked like the entire household lined up to welcome Emma—or to gawp at her and take an immediate dislike to her.

If he'd had any space left in his heart to pity anyone beyond his sons, he'd have been feeling very sorry for Emma right now.

Alex looked at his boys and then he looked at the chaise. He didn't want to betray or upset the boys by appearing to be too close to Emma. But he also didn't want to let them down by setting them a bad example.

He pressed his fingers to the bridge of his nose for a moment—he was beginning a thumping headache—and then moved forward to open the chaise door and hold his arm out to Emma.

'Thank you.' She leant on him only very lightly, and then almost immediately let go, and walked over to his butler, Lancing, and Mrs Drabble, at the head of the line of servants, directing a bright smile at them and holding her hand out.

As Mrs Drabble bobbed the tiniest of curtseys without meeting Emma's eye, Alex realised that he was almost holding his breath.

'I'm so pleased to meet you,' Emma said. 'I'm afraid that, although I ran my father's household, I have no experience in running a household of this exact nature and will need to rely heavily on your expertise.'

Having known Mrs Drabble for over twenty years,

Alex knew a chink in her armour when he saw one, and she definitely twitched—in a good way—before returning to her '*It'll take more than that to win me over thank you very much*' stance.

'Indeed, Your Grace,' she said, moving her eyes to Emma's face for the merest of moments before resuming her stare over her left shoulder.

'That was a long journey,' Emma said, for all the world as though Mrs Drabble wasn't being stunningly unfriendly. 'I wonder whether, after I've been introduced to the household, you would be able to show me to my chamber so that I might freshen up before dinner?'

'Of course, Your Grace.' There was that little twitch from Mrs Drabble again.

There was a scuffle from behind Alex, and he looked round to see John with Harry in a headlock.

'Boys,' he said in his deepest, sternest voice.

John let go, and Harry aimed a kick at him as he did so. Freddie was standing a couple of feet away from his brothers, glaring in the direction of Emma. Alex swivelled his eyes between them all and sighed internally. In time, Emma might perhaps be able to perform the miracle of winning Mrs Drabble over, but would she be able to win the boys over?

That would probably be a miracle too far for anyone.

'I should introduce you to my boys,' he said to Emma, who whipped straight round, almost overbalancing.

'I'm so sorry,' she said, moving towards them, her arms outstretched. 'I didn't see you there in the dusk.'

John and Harry immediately stood behind Freddie and looked at him, as though to see how he was going to react. And Freddie... Well, it was almost like looking in a mirror. Alex had glimpsed himself from time to time in lavishly mirrored ballrooms when faced with someone to whom he really didn't want to talk, and knew that he did the same straightening of the shoulders and complete lack of facial expression.

'How do you do?' Freddie barely moved a muscle as he spoke, but then held his right hand forward.

Emma diverted her outstretched arms—clearly intended for a hug—into shaking hands with Freddie. As they shook, the merest hint of distaste—a tiny curl of the lip and very slightly raised eyebrow—crossed Freddie's face, before he withdrew his hand just a fraction too quickly.

If he hadn't been torn between deep misery on behalf of his sons, mortification at Freddie's rudeness and sympathy for Emma, Alex would almost have been impressed. As it was, he felt as though he ought to try to improve the situation.

He took a step forward and put his arm around Freddie's shoulders, just as Emma said, 'I can't imagine that you want to waste any time talking to me when your father is just home after his stay in London. You must have so much to tell him. Why don't the four of you spend some time together while Mrs Drabble begins the mammoth task of introducing me to the house?'

She looked at all of them with a very bright and, to Alex's eyes, very forced smile, and then continued, 'In fact, I am very tired after such a long journey. I wonder if my dinner might be brought to me in my chamber just for this evening, after you've shown me around a little, Mrs Drabble? If that wouldn't inconvenience anyone too much?'

Freddie's shoulders relaxed very slightly, Mrs Drabble's

mouth twitched at the corners, as though she was on the brink of smiling, and Alex almost wanted to hug Emma.

He barely saw her again for the rest of the evening, other than a couple of glimpses of her rounding corners with Mrs Drabble and occasional snatches of her voice in conversation, and spent an enjoyable time immersing himself in the world of his children again, eating supper with them in their nursery.

Freddie didn't mention Emma at all, and neither did John or Harry. Instead, they filled him in on the dam they'd been building in a little river to the west of the estate, and the fish that they'd seen in the river, and the big fight that John and Harry had had, during which John had made Harry's nose bleed and after which Mrs Drabble had given Harry an extra custard tart to make him feel better.

It was the best evening Alex had had since before he'd left for London. In fact, now that he was back here, it was almost possible to believe that the entire marriage was a nightmare that had never really happened, until— weary after last night in the inn tossing and turning thinking about Emma, their situation and their kiss— he took himself off to bed and looked at the connecting door between his and Emma's suites and began to think, really hard, about the fact that she was just on the other side of the shared sitting room that that door led to. Probably in her nightgown.

God.

After another less than optimal night's sleep— hopefully he'd get used to Emma's presence in the house quickly—Alex was up early to break his fast before Emma could feasibly be expected to be awake, let alone ready to descend for her own breakfast. He'd see the boys and then take himself off on business around the estate. There was always more business in which he could involve himself, so it wouldn't be difficult for him to be so busy with his work and the boys that he would have little time to spend with Emma.

By the evening, his mood had calmed. Once they'd got used to the situation they would easily be able to achieve an amicably distant marriage; many aristocratic couples managed it. They could establish a routine similar to the one they'd had today, and then Emma would move to the dower house, and all would be well. She would essentially be just another pleasant person whom he knew and saw for short periods reasonably regularly. He was surrounded by people all the time, after all.

Before going to see the boys while their nurse began their evening routine, he sat down at his desk to write a quick note to let Emma know that he would unfortunately not be able to dine with her this evening. He'd contemplated sending her a message via Lancing, but that had seemed a little rude.

Oddly, it was difficult to find exactly the right words.

He screwed up the fourth piece of paper he'd started and dipped his quill into the ink for perhaps a tenth time. What was wrong with him? All he needed to say was that he was paying a long overdue visit to a neighbouring friend. There was nothing wrong with that. They'd agreed that they would lead separate lives. He hoped she wouldn't be lonely, though.

He looked at the stack of invitations to one side of the desk. Perhaps they should accept a few of those, sooner rather than later, and attend them as a couple, so that Emma had the opportunity to make friends in the neighbourhood.

It wouldn't be a problem attending dinners and dances together; it would be very different from spending time together at home.

Back to his message to Emma. What should he say?

Eventually he finished the two-sentence note—time spent on it approximately two minutes per uninspired word—and rang for Lancing to pass it to Emma, telling him that he was unavoidably required to go out this evening.

Lancing looked at him for maybe half a second longer than would have been usual and then said, 'As you wish, Your Grace.'

He was without question criticising Alex for not staying at home with his—no, Alex couldn't even *think* the word 'wife' without qualification—with Emma. This was the problem with devoted lifelong retainers. Obviously they were wonderful most of the time, but sometimes, when you just needed a bit of privacy and no criticism for your actions, you could do without them. Much like certain members of your extended family, really.

'Thank you,' he said firmly, and Lancing gave him another slightly too long look before leaving with the note.

The boys were eating their dinner when Alex reached the nursery. Emma was sitting at the table with them, helping Harry cut up his food, while Freddie and John both sat somewhat unnaturally far from her.

'Good evening,' she said to Alex, standing up. 'I hope you've had a good day. I will leave you to spend some time with the boys and bid you goodnight.'

'Goodnight,' said Alex, feeling guilty that he was effectively abandoning her to an evening of solitude.

Once she'd left the room, the boys, as always, had a lot to say—or shout—about what they'd been doing today. And Alex, as always, wondered if he should be making a better job of fatherhood.

Perhaps Emma would be able to instil a little more discipline into them, while not squashing their personalities. It was a difficult balance, and one that he didn't feel he'd achieved very well, because his main aim since they'd lost Diana the day Harry was born had been to make them feel loved, with no great regard for anything else.

'Emma took us for a walk,' Harry told him.

'She knows a lot about frogs,' John said. 'And she wanted to know about our studies and what we like doing best.'

Freddie didn't say anything for a while on the subject of Emma until, when pressed by John, he conceded that she wasn't the worst governess they'd ever had and did know a lot about animals.

'But she won't stay. They never do.'

Alex hadn't understood until he had his children quite how much being a parent could break your heart. Telling his children that they'd lost their mother and seeing the anguish of the older two had magnified his own grief immeasurably. Right now, he just wanted to hug all three of them. He also wanted to reassure them and tell them that Emma *would* stay, because she was different from the many governesses who'd left because they... Well, he hadn't *married* them. Difficult to put that into words, though, without discussing things best left undiscussed.

'You know you're the best three sons in the world?' he said instead.

'So can we have extra pudding?' John asked.

* * *

Two hours later, Alex, seated in front of a fire in the library at the great baronial hall of his friend and neighbour Gideon, Viscount Dearly, reflected again that it was good to see Gideon. They'd known each other since they were in leading strings, as their estates backed onto each other and their fathers had been friends, and then they'd been to both Eton and Oxford together; and they shared the same sporting interests and genuinely liked each other. It was a real relief after all the fakeness and plotting and, frankly, nastiness of a London Season, followed by his surprise marriage, to be home relaxing with his closest friend.

Until, inevitably—as he should have realised it would—the conversation turned to the rumour Gideon had heard about Alex's marriage.

'It's actually *true*?' Gideon said.

His incredulity wasn't surprising. Under normal circumstances there would have been no possibility of Alex's marrying without Gideon being involved.

Alex nodded. He didn't have any words. He couldn't say *Yes* without qualifying it with *unfortunately*, but that felt incredibly rude and something else—disloyal, perhaps, to Emma.

'Congratulations?' Gideon raised an eyebrow.

Alex didn't twitch. 'Thank you.'

'Please don't feel that you have to say anything, but if you do wish to talk, you know I'm the soul of discretion.'

That was true. Gideon was an excellent person in whom to confide. He was not only very discreet, but also very understanding and supportive. Perhaps that was why Alex had decided to come here this evening, he thought. Had he subconsciously wanted to talk about it?

'You got married only a couple of days ago and yet you're here with me this evening. Rumour has it that the young lady's aunt forced you into the marriage?'

Alex looked at Gideon's wide, so familiar, and currently very concerned face. And then he thought of Emma's face, and the way she looked when she was laughing, or smiling, or had concern in her eyes. Funny how you could quickly get to know someone quite well. And, God, what was he thinking? He really did *not* know her well. He couldn't betray her, though, even to his oldest and dearest friend.

'No, her aunt didn't force me into it,' he stated. 'I...'

Gideon said nothing; he just poured them both more brandy.

Alex really did want to talk about it, he realised, but he didn't want to say anything bad about Emma.

'Basically, I saw Sir Peter Fortescue trying to compromise her into marriage. He managed to tear the bodice of her dress and summon a huge crowd of people to witness the whole thing. She would have been ruined if she hadn't finished the evening betrothed, and I couldn't abandon her to that fate. So I asked her to marry me.'

'I see.' Gideon nodded. 'And that was that?'

'It actually wasn't. She tried very hard to refuse me. She's an extremely honourable woman. One of the few young ladies I've met who wasn't desperate to become a duchess, and she didn't want to see me trapped into a marriage she knew I didn't want. I had to convince her that I needed her as governess to the boys.'

'And do you think you could be happy with her?'

'No.' The answer shot straight out of Alex's mouth. 'I will never be happy with another woman. I don't want to be.'

'Because?' Gideon stared. 'Oh. You're scared of losing someone again.'

Alex nodded, not surprised by how perceptive he was.

'I'm sorry. That's a very difficult situation.'

Alex nodded again. And then he said, 'A game of piquet?'

Because now he'd told Gideon everything—pretty much everything anyway—and why was he thinking about their kiss at the inn again—there was nothing more to say.

Difficult situation summed it up well.

Chapter Eight

Having visited the kittens in the stables, and then eaten a lonely dinner, Emma plonked herself down in the chair at the writing table in the very lovely boudoir that Mrs Drabble had informed her was now hers. She pulled open the drawers to each side. They were filled with paper, envelopes, quills, ink, everything a duchess might need for her correspondence.

Had they belonged to the last duchess?

What had Diana been like?

Emma was never going to be able to compete with her in anyone's affections. She didn't *want* to compete with Diana, and she didn't *want* a marriage filled with grand passion, but she *did* want to be held in at least a modicum of affection by someone in her new life, or she'd have a very lonely existence.

She took out a piece of paper. Sitting by herself doing nothing wasn't going to do her any good, and writing to someone would engage her mind. Perhaps she'd write to her great friend Lily, whom she'd met at her Bath seminary and with whom she'd maintained a regular correspondence ever since, through Lily's marriage to a very respectable squire who resided in the county of

Hampshire and her subsequent speedy production of three little girls.

Perhaps she could go and visit Lily. Hampshire was nearer to Somerset than London, and a duchess could certainly travel without her duke as long as she took a maid and a footman.

A few minutes later she put her quill down. She didn't have the words now to describe to Lily her meeting with the duke and subsequent marriage to him. She *should* write to her soon, in case Lily heard about the wedding and was hurt that Emma hadn't told her herself, but it wouldn't make any difference if she left it until tomorrow.

She would do some embroidery. She'd brought with her the slippers on which she'd been working at her aunt's. Maybe she should get those out.

She hated needlework. She'd been embroidering these slippers since the beginning of the Season and had accomplished very little. There were advantages to being a duchess, and one of them had to be not doing embroidery very often.

She would read instead. Maybe she'd go and sit in the shared sitting room between her bedchamber and the duke's and read there before getting into bed. It would be too depressing to sit in her own chamber for the entire evening. She'd better allow Jenny to help her into another one of the bridal nightgowns she had, and then tell her she wouldn't have any further need of her services tonight.

Jenny insisted on brushing out Emma's hair and arranging her near-transparent nightgown just so, for Emma's imagined night-time encounter with the duke. When she'd finally finished, Emma locked her bedroom door, hauled a robe around herself and went into the sitting room, locking the door from there to the corridor outside too. She really didn't want to see Jenny again this evening. It was too wearing—and if she was honest, also depressing—parrying all her comments about what Emma and the duke would be getting up to tonight.

She tried very, very hard and eventually managed to concentrate a little on her book, to the extent that she even turned some pages and became quite interested in what might happen between the book's heroine, Emma, and her neighbour Mr Knightley. Normally, she absolutely adored this author's writing, but she wasn't in the mood for reading this evening.

She could just go to bed. She wasn't at all tired, though. Maybe she should start again from the beginning of the book and concentrate better this time.

She was still awake, curled up in the corner of the sofa, when sounds from the duke's chamber alerted her to the fact that he must have returned home and retired for the evening. She'd better go and get into bed immediately; it would be mortifying if he came in here and found her, as though she'd been waiting for him, when he so clearly didn't want to see her this evening.

Perhaps he didn't want to see her any evening. That was a lowering thought, although it was of course exactly what they'd agreed.

In her haste to jump up, she caught her foot in the end of her robe and tripped and fell onto the floor. As she picked herself up, the connecting door into Alex's chamber opened and he appeared in the doorway.

'It's you,' he said. 'I just wanted to see what all that clattering was.' He moved forward and unnecessarily held out his hand to her.

'Thank you,' Emma said, not taking the hand. She

didn't want to look as though she was desperate for physical contact with him. 'I tripped. I was reading in here.' She held her book up as though it was evidence. 'And now I'm going to bed. Goodnight.' She put her hand on the sofa to lever herself up.

Alex took a step backwards and said, 'I trust that you are unhurt?'

'Yes, indeed I am.'

Now that she was back on her feet, trying not to wince at where she'd landed heavily on the side of her bottom—she'd have a big bruise there in the morning—she could see that he was struggling to keep his eyes on her face. They kept straying down to her décolletage. She looked down and realised why. Her *robe de chambre* was open and the frothy lace at her bosom had fallen down, so that her nightgown was far too low, only very barely skimming her nipples, and, in fact, it was so close to see-through that she might almost be naked.

Her entire body suddenly felt warm, and all she could think about was the way his eyes were on her and the look of appreciation in them. The room was cooling now, and the air on her skin, together with his gaze, almost made her feel as though he was touching her.

He swallowed and she took a deep breath. Suddenly, she realised that she was standing still, half-naked, being gazed at by a man who, while he *was* her husband, had explicitly stated that he did not wish to engage in husbandly activities with her.

She whipped the robe around herself, making sure that it covered her up to her neck, and said, 'So, goodnight.'

If there was one tiny note of satisfaction in the incident, it was that Alex's voice was definitely hoarse when he replied, 'Goodnight.'

* * *

Emma struggled to get to sleep because it was very difficult not to think far too much about both her boring evening—the first of many to come, presumably—and Alex's eyes on her body in her nightgown.

She was still eating a relatively late breakfast when Lancing informed her that His Grace would be grateful if she would go and see him in his study when she was ready.

'Thank you so much for coming,' he said when she entered the room.

It suddenly felt very similar to the occasions during her teenage years on which she'd been required to go and see the head of her seminary, when she'd behaved in a manner 'unbecoming to a young lady of quality', in the head's words, for misdemeanours ranging from running in the garden to giggling with Lily during lessons to exchanging notes with the very attractive piano master.

Emma was not going to enter into a head-of-seminary-versus-naughty-schoolgirl relationship with Alex, so instead of standing in front of his desk, which was what he seemed to be expecting, she took a seat in a comfortable armchair to one side of the desk, so that he was forced to turn to look at her.

'Not at all,' she said when she was comfortable in the chair. 'Did you have something you wished to discuss with me?'

'Yes. I wanted you to know that I've asked my man of business to settle on you formally the fortune and other assets comprising your dowry, so that whatever might happen to me you will be financially independent for life.'

'Thank you.' Emma realised that she wasn't at all surprised; Alex had already demonstrated himself to be both kind and a man of his word.

'Also, I thought you might like an introduction to the estate. If you would like, I could drive you around it this afternoon.'

Emma genuinely couldn't imagine anything she'd rather do today. She needed to get to know her surroundings, and during their journey from London Alex had proved to be a very pleasant companion. He would, of course, be the ultimate expert on his own land, and she certainly didn't wish to spend any more time than she needed to alone.

'I'd like that very much,' she told him.

'Excellent.'

And then he didn't say anything else, which gave her the impression that, much as when her seminary headmistress had finished telling her off each time, she was being dismissed.

She didn't want to be dismissed. Obviously, Alex had been extremely kind to marry her, and this situation was not of his choosing, and she had gained a lot from it while he had gained nothing, but they were still going to have to find a way of dealing with each other with which they could both be reasonably happy. And Emma could not be remotely happy if Alex treated her as though he was in charge.

'Would two o'clock be acceptable for us to set off?' she asked.

'Yes, I...suppose so.' He seemed like an inherently kind and decent man who had, however, fallen into the way of being a duke and got used to things being on his terms, including what time they might set off anywhere.

She beamed at him. 'Perfect. Well, if you'll excuse me, I need to go and see the boys now.'

Emma was ready, in one of her smart new pelisses, a dark green velvet one, covering a pale grey walking dress in worked muslin, also new, in good time for their drive, and arrived in the castle's great hall at the same moment as Alex, who was wearing a greatcoat, which showed his shoulders to excellent advantage and made him look very, well, big.

'Good afternoon,' she said, trying to ignore the shiver that just seeing him seemed to have caused.

That kiss had a lot to answer for.

'Good afternoon.' He did have a very nice voice. Deep and kind of...*throbby*. In a very alluring way.

For goodness' sake. She was losing her wits.

'I have had my curricle brought round to the front,' Alex said, indicating the door ahead of them.

'Thank you,' Emma said, and they walked out of the castle together, for all the world like a normal couple.

'I'll take you out in a gig another day, so that we can go cross-country, but today I'd like to give a recently acquired pair an outing,' he said, holding his arm out for her as they descended the wide steps down from the castle's main entrance.

'How exciting to see a new pair being put through their paces,' she said, wondering if there was any chance that he'd allow her to drive for any part of this afternoon.

Alex handed her up into the curricle and gave her a blanket for her to wrap around her legs, before leaping up himself and taking the reins.

He was a good driver, Emma noted as they set off. Fully in control, but not forcing his horses in any way.

He was also a man who knew and loved his land, it seemed.

'There's been a settlement here since the turn of the twelfth century,' he told her as they skirted the nearest village after he'd—very proudly—pointed out the school he'd had built and told her that the village girls as well as boys were educated there.

'We're heading up towards some of my farming tenants now. The earliest farmers here were Normans. The land's particularly good for sheep and wheat, but we farm as great a variety of crops as we're able, for the nutrition of the soil and the health of the crops.'

He definitely had his tenants' interests very much at heart. The properties that she saw were all well-maintained, and Alex had a lot to tell her about the hospital that he'd had built over the past few years. He was also very enthusiastic about agriculture.

'I presume that there must have been a revolution in farming techniques with the invention of so much new machinery in recent years?' Emma asked.

'Yes, very much so. My own father, as a landowner, was resistant to it, as are some of the farmers. Others worry that the introduction of mechanised labour will result in the unemployment of workers. But my view is that it's very much a good thing—and indeed we've seen that workers' activities are now merely diverted to other uses relating to crop rotation and field enclosures, for example, which expands our economy rather than causing unemployment.'

Emma nodded. 'It's similar in the textiles industry. My father was a very early adopter of new machinery and practices, and we intend to continue that in the factories. We have adopted additional security in case the Luddites' attacks spread to our region.'

'*You* intend to continue that? *You* have adopted additional security measures?' Alex asked, without looking at her, concentrating on negotiating a tight bend in the lane.

'The manager of the factories—my cousin—asked me to continue advising him by correspondence. He and I worked closely together before my father's death. I would like to visit the factories and the villages where the workers are housed from time to time. My father was quite devoted to his employees and ensured the safest possible working conditions and good pay for them, and my cousin and I intend to continue similarly. I am very grateful to you for settling my father's assets on me so that I might continue to be involved in a more formal manner.'

'It sounds as though you and I might both benefit from an exchange of information in our different ventures.' Alex turned his head briefly to smile at her before refocusing on his driving.

'Yes, I think we might.'

Emma had to admit to herself that she was impressed at Alex's ready acceptance of her intention to continue her involvement in the running of the factories. A lot of men would have been horrified by her links to trade, and by the fact that she, a woman, thought she had anything of an intellectual or managerial nature to offer.

Maybe he would be open-minded enough to allow her to drive him.

'I was thinking of buying myself a carriage,' she said. 'Perhaps a phaeton.'

'Indeed?'

'Yes. I drove a lot in Lancashire and missed doing so while in London. I love driving.' She paused for a moment and then said, 'Today is a very good day for driving.'

Alex slowed his horses and looked at her. 'Are you suggesting that you'd like to drive now?'

'Yes.' Emma smiled at him.

He didn't look as though he was keen to hand the reins over. 'This pair are particularly lively,' he said. 'And strong. And this is a curricle.'

'And I am a good driver,' Emma said.

'Although unpractised in recent months. Have you driven a curricle before?'

'Yes, I drove my father's curricle, on his instruction, and while I *am* unpractised in recent months, I was so practised before—over many years—that I don't think the lack of recent practice will have made any discernible difference to my skill.'

'Really?'

'Yes.'

Alex turned to study her again for a moment. He didn't say anything for a few seconds, and they both sat and looked ahead at the horses and the lane in front of them.

Then he said, 'I'll take you to a quiet, straight length of road and you can drive. I must warn you again, though, that these horses are wonderful, and very well-matched, but require an experienced and strong driver.'

'Thank you—and thank you for the warning. However, I think we and the horses will survive my driving very happily.'

When they got to a part of the road that Alex told her he judged to be a suitably easy place to drive, he handed her the reins.

Emma found herself smiling just at the feel of them

in her hand again. She moved her fingers very lightly, to get the measure of the horses, how they would respond. They did indeed feel very lively, and very well-matched. She would of course have expected nothing less of Alex's horses.

Once she was sure that she was ready, she set off. Soon she increased their pace, conscious the entire time of Alex hovering very close to her, clearly not at all confident that she could handle his team.

'You drive well,' Alex said after a few minutes.

'Why, thank you,' Emma said, slowing very slightly for a corner. 'You will note, however, that while I do think that you drive very well, I did not comment on your driving as I did not wish to patronise you.'

'You will perhaps have noted that most men of the *ton* do drive but the majority of women do not.'

'Well, I told you that I am a good driver.'

'And you are.' He nodded. 'Very good, in fact,' he added as Emma negotiated a sharp double bend in the road at speed.

'You are a very good driver too.'

'Er, thank you. I feel I should perhaps apologise for prejudging your driving.'

'Not at all.' Emma accompanied her words with her best sarcastic eye-roll, all the while focusing on the horses and the road, and Alex laughed.

They had come to another more open, straight section of road, and Emma increased their speed again.

'I might have been a little patronising before,' said Alex, 'but now I'm not being patronising. I'd say this to anyone—man or woman—you're driving so well that I'm literally relaxing in my seat. That is not something that happens when anyone else drives me. In fact, it's very rare that anyone *would* drive me. Not even my best friends, all of whom are good drivers. And, as I say—and as you are obviously aware—these horses require an experienced handler. I care very much about my horses, and I would not like anyone to job their mouths. Before you drove, I obviously had no idea whether or not you were any good, other than your clear belief that you were.'

Emma laughed. 'I'll take that as a compliment. Thank you for trusting me enough to allow me to drive them in the first place.'

'If I'm honest, I was prepared to take the reins if necessary.'

'Oh, really? I didn't notice you hovering and breathing down my neck at *all*.'

Alex laughed again, Emma gave him a sideways smile, and then he said nothing about re-taking the reins himself, and she drove all the way back.

Jim, the head groom, came running out as they came into sight. 'Are you injured, Your Grace?' he shouted.

'I'm very well, thank you, Jim,' Alex called. 'He's never seen anyone drive me before,' he told Emma, 'so he naturally assumed that a disaster had befallen me.'

'It seems I must thank you again.'

'Not at all. I was merely trying to compliment you again without patronising you. And, yes, I do think you should buy your own carriage. And horses. Should you like to arrange the purchases yourself, or would you like to discuss them with me? Or you will be very welcome to drive any from our stables here.'

'That's very kind.' Emma hadn't felt this contented for months. 'I believe that I should draw on your local expertise.'

'At your service.' Alex gave a mini salute and she laughed. 'Do you also ride?' he asked.

'I do ride, but only very averagely,' Emma said, rising with reluctance to alight from the curricle.

'You know, I begin to think that little about you is average.' Alex held his arm out for her and she took it lightly.

'I'm going to take that as another compliment,' Emma said.

'It is.' Alex smiled at her and she felt even more contented than she'd felt a couple of minutes ago, if that were possible. 'Now, I hope you don't mind, but I have some more papers to look through before I go to see the boys. I thought I might eat with them in the nursery this evening.'

Oh. A very clear message that for the second evening running he wasn't going to eat with Emma.

And just like that, her mood deflated.

She had her pride, though. 'Perfect,' she said. 'I'm very tired and thought I might take my supper in my chamber again.'

'Ideal. I will see you tomorrow, then.'

'Indeed.'

And so, after what had felt like a wonderful afternoon, she walked inside to begin another miserable evening.

Chapter Nine

Alex felt extremely guilty watching Emma go. He shouldn't abandon her like this.

On impulse, he called out to her. 'Emma. Why don't you join the boys and me in the nursery for supper? If you like?'

She stopped, and even from a distance he could see that her shoulders grew a little rigid, and then she turned round to face him.

He moved closer to her so that he'd be able to hear her response, as she said, 'Thank you, but I do not wish to intrude on your time with your boys.'

Alex opened his mouth to tell her that it wouldn't be an intrusion. Except that wasn't true and he couldn't say the words because he was obviously going to put the boys' happiness above Emma's, and he was fairly sure that they benefited from time alone with their only parent.

He could see her features settling into what looked to him to be a careful mask, to hide any emotion she might be feeling. He recognised it because he often wore such a mask himself. And he realised that he couldn't do this to her. On the occasions he'd seen her with others she'd

seemed very friendly. He couldn't consign her to loneliness every single evening.

When he'd asked her if she'd like to go for the drive
today it had been because he'd felt—had known—that
he had a responsibility to ensure her happiness as far
as he could, without engaging too closely with her. The
drive had been perfectly enjoyable; it wouldn't be a terrible hardship to eat dinner with her two or three times
a week.

'I realise that I am not yet particularly hungry,' he
said. 'I don't think I will eat with the boys, therefore, but
will instead take dinner in the dining room later on, after
I've spent some time with them in the nursery. Would
you care to join me?'

Emma was standing very still, clearly reflecting. After
a few seconds, she said, 'I'd enjoy that, thank you.'

'Excellent. I'll see you then.'

She came down for dinner wearing a pale pink dress
that he didn't think he'd seen before, and against which
her dark hair and light brown skin looked very beautiful.

'I believe that Martin—I presume you've been introduced to our chef—has produced some particularly
delicious dishes for this evening,' he said.

It felt important to keep the conversation on mundane matters, because he'd been enjoying her company
far too much and had struggled greatly to banish from
his mind the image of how she'd looked last night in
her nightgown. He needed to regain some self-control.

'I look forward to tasting them.'

As they finished bowls of velvety chestnut soup, Emma
said, 'The boys are wonderful, a credit to you.'

'Thank you.' Alex smiled at her and then, almost to his own surprise, added, 'Much credit must go to their mother, for her influence in the early years with the older two.'

Where had that come from? He didn't usually choose to mention Diana.

Emma nodded. 'Tell me about her? If you'd like to?'

Alex knew that he didn't have to reply—knew that although she would be interested in his answer she would understand if he chose not to say anything—but, actually, found that he did wish to tell her.

'She loved our children. She loved dancing. She loved to laugh. She loved playing backgammon. She hated apples, of all things. And she was beautiful. And funny.' He felt a little choke in his throat and clenched his jaw.

'She sounds wonderful. I'm so sorry for your loss.'

'Thank you.'

Oddly, Alex felt as though some of the emotion washing over him was due to the sincerity in Emma's regard, not just his bereavement.

He really should try not to become too close to her.

He did his best to keep the conversation on food, a potted history of his family and questions about Lancashire for the remainder of the meal, and, other than a couple of occasions on which Emma caused him to laugh out loud, it wasn't particularly different from making mild conversation with a pleasant acquaintance. He could certainly do this, remain emotionally and physically aloof from her while being polite and not ignoring her. He hoped that they could rub along very happily together like this.

After Emma rose from the dinner table, Alex had half a glass of port in boring isolation, and then went to join her in the drawing room, just to bid her goodnight out of politeness.

She was sitting next to the fire, her dark head bent over some embroidery. It was a slightly incongruous picture, in that it was difficult to imagine someone as energetic and vibrant as he'd learnt that Emma was spending hours with a needle.

'What are you making?' he asked politely.

'Gentleman's slippers,' she said, holding up the one she was working on. 'They were initially intended as a gift for my uncle, but since they aren't going to be worthy of parcelling up and sending by post I think they might have to be for you.'

'That is very kind,' Alex said, stunned.

So far in their acquaintance she'd demonstrated herself to be very competent at a wide range of things, everything he'd seen her do, in fact. Until now. She was *not* a gifted embroideress.

'They are…' Good God. Would he have to *wear* them? 'They are, sadly, relatively small.' Thank heavens. 'Sadly, I have very large feet.'

'Oh, don't worry.' Emma bestowed a sunny smile upon him. 'I'm sure that with my needle skills I'll be able very easily to alter them to fit you. I could perhaps sew an extra piece on the end.'

She *had* to be joking. She looked deadly serious, though.

'Thank you,' he said while she continued to sew, very slowly and, to Alex's eye, very unevenly.

'Perhaps a brocade strip,' she said, eyeing his feet.

'Wonderful.' Alex shifted slightly in his seat. How was it possible that, while sitting opposite a woman mangling a pair of slippers that she was threatening to make him wear, all he could think about was the fact that she was looking at his feet, and how she might look at the rest of him? Really, how was that possible?

She raised her eyes to his and smiled at him. 'You're genuinely scared, aren't you?'

'I'm not scared,' he said.

She leaned towards him and he leaned forward too, in a reflex action.

'I'm not going to make you wear them,' she said.

'I knew that,' he told her.

Emma laughed, a lot, and then Alex laughed a lot too.

'I might have been worried for a minute,' he admitted eventually, which made her smile in a very victorious manner, and that made Alex smile too.

And now neither of them was speaking, nor smiling. They were just looking at each other. Alex could see the rise and fall of Emma's chest, a tiny pulse beating at the base of her delicate neck. She moistened her lips, the lips that he'd kissed two nights ago in the inn.

No.

His mind was going to places it really shouldn't, and if he wasn't careful he might act on his thoughts.

'I think that, if you don't mind,' he said, 'I will retire now.'

It should be up to Emma to decide first to retire, but two people who'd just become legally married shouldn't have to stand entirely on ceremony with each other.

'Indeed,' she said immediately, 'I too am tired.'

They didn't speak at all as they went upstairs together. When they reached the corridor outside their rooms, Alex indicated their shared sitting room with a small nod of his head, and Emma nodded in response.

He opened the door and held it so that she could pass

inside the room, before closing it behind them. Emma had come to a halt a few feet away from the door and was standing looking at him, her hands clasped in front of her, her chest rising and falling more rapidly than usual.

Alex wanted to go straight to bed. He didn't want to be seduced into doing something ill-advised, or even just to be thinking ill-advised thoughts, like how much, all of a sudden, he wanted to kiss her plump lips, pull her against him, make her moan with desire for him, begin to sate his own physical desire for her.

He didn't want to think about that at all.

Emma bit her lip, and then lifted a hand and pushed back a ringlet that had escaped the ribbon holding back the rest of her curls. The ringlet fell forward again. As though propelled by an unseen force, Alex stepped towards her and, very gently, tucked it back into the ribbon, his hand brushing the softness of her cheek as he did so.

He wasn't gentle enough; apparently the hairstyle was quite fragile. His fingers had dislodged the ribbon and now her hair tumbled around her shoulders.

And it was as though his fingers had a mind of their own. He *should* have taken a step backwards and bidden Emma goodnight, but instead he found himself running his hands through her curls, then tugging her hair very gently and cupping the back of her head. And then, as though some invisible cord was pulling him, he was reaching down to brush her lips with his.

Emma sighed against his lips, and the small sound was the undoing of him. He kissed her again, lightly, and then deepened the kiss, parting her lips with his tongue. Emma sighed again, then ran her hands up his chest and around his neck. She was soft, pliant, warm, eager, *perfect*, against him.

He wanted more of her, he wanted to lift her, carry her into his room, place her on his bed…

The marital bed.

He didn't want a real marriage with her. What if she got pregnant? Died in childbirth as Diana had? He didn't want to do that to another woman. And, for himself, he didn't want to grieve again.

As images of the aftermath of Diana's death crowded into his mind, he let go of Emma.

He heard her say, 'Oh,' and dragged himself back to the present.

'I…' He looked at her, beautiful, with her tumbled hair and swollen lips and still half-closed eyes. He wanted to say something nice to her, not hurt her feelings in any way. But he didn't have the right words.

She opened her eyes slowly and smiled uncertainly at him. He found himself shaking his head very slightly. Her smile dropped and she pressed her lips together. She looked…shocked. And—from the way she was now wrapping her arms around herself—maybe as though she had realised that he was shutting her out and was trying to protect herself.

God. He really didn't want to hurt her. But, however much he wanted to say something, he just couldn't talk now.

'I'm sorry. Goodnight.' He took the few steps necessary to enter his chamber and closed the door firmly behind himself without looking back.

That should not happen again.

He made sure that he breakfasted early in the morning, having noticed that Emma was not a particularly early riser. There was no point in laying himself open to disturbing thoughts—any kind of temptation—when he didn't have to. Sharing his meal with a newspaper rather than Emma was a much better way of spending his time.

He went up to the nursery after he'd finished eating. A few minutes after he'd sat down with the boys, Emma came into the room.

'Good morning,' she said.

All three of the boys' heads shot round and they all chorused, 'Good morning,' very over-eagerly.

Alex frowned.

'I hope that none of you are scared of spiders,' Emma addressed the boys.

Harry immediately giggled, and Freddie kicked him under the table. Alex opened his mouth to reprimand him, but Emma was still talking.

'If so, you'd better be very careful because there were a lot in my bedchamber last night.'

Harry giggled again.

Alex glared at him The boys were clearly involved in this, but maybe he should speak to them when Emma wasn't there.

'I'm so sorry,' he said. 'I'll call Mrs Drabble immediately.'

'There's no need,' Emma told him. 'I got rid of them all myself out of the window. Fortunately, I'm not at all scared by spiders. Indeed, I like them, and count myself quite an expert on the different varieties we have in England.' She sat down next to John and put a monogrammed handkerchief down on the table in front of him. 'I believe that this is yours.'

John's eyes widened and he said, 'Oh.'

'I must tell you,' Emma said, 'that it would be polite to thank me for the safe return of your property. Something else I must tell you is that I now have a spy watching my door. One further thing: if any other small creatures should find their way into my chamber, assisted by anyone, I might lose my temper. And I am *fearsome* when I'm angry.'

She smiled sunnily at the boys, and as one they all shrank backwards.

Alex nodded, impressed. *Masterful*, he mouthed at her. She turned her still-sunny smile on him and he couldn't help laughing.

'I'm going to leave you all to it now,' he said, 'and I shall look forward to hearing whether or not any of you make Emma angry.'

As he closed the nursery door, he decided that he would have a polite dinner with Emma this evening, but other than that would not see her today.

Later, as he was eating a quick luncheon in the library, Lancing brought him a note from his aunt—his late father's older sister—informing him that she would be visiting that afternoon as she was desirous of meeting the new duchess, of whose existence, she wrote, she would have liked to have been notified by Alex.

Alex in turn sent word to Emma, and then, reckoning that he had two clear hours, took himself off to the stables to discuss possible horse purchases for Emma with Jim.

Almost exactly two hours later, Alex and Emma were waiting together in the grand saloon next to the castle's great hall when they heard the unmistakable noise and bustle of an arrival.

Lancing flung open the doors and announced, 'The Countess of Denby.'

Alex watched Emma as his aunt walked slowly into the room, wanting to see her reaction. His aunt was an elderly woman and, having embraced and apparently loved the elaborate fashion of the later eighteenth century, had made no concession to the less ostentatious modes of dress favoured by women for the past thirty years.

It wasn't every day that you saw a lady dressed for a country afternoon call in the enormous panniered skirts and huge wigs that had characterised pre-French Revolution fashion, but Emma barely twitched at the spectacle before her and walked forward and took his aunt's outstretched hands.

Alex was impressed; most people reacted more overtly to his aunt on first meeting her.

'Good afternoon, young lady.' His aunt had no regard for convention, and in Alex's experience it was highly unlikely that she would treat Emma as anything other than a much younger lady to whom she would offer a great deal of probably unwanted and possibly incorrect advice.

'Good afternoon.' Emma smiled at her.

'I need tea.' Alex's aunt strode forward, her immense skirts rustling around her, and arranged herself on a sofa in the middle of the room. 'Sit near to me, girl. Alexander, where's that butler of yours? Tea!'

'Of course, my lady.' Lancing had materialised out of nowhere.

Alex was sure that his household, led by Lancing, would magic up all manner of sandwiches and cakes very quickly.

'So what's this I hear about you compromising my nephew into marriage?' his aunt asked Emma, who frowned only a very tiny bit before producing what might almost have passed for a serene smile.

'It's nonsense,' Alex said. 'Emma and I met in Hyde Park and fell almost immediately in love, but kept our relationship secret for a while.'

'Sounds like a complete faradiddle to me,' his aunt boomed, adjusting her ear trumpet. 'But so does the compromise story.' She poked Emma with the black fan she'd been holding. 'I like the look of you. I don't see you behaving badly.'

'Thank you,' Emma said.

'What?' Alex's aunt turned the ear trumpet again.

'I said thank you,' Emma said loudly.

'You have a very quiet voice. Now, tell me about your family. I knew your mother. Bad business when she ran off with your father.'

Emma replied slowly, and loudly, repeating herself when asked, answering an extraordinary number of questions, smiling throughout, even in the face of some quite remarkable incivility.

'So your grandmother was Indian? Your beauty is very unusual. Quite out of the common way. I like it, though.' Alex's aunt smiled at Emma, as though bestowing upon her an enormous favour rather than enormous rudeness.

Emma said, 'I'm honoured,' sounding as though she was trying not to laugh, which was a relief, because a lot of people would just have been offended.

Alex stood up, though. Enough was enough.

'Would you care to take a turn about the gardens, Aunt? And see the boys? Your great-nephews would be delighted to see you.'

'How old are they now?' his aunt asked, not moving from her sofa.

'Nine, seven and four.'

'No,' she said. 'Too young. I don't like young children. Perhaps the oldest. Frederick. Perhaps not, though. I've been feeling rather bilious recently.'

'The garden, then?' Alex persisted.

'No. Too cold. I have my own gardens, you know. One garden is much like another. Sit down, young man.'

'Of course,' Alex said.

He glanced at Emma out of the corner of his eye. She was definitely struggling not to laugh now, which made him smile. A good thing, he realised, because normally an hour into a visit from his aunt he'd be feeling irritated, at best.

'I'm tired,' his aunt said abruptly. 'I think I'll have to spend the night here with you.'

Alex's eyes swivelled straight to Emma's. She was looking as horrified as he felt. Neither of them spoke for a moment, and then Emma, projecting her voice magnificently, said, 'Oh, how wonderful. You'll be able to see the boys properly. We always eat dinner with them in the evenings.'

'They should be in the nursery.'

'I'm afraid that Alex is a very modern parent, and I, of course, follow his…lead. We cannot consign them to the nursery.'

'Help me up,' Alex's aunt said to him. 'I must leave before it gets dark.'

'Masterful again,' Alex whispered to Emma over her head.

'Masterful what?' his aunt asked.

Alex stared at her. Was she in fact not really deaf? Or had he just been unlucky?

'It's been so wonderful to meet you,' Emma said, diverting his aunt's attention in—yes—a masterful manner.

She offered her arm to the older woman, and they passed out of the room together.

'I can only apologise,' Alex said to a laughing Emma, when his aunt's eighteenth-century landau had passed out of sight.

'Not at all. I'd like to think that if I become old and infirm I shall take advantage of it in exactly the same way. I'm sure she has a kind heart.'

'I think it might be your own kind heart imagining the same in her.' Alex smiled at Emma and tried to imagine her old, infirm and rude. She'd still be beautiful if she became old and, please Lord, she would indeed attain old age, unlike Diana. God. He forced his thoughts away from Diana's early death and tried to recapture his previous train of thought. Infirm, that was it. Well, that wasn't a particularly pleasant thought either: he'd hate to think of Emma becoming infirm. He turned his mind to rudeness: it was impossible to imagine Emma becoming rude.

'Perhaps we should indeed both eat with the boys this evening?' Emma suggested. 'So that we didn't take their names in vain.'

Alex nodded, relieved to have his thoughts diverted from hoping that nothing would befall Emma and that she would indeed become an old woman in due course. 'I think you're right.'

He began to regret agreeing to her suggestion within minutes of the meal starting. John and Harry seemed to have thawed dramatically towards Emma, but Freddie,

well, Freddie was behaving as though he'd inherited his
social skills from his great-aunt.

'I don't want to sit next to Emma,' he began.

'I'm very happy to sit here.' Emma sat down between
John and Harry.

'Did you enjoy your walk with Nurse this afternoon?'
Emma asked.

'Better than walking with you,' Freddie muttered.

Alex opened his mouth to tell him to apologise immediately, but Emma hurriedly began to talk to John and
Harry about frogs and tadpoles. She lifted her eyebrows
and indicated Freddie with her eyes, all the while smiling
and continuing to talk to the other two, and eventually
Alex deduced that she thought he should talk to Freddie.

When they'd finished eating, Emma pushed her chair
backwards and said, 'I'm quite exhausted by my busy
day today. I'm going to retire to bed now.'

Perfect. If they retired to their chambers at different
times, there should be no danger that Alex would succumb to temptation and kiss her again.

'I'll see you in the morning, boys. Alex, I wonder if
I could speak to you for a moment outside before you
read together?'

'Of course.' Alex stood up and followed her outside.
Perhaps she was going to tell him that she couldn't bear
to look after the boys any more. He really hoped that
wasn't it. 'I'm so sorry about Freddie's rudeness. I'm
going to have a very firm word with him now.'

'Without wishing to dictate to you about your children, I'd like to say that I really don't think you should
tell him off,' Emma said. 'I think something's happened.
I think you ought to ask him what's wrong. When he's
on his own.'

Not at all what he'd been expecting her to say. Alex reflected for a moment; maybe she was right.

Half an hour later, as John and Harry were engrossed in a game of sticks, Freddie suddenly blurted out, before Alex had had the opportunity to ask him anything, 'So, are we going to get another baby in our family?'

Well. It seemed as though Emma was right; Freddie didn't sound happy.

'No,' Alex said cautiously. 'Did someone tell you that we would?'

'Mikey said.'

Damn. If Freddie was going to visit the stables, why couldn't the grooms just have done their usual swearing and letting Freddie throw fallen orchard apples and ruin the head gardener's prized ornamental lawn?

'No. We are not,' he said firmly.

'But Mikey said when people get married, like you and Emma, they usually have babies.'

Alex frowned, realising all of a sudden just how carefully he was going to have to tread in setting an example for his children. He wanted them to experience strong, loving marriages as adults, the kind he'd had with Diana and his parents had had. So it wouldn't be good if they witnessed him and Emma in a soulless marriage. But he couldn't allow himself to develop feelings for her, both for his own sake, in case something happened to her, and for the boys, because he couldn't have them thinking that their mother had been replaced.

Should Emma perhaps move to the dower house sooner rather than later so that any gossip could happen and be overcome? And so that the boys would understand that this was a different type of marriage from the one he'd had with Diana? Or should he work hard to get over the ridiculous physical attraction he knew he felt towards Emma? Get used to the fact that they had adjacent bedchambers and be friends with her while she remained in the house?

Whichever, they should begin to attend social events together, so that he could signal to people that, whatever their living arrangements might eventually be, he expected her to be treated as his duchess socially, and so that she could make some friends with whom she could remain friendly in the event that she did move to the dower house.

He had an idea. They should go to a ball, or a dance, and he would dance with her. That would serve a dual purpose. It would send a strong signal—the entire neighbourhood was aware that he wasn't a keen dancer, and indeed had almost never danced with any woman other than Diana—and Emma would meet some of the other ladies who lived locally.

In the meantime, he needed to address this issue, and now John and Harry were listening too.

'Not everyone has babies,' he told the boys. 'Instead of having babies, Emma and I will…dance.'

What? What was he talking about? And why had he just imagined holding her in his arms on a dance floor and liked what he'd imagined?

'Emma likes dancing,' John said.

'How do you know?' Alex asked, surprised.

'She told us in the apple orchard yesterday. And then we danced, and we laughed and laughed,' John said.

'I like Emma,' Harry said.

Damn, this was complicated.

The next day, thinking while he breakfasted alone that he would ask Emma over dinner that evening if she'd like to go with him to some local dinners and dances, Alex realised that they were already falling into a pattern of not really seeing each other during the day, but having dinner together in the evening. If he was honest, the companionship was pleasant. If he could just get over his physical attraction to her—which he was sure he would in time—they could rub along more than happily, from his side, anyway.

'I'd love to,' Emma said, when he broached the subject that evening as they both tasted a particularly good turbot and gooseberry dish.

'Excellent. We have an invitation to a dinner dance tomorrow evening, with some neighbours who live about ten miles away. I think several amongst my acquaintance will be there and think you might enjoy it.'

'That sounds wonderful.'

Chapter Ten

'The Duke and Duchess of Harwell,' said a footman, flinging open double doors as though he was auditioning for a role in the royal household rather than announcing guests at a country squire's evening dance.

Emma smoothed the skirts of her gauze overdress for the third time since they'd left their carriage.

'You look immaculate,' Alex told her, and put his arm out for her to take. 'Beautiful, in fact. Nothing to worry about.'

Emma tried not to grimace at him. She'd never felt like this in London, but in London she hadn't really cared. Now, though, she felt as though this mattered, since she was likely to be seeing these people regularly, and she'd like to have some local friends.

They took a step forward together, and Alex said a resigned, 'And *smile*,' into her ear, while doing a big, obviously fake, smile of his own, which *did* make her smile as they entered the drawing room, interested eyes watching them from all angles.

He stayed with her and introduced her to almost everyone in the room, for all the world like an adoring new husband. Quite a contrast to how he was at home. There, while he was unfailingly polite—and indeed thoughtful in a number of his suggestions to make her life more comfortable, including taking dinner with her, showing her around the estate in his curricle and accepting the invitation to this dance to enable her to meet their neighbours—he clearly didn't want to spend a lot of time with her.

Which, of course, she was completely happy with. Neither of them had wished to marry the other, and they'd been clear that their marriage would be a bargain that did not include close friendship or anything more intimate. And Alex's behaviour since the second of their two kisses had made it very obvious that he didn't wish anything intimate to happen between them again.

If she was honest, Emma was still struggling not to be upset—deeply hurt, in fact—that Alex clearly regretted their quite earth-shattering second kiss, and was finding it difficult not to be spine-tinglingly aware of him whenever he was anywhere near her. But she must not complain, not even just internally. Alex had been completely open with her from the beginning and this was the bargain they'd made.

'And this is my oldest friend, Gideon,' Alex said, as a large man with red hair and a smile almost as wide as his very broad shoulders shook Alex's hand vigorously.

'Delighted to meet you.' Gideon bowed and then said, 'May I have the pleasure of a dance with you? Only so that I can tell you scurrilous stories about Alex, of course.'

Emma laughed, immediately liking him. 'I'd be delighted.'

'If we're allowed to dance with the duchess, I'd like

the honour of staking my claim now,' another man said, and within a minute or two they were surrounded by several men, all wishing to stake dancing claims.

To Emma's surprise, Alex didn't relinquish her hand, but remained at her side throughout the clamour that ensued, and then raised his voice just slightly, so that the other men fell silent, and said, 'My wife isn't available for the first dance; that pleasure is mine.'

Emma nearly squeaked out loud at the thought of dancing with Alex. Firstly, it was deeply unfashionable for a married couple to dance, even at a private party like this, so it would be a strong signal to the assembled guests that Alex was a devoted husband. And secondly, if she was honest, she'd already imagined dancing with him last night, when she'd been struggling again to get to sleep, thinking about their kisses and him in his bed two doors away from her. But she hadn't expected *actually* to dance with him.

She realised now that when she'd imagined dancing with him she hadn't done him justice. Resplendent in simply cut, sombre-hued and yet glorious evening wear, he eclipsed every other man here tonight. He could be the worst dancer in London, and yet it must feel like an honour to be on his arm, because he *looked* like the best dancer a man could be.

'If the duke and duchess are to dance together, then the first dance must be a waltz,' announced Lady Felicity, the squire's wife. 'Followed by a series of quadrilles and a *danse espagnole*. You will find us bold in this county, Your Grace.'

'Indeed,' said Emma, torn between a giggle exacerbated by the loud grumbles from several disgruntled misses who would now not be able to join the first dance of the evening, as they didn't yet have permission to waltz, and thinking, *Oh, my goodness, I'm going to waltz with Alex.*

The string ensemble at the end of the room struck up and all the women who were dancing stepped into their partners' holds.

Emma had waltzed many times before—her aunt had ensured that she got the permission of the Almack's hostesses early in the Season—and her emotions had ranged from annoyance, or even disgust that she had to dance with a particularly unpalatable partner, through mild irritation, or pity that a perfectly pleasant man was an incompetent dancer, to enjoyment of a partner who had the winning combination of good conversation and competent dancing skills.

She had never once felt any kind of a stomach-flutter or *tingle*. Now, though... Now it was as though all her senses were coming alive for the first time.

As Alex held her right hand lightly in his left, with his other hand skimming the small of her back, it was as though every nerve in her body was attuned to where his body was and where they might touch as the dance progressed. She could smell his deeply masculine scent, sense the rise and fall of his chest almost brushing her own chest, feel the warmth and hardness of his body so close to hers... On the face of it, he was far too tall for her, but somehow it felt—from her perspective, anyway—as though they were the perfect match physically.

They were completely silent as they moved, but the silence wasn't awkward; it was as though their movements were doing the talking. The way they were dancing felt both deliberate and yet entirely natural, as though they couldn't help themselves giving in to the music.

It was wonderful.

Emma loved it when they moved slowly together in the slow parts of the dance, and she loved it when they danced in perfect time with each other in the faster parts.

She only realised the music had stopped because of the sudden movement and chatter around her of others stopping their dance and then leaving or joining the dance floor.

She looked up at Alex. He was still holding her hand and her waist, and was gazing down at her with partly closed, glazed eyes.

He began a slow smile, which Emma felt right to her centre, and suddenly she was feeling hot and as though her insides were liquid and as though she could barely stay standing without the support of Alex's arms.

'I…' he began. And then suddenly Gideon was next to them, and Alex stopped talking. Emma *really* wanted to know what he'd been about to say. Probably nothing… but maybe something.

'And the next dance is mine, I believe,' said Gideon with another of the broad smiles Emma was already beginning to expect from him on the strength of less than one hour's acquaintance.

'Um.' Alex pulled his eyes from Emma's and turned them to Gideon with what looked like a big effort. After a long moment, he said, 'Of course.'

'Thank you for the dance,' Emma said, and then thought how utterly ridiculous that sounded, given that he was her husband. Legally, anyway.

'I enjoyed it,' Alex said, very simply, and Emma's cheeks warmed as Gideon led her away.

* * *

Gideon was a very good conversationalist, with all sorts of harmless gossip and useful, often funny information to impart. He was a perfectly good dancer into the bargain, and yet Emma found herself a little distracted throughout their quadrille.

At one point, during another dance, she realised that she was looking away from her temporary partner, Sir Robert—the squire, and their host for the evening—in an attempt to see where Alex was.

She snapped her head back and beamed at the squire, and said, 'Oh, *indeed*,' in response to his comment on the beauty of an apple orchard in full bloom.

She did love dancing, and she did enjoy the fourth and fifth dances, with the squire's younger son and the single and very charming Viscount Bagley respectively, but it was as though they were just rehearsals for the sixth dance, which—almost scandalously, really, given that they were a married couple—she'd agreed would be with Alex.

And when he made his way to her side the second the dance finished, she felt her whole body lightening and a big beam beginning on her face. Alex was smiling too, seemingly oblivious to the people around them. If she hadn't known better, she'd have thought he was genuinely very pleased to see her. He was clearly a very good actor.

Someone was clearing his throat next to Emma and she gave a start, then realised to her horror that it was her last partner, Viscount Bagley. This was awful. She was behaving like an infatuated debutante, ignoring everyone around her other than the subject of her dreams. What was *wrong* with her this evening? It had to be the shock of their very sudden marriage catching up with her.

The one saving grace was that the viscount was so charming, good-looking and reputedly rich that he must be fawned over by the majority of his dance partners, and his feelings would surely be robust enough to cope with Emma's distraction.

'Thank you,' she said to the viscount, who was now bowing deeply over her hand.

'I very much enjoyed our dance,' he said, still holding on to her hand.

Alex cleared *his* throat, and Emma and the viscount both looked up. Alex's face held a remarkably forbidding expression all of a sudden, and the viscount dropped Emma's hand very quickly. Then, quite ridiculously, Alex immediately took it.

Emma really wanted to tell him that he was over-acting, looking not so much like a fondly loving husband as a jealously obsessive one. If she was honest, though, she was thoroughly enjoying the over-acting. In fact, she was thoroughly enjoying the entire evening.

Still holding her hand, Alex moved with Emma towards the middle of the dance floor to join the next quadrille set.

'Your husband is clearly besotted,' their hostess trilled, dragging Gideon past them. 'I can't remember the last time he danced. Probably not since the last time he danced with Diana.'

She bestowed a huge smile upon the two of them and Emma decided that she had very large teeth and she didn't like her. Really, who would bring up someone's late wife at a moment like this?

'Ignore her,' said Gideon to Emma, just before the

squire's wife dragged him off. 'She had high aspirations for her sister to marry Alex. It's jealousy.'

It might be jealousy, but it wasn't particularly nice to know that, in addition to everything else he'd been forced to do on her behalf, Alex was now being forced to dance when he clearly didn't want to.

She looked up at him and said in a low voice, 'Please don't feel that you have to dance with me.'

'I enjoyed our first dance and I'm looking forward to this one.'

'Really?'

'Really.' He spoke into her ear, so that only Emma could hear him. 'Lady Felicity said that entirely to make you feel uncomfortable. It seems a lot of people are a little jealous of a new duchess. I've been enjoying dancing with you. But even if I didn't, it wouldn't hurt me, would it? So, you shouldn't feel guilty. And I did enjoy it. And apparently I'm talking in circles.'

He smiled at her, and she laughed and said, 'Thank you. And it is true. Dancing twice in an evening is not the biggest hardship for even the most hardened of anti-dancers.'

Certainly it was nothing in comparison to getting married when you didn't want to.

A couple of seconds later, she was whisked into the start of a very energetic country dance. And, *oh*, the gorgeous anticipation of knowing, as she was twirled around by a succession of partners, that she would end up holding Alex's hand again. They smiled, they laughed, they danced in perfect time together, and for the duration of the dance it was bliss.

'I really did enjoy that.' Alex was still laughing slightly, as they all had been, at the antics of a couple of the other men, which had annoyed Lady Felicity considerably, going by her pursed lips and wagging finger.

'A final quadrille set,' announced Lady Felicity, 'and then we go next door for supper. I've planned the night along London lines, Your Grace—' she nodded at Emma '—so that you will feel at home.'

'Thank you so much,' said Emma.

'I'll be back to escort you.' Alex smiled at her as she accepted the arm of her next partner, a very pleasant-seeming man named Mr Scott, and moved away from her to join the squire and another man in the corner of the room.

Emma spent the entirety of the next dance wondering whether Alex would stay with her throughout supper and feeling annoyed that she couldn't stop thinking about him.

When the dance ended, Alex was nowhere to be seen.

'Allow me to escort you?' Mr Scott asked.

'I…' Emma couldn't believe how disappointed she felt. She should really stop this. She and Alex had a non-romantic arrangement and this evening he was doing her a huge favour and she should remember that. 'Thank you.'

'Emma. Scott.' Suddenly, Alex was bowing in front of them, and equally suddenly Emma felt as though the evening had brightened. This truly was ridiculous. She almost wanted *not* to go with Alex, just because she shouldn't be feeling like this. Also, though, she really wanted to go with him.

He held his arm out to her and she took it, and within a short space of time they were seated at a small table in the room next door with two other couples.

'I'm going to perform the introductions again,' Alex

said. 'You met so many people earlier that I'm sure you won't have retained all their names.'

'I'm Letitia,' said the lady nearest to Emma. 'I'm Gideon's sister.'

Emma could see the resemblance—the same hair colour and the same ready smile—and liked her as much and as quickly as she'd taken a liking to Gideon.

'And I'm Maria.' The other lady leaned round her husband and grinned at Emma.

'Or Lady Merrick. As you can see, she's a complete hoyden,' Letitia said, smiling at her friend. 'Well, we both are, but it's all right because we're both respectably married. Like you. So, tell me, have you fallen foul of Lady Felicity yet? She was *desperate* to get her sister married off to the duke, which was never going to happen, because she's one of the rudest people anyone's ever met, and Alex is *not* rude, although he does live up to his Ice Duke name when he's annoyed.'

'I'm not rude? Did I hear you say that?' Alex was grinning at all three of them, looking about as far from icy as the sun.

Supper time flew by, and by the end of it Emma genuinely felt as though she had new friends in Letitia and Maria. Which, of course, she realised, had been Alex's design in escorting her into supper and ensuring that they sat in that group. Again, she couldn't fault his kindness.

'Don't dance every dance if you haven't already committed to doing so,' Letitia said to her as Lady Felicity urged them to return to the other room to continue with the dancing. 'Sit at the side with us and have a good gossip. It's one of the advantages of being sensible married women.'

'Sensible!' scoffed her husband, smiling at her good-naturedly.

Never mind the music, Emma wanted to dance at the thought that she had these lovely new friends.

Letitia and Maria were as good as their word in terms of gossiping by the side of the dance floor, and within fifteen minutes Emma had heard excellent stories about almost everyone in the room.

She was enjoying herself so much that when Alex approached her to ask her to dance Lady Felicity's much-trumpeted *danse espagnole* with him, she was almost annoyed. Not entirely, though: the idea of a third dance with Alex was extremely enticing.

'Three dances in one evening?' Lady Felicity remarked very loudly as they passed her. 'I declare you have your husband quite under your thumb, Your Grace.'

'Not at all.' Alex had a touch of the Ice Duke in his tone all of a sudden. 'My wife was enjoying a comfortable cose with her friends, but I begged her to dance with me again.'

'That was satisfyingly fierce of you,' Emma said as they took their places.

'She was very rude.'

'True. Thank you for introducing me to your friends. They're lovely.'

'I thought you'd like them.' He produced an exaggerated look of smugness, which made Emma laugh. And they laughed together through most of the dance, which Emma thoroughly enjoyed.

'I did not realise that it was now acceptable for married couples to dance thrice together in one evening,' the vicar's wife, Mrs Hardy, said very loudly to her husband, just as the dance finished.

Apparently complaints about marital triple dancing were the order of the evening.

'Ignore her,' Letitia said, materialising at Emma's elbow as Alex moved away. 'She had designs on Alex herself a few years ago, and is still put out that he did not succumb to her lures.'

Goodness. No wonder he'd felt hounded by matchmakers.

'And as for a married couple not dancing three times together when we all know what they do in the privacy of their own bedchamber...'

'Letitia!' Emma was trying to laugh, but all of a sudden she felt completely deflated. How would this relationship of hers and Alex's develop? Would they be pretending like this for ever? When she was forty and childless, and had never had intimate relations with a man, would she still be pretending? Suddenly, she just wanted to leave, go home—if the castle could be called her home—and go to bed. Clearly alone.

As if by magic—or maybe just through excellent observation or a coincidental sudden desire to go home himself—Alex reappeared in front of her.

'Are you ready to leave, Emma?'

'Yes, indeed. I find myself very tired this evening. I think perhaps all the country air has exhausted me.'

'That or the fact that it's three o'clock in the morning,' Alex said.

They said their goodnights and thank-yous, and then Alex led the way out to their carriage, holding Emma's arm in what felt like an extremely *polite* way. Especially when she could make out Letitia and her husband getting into their own carriage ahead of them, definitely being a lot more tactile in a much less polite but much more romantic and lovely way that demonstrated an easy and close affection.

Emma swallowed a sigh and sat down on the forward-facing seat of the carriage, slightly to one side in case Alex might be tempted to sit next to her. He sat down opposite her, right in the middle of the seat. Of course.

'Did you enjoy the evening?' he asked as they set off.

'Yes, thank you, very much.' Most of it, anyway, apart from the references to Diana and the reminder just now that he and Emma would never be more than friends. 'Did you?'

'I did, thank you. Despite the scandal I have caused by dancing with you three times.' He smiled at Emma. 'You seemed to get on very well with Letitia and Maria.'

'Yes, I did. I plan to call on them this week.'

'Very good.'

Clearly, he'd been feeling guilty about leaving her to her own devices during the day, and had hoped to provide her with some friends by introducing her to their neighbours, which was very kind of him.

A few minutes later, they were still chatting about the evening and some of the neighbours—Alex had a very good story involving the vicar, a croquet mallet and some cheese, which made Emma almost snort with laughter in a very unladylike fashion—when the carriage drew to a sudden halt.

Emma flew forward from her seat and put her hands out to save herself. They met a solid wall of chest, and she was saved from being flung any further by Alex's hands gripping her arms.

'Ermph,' she said into his chest.

'Are you all right?'

Was she? Yes, except she felt slightly as though she'd lost her wits. All she could think of was the muscly hardness of his chest and the way she was pressed up against him, almost sitting on his lap.

'Yes, thank you,' she managed to say.

'Good.'

Alex let go of her arms and put his hands on her waist and moved her very gently to the side while Emma fought with herself not to give in to the temptation of sinking right into him as he held her for this moment in time.

'I should check that all is well,' he said after a second.

'Of course!' Emma moved away fast. He'd clearly been experiencing *no* temptation, and just as clearly was *not* still thinking about where their bodies had just touched and feeling almost singed by the contact.

The coachman appeared at the door of the carriage just as Alex opened it. 'A deer in the road, Your Grace.'

'Did you hit it?'

'No, Your Grace, we stopped in time.'

'Excellent. Thank you.'

Emma moved back to her side of the carriage as the door closed and then they sat in silence for a few seconds until, slightly desperate to break the tension that seemed to have sprung up between them, she said, 'Do you have many deer on your land?'

And they passed the rest of the journey determinedly talking about livestock.

When the chaise drew up at the castle's main entrance, Alex descended first and then helped Emma down. He thanked the coachman and then led Emma towards the front door, still with her hand tucked through his arm.

'The stars are amazing.' Emma pointed upwards with her free hand. 'That was something I missed in London. Every night in the countryside I think how magical they are. Look. Argo Navis is so clear tonight.'

'I'm impressed. I don't think I could have named that one.'

'I've always loved the constellations. Which is a good thing, given that I'm educating your boys.'

'Very true.' Alex nodded, and then smiled at her. They'd reached the steps up to the wide front doors. 'I hope Lancing has gone to bed,' he said in a low voice. 'I always tell him and Graham not to wait up for me on occasions like this, but I appear to have little authority in my own home, because they often completely ignore me.'

Emma laughed. If there was one person who, apparently effortlessly, seemed to have a lot of authority, it was Alex. And not just because he was a duke, but because he was *him*.

Her arm was still in his as they went into the empty hall together.

'I see Lancing has abided by your wishes,' Emma whispered.

'Indeed. He's left a candle for us here, look.'

One candle. For them to share. Emma suddenly felt very tired. This pretence was…hard. Although clearly she shouldn't complain, even inside her head, because if Alex hadn't married her who knew what she might be doing now? Almost certainly something worse than pretending to be sharing a bedchamber with a very attractive man.

Alex picked the candle up, and Emma realised that she was still holding his arm.

'Are you ready to go upstairs?' he asked, and she nodded, not sure whether or not to pull her hand away.

In the end she didn't, and they began to move towards the staircase together.

The darkness licking around them, the shapes of furniture and paintings distorted by the candle's flickering light... All of it would have felt eerily intimidating without Alex's solid presence beside her. Emma found herself wanting to continue to hold his arm, just to reassure herself that he was there apart from anything else. She'd always hated the darkness. And, yes, of course it was just *nice* being arm in arm with him.

'We should probably enter our sitting room together, rather than going into our bedchambers separately from the corridor.' Alex's whisper brushed her ear, and she shivered. 'Walls have ears. Well, eyes.'

'You're right,' she whispered back, hoping that her voice wouldn't vibrate as much as her body seemed to be doing.

They carried on up the stairs in silence, arm in arm, Emma almost breathless from her awareness of Alex next to her.

When they finally reached the top of the stairs, rounded the ornate newel post at the top of the banisters, walked along the corridor and arrived in front of their sitting room door, it was almost a relief to be able to let go of him.

Emma removed her arm from Alex's and took the candle from him so that he could open the door quietly, to avoid waking the rest of the household, and in they went.

'So neither Jenny nor Graham waited up for us,' Alex said, once he'd closed the door.

'No.' Emma cleared her throat to get rid of the croak that had come from nowhere. 'No.'

She and Jenny had fallen into a routine where Jenny helped her get ready for bed—usually into a frothy confection of a nightgown with which Jenny presumably imagined Emma would impress Alex—and then left Emma for the night. Emma was sick and tired of all the night-time pretence, and thoroughly relieved that Jenny wouldn't be there tonight.

'So.' Alex cleared his own throat. 'Goodnight, then.'

'Goodnight.'

Neither of them moved.

Then Alex said, 'I should, that is to say, would you like me to light your candle with this one? Or perhaps you'd like to light it yourself?'

'Of course. Thank you.' Emma took the candle from him. Their fingers brushed as she did so and she nearly dropped it.

'Can you manage?'

'Yes! I don't know what happened there. Very clumsy of me. I'll bring it back directly, so that you may use it in your own chamber.'

It took her three attempts and a further near-drop of the candle before she had her own properly lit. Alex was having the most extraordinary effect on her this evening.

'Done,' she said as she returned to the sitting room.

Alex was at the window, looking out into the moon-lit garden.

'It's beautiful in the moonlight, isn't it?' she said.

'It's beautiful at any time. Although I don't really feel

as though it's my land, rather that I am a custodian of it for future generations, and I feel very fortunate.' He turned and walked towards her to take the candle. 'We really should bid each other goodnight now that you have your candle lit; it's very late. Almost time for an early breakfast, in fact.'

'Yes.'

Again, neither of them moved.

Alex looked dark, brooding, very serious in the candlelight.

'You…' Emma began, and then stopped, not sure what she had been trying to say. 'Thank you for this evening. I very much appreciate your kindness in introducing me to your friends and in demonstrating to everyone that we—'

'You have nothing to thank me for.' His voice was rough.

'No.' She wasn't really sure what she was saying because all her focus was on his face lit by the candle between them, the shadow of his beard growth, the *size* of him standing there in front of her.

Alex took the candle and placed it on a chest to one side. 'We don't want to get burnt.'

'No,' Emma said again.

She might not get burnt by the candle, but she felt as though she was being burnt by *something*. She could feel heat in all sorts of places.

Alex took a step closer to her, and she moved closer too, taking a deep, shuddering breath as they drew together. Memories, images from when they kissed at the inn, were playing in her mind now.

'I enjoyed our dances,' he whispered.

'Me too.' Emma was whispering as well.

Alex was so close now she could barely breathe from anticipation.

He lifted one hand and very gently traced a finger down her cheek. 'You look beautiful in that dress.'

Emma couldn't speak. All she could do was smile and tilt her head up towards his. He was going to kiss her again, and it was going to be the perfect end to a wonderful evening.

Chapter Eleven

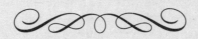

Alex allowed his fingers to wander down the smooth skin of Emma's cheek and to trace the shape of her lips. So soft, so beautiful. The tip of her tongue peeped out and she moistened her lips, and he felt a shudder throughout his entire body. He found himself moistening his own lips in response, and leaning his head nearer to hers.

Their mouths were less than an inch apart now, and they were edging ever closer to each other, heads tilted one way and then the other, mirroring each other like two pieces of a puzzle that were about to fall into place.

He could feel the anticipation building inside him. He knew from their first two kisses how Emma's lips tasted, how well she fitted against him, and he was desperate for more.

Their lips were so close now that he could feel her breath against his mouth. She murmured something unintelligible and suddenly he pulled her against him into a hard kiss. She gave a deep shudder and returned the kiss, threading one arm around his neck, pressing her other hand tight against his chest.

Holding her against him with one arm and continuing

their kiss, ever deeper, he ran one hand from her hip to her waist, and then up to the swell of her breast, feeling her shiver as he touched her. He nipped her lower lip with his teeth and then allowed his thumb to skim her hardened nipple through the fabric of her dress and felt her shudder again against him.

Damn, he wanted her. He wanted to taste all of her, feel her softness against his hardness, explore her body, work out what made her come alive, make her shudder and shiver again, be entwined with her, enter her, be as one with her.

As one with her.

Like man and wife.

Like he had been with Diana.

He stilled. He couldn't do it.

It wasn't even the thought of betraying Diana, because it wasn't a betrayal, was it? She was gone and she'd have wanted him to be happy.

He dropped both his hands and lifted his head.

He knew what it was. It was the fact that he *did* want to be happy. And the thought of allowing himself to care that much again for a woman, even a fraction of that amount, was too frightening. If he allowed himself to love Emma and anything happened to her, he'd be plunged into the depths of despair again, and he didn't want that, couldn't cope with it. He just wanted contentment, a happy, serene life without the possibility of any further grief.

He definitely wasn't doing this.

He took a step backwards and said, 'It's late. We should probably go to bed.'

Emma was just standing there, unmoving, staring at him with a dazed look on her face, as though she couldn't understand what was happening.

He shook his head. 'I...' He should apologise, some-how. 'I'm not... I can't...' He drew a breath and then said, 'I'm sorry. This isn't right for me.'

It was as though his words snapped Emma out of the near-trance she'd been in. 'Of course. Goodnight. Thank you for a lovely evening.'

And then she gathered her skirts and whisked herself through the door into her bedchamber.

Alex stared for a couple of seconds at the closed door before turning to go into his own chamber.

He'd absolutely done the right thing. It was right for both of them. So he should be feeling pleased, positive.

He didn't feel happy at all.

He was sure he would tomorrow, though.

Alex awoke later that morning not feeling remotely refreshed. Despite the late hour, he'd been unable to sleep, and had tossed and turned for what had felt like most of the remainder of the night, replaying the evening in his mind. He'd danced with Emma in order to dem-onstrate to his friends and neighbours that she was very much his wife, whatever rumours they might have heard to the contrary, for the same reason that he'd kissed her at the inn, and both times it had turned into something unexpected and quite unwelcome.

There was an obvious solution: avoid her as far as was polite when there were no onlookers to be impressed, and avoid actual physical contact when there *were* onlook-ers. In due course he'd have his physical impulses under control—he hoped really quite soon—and then Emma would be an accepted presence in his life, and they could continue as friends living under the same roof.

So he hauled himself out of bed and down for a quick

breakfast and out for the day before a polite dinner with Emma in the evening.

It worked. It definitely worked.

After their polite and pleasant dinner, they retired upstairs together, entering their bedchambers via their shared sitting room, as was now becoming their custom, and Alex found the strength of mind to go straight into his bedchamber without allowing himself to linger, or dwell on just how much he'd like to...

No, he shouldn't even allow himself to think that behind closed doors. That way lay insanity. It was fortunate that he was so tired after only a couple of hours' sleep last night that he actually nodded off quite quickly, thinking about how he and Emma had joked together over dinner, and her infectious laugh. But it was perfectly normal to go to sleep thinking about your evening...

The next afternoon, having received an invitation from Gideon's sister Letitia, Alex decided to visit the nursery, firstly to spend a little extra time with the boys, and secondly to ask Emma if she'd like to attend an impromptu dinner at Letitia's house the next evening.

Emma was in full flow when he let himself into the room, and the boys were rapt, which was the first time he'd ever seen them like that with a governess.

They were so rapt that they didn't appear even to notice his arrival.

Emma was doing an excellent imitation of a tiger, insofar as it was immediately recognisable, if not accurate, complete with a description of where tigers liked to roam, hunt and sleep.

'Do tigers eat people?' asked John.

'Not very often,' Emma said.

'Do they eat fish?' Harry asked.

Emma's answer morphed into a discussion about the apparently very many rivers in India.

'Papa!' Harry suddenly interrupted Emma, having finally noticed his father.

'Shh.' Alex put his finger to his lips. 'Emma's talking.'

'What's the longest river in India?' Freddie asked, the most animated Alex had seen him about anything other than the stables and horseplay for a long time.

'Have you heard of any of the rivers?' Emma asked. 'What do you think it is?'

'Something beginning with G?' Freddie said.

'That's right,' said Alex.

Simultaneously, Emma said, 'That's what a lot of people think, but in fact it isn't.'

Alex raised an eyebrow and Emma smiled at him and said, 'I believe that the Ganges is the third longest river in India and the longest is the Indus.'

He smiled back at her, impressed.

'Your knowledge of geography is certainly better than I could ever have hoped for in my boys'…' His boys' *what*? He couldn't call her a governess in front of them. She was, after all, legally at least, their stepmother. 'In any instructor of my boys. Or indeed anyone I know, frankly.'

'My grandmother was Indian, and during my childhood she told me a lot of stories about her own childhood. I've been fascinated by the country ever since and have read as much as I can on the subject.'

'Did she live in England?' Freddie asked.

'Yes, in Lancashire with my grandfather.'

'How did she come to live here?' Freddie's questions were almost too much, but Alex decided not to reprimand him.

He was still very young, and also Alex was very interested himself in Emma's answers but didn't want to discuss his own affairs, particularly Diana, and so he couldn't reasonably ask Emma too much about her background.

'My grandfather owned a textile business and travelled to India to find new fabrics. He was asked to dinner by my grandmother's father, who wished to sell him silks from his land. He was a maharajah, and my grandmother was a princess. She met my grandfather and they fell in love, and she embarked on the long journey across the Near East by land and then over the Mediterranean Ocean and all the way to the North of England with him.'

'That's a really long journey,' John said.

'It is.' Emma smiled, and something about her—something wistful in her eyes—told Alex that her interest in India was more than academic.

'Do you perhaps wish to travel there yourself one day? If you don't mind my asking?' he said.

Emma hesitated, and then said, 'Yes.'

Alex nodded, surprised by how unsurprised he was. Women rarely undertook such journeys, but the more he learned of her, the more he realised that Emma was a rare woman. A woman who was very different from him.

'Have you travelled?' she asked.

'I was fortunate enough to do a Grand Tour. Europe. I very much enjoyed it and saw some wonderful sights.'

'But?' She had one eyebrow fractionally raised.

'I like my corner of Somerset,' he told her. 'I enjoy being here, doing my best to be an attentive landlord.'

He counted the schools and the hospital he'd built in recent years as far greater achievements than swanning around the continent as the idle, rich young man he'd been at that stage of his life. And of course his sons were here. His *life* was here.

Emma nodded almost imperceptibly. 'I can see that.'

Their eyes met. She looked as though she was weighing up what she saw before her, much as he was. She nodded again, and he did too. He had the feeling that her urge to travel was as great as his to remain at home.

They were indeed very different.

Emma hesitated for a moment, and then said, 'I would very much like to travel extensively.'

He realised that she'd probably been waiting for the right moment to tell him that. Well, he certainly wouldn't stop her. Indeed, perhaps it would be for the best for both of them that she travel, as long as scandal did not attach to anything she did. When she returned home, any residual attraction between them would hopefully have been erased by time spent apart.

And if the thought of Emma travelling simultaneously scared him and made him realise that he would miss her company, all the better that she go.

'That will be your prerogative,' he told her.

She didn't smile, but just said, 'Thank you.'

Alex felt as though he'd taken a test, but he couldn't tell whether he'd passed or failed. He did know that following their conversation he felt a little miserable.

Emma opted to take her dinner in her chambers that evening, citing a headache, and again, Alex wasn't sure why. He also wasn't sure whether or not he was pleased.

The next morning, the routine into which they seemed already to have fallen since the addition of Emma to the household was disturbed, as they all woke up to a beautiful thick blanket of snow covering everything within sight. The boys were desperate to get outside, and the adults in the household were split between those who agreed with them and those who didn't want to get cold and wet.

The small child in Alex adored the snow, but as Parsons, his man of business, kept telling him, he had a huge amount of bookwork to do.

'Perhaps I might have finished by late morning,' he said, wondering if to Parsons' ears he sounded like a child, pleading to be allowed out to play.

'I hope so, Your Grace,' Parsons said, his creased face impassive.

Alex was still toiling away—how was it possible that these numbers totalled a different amount every time he looked at them—when sounds of shrieking and laughter reached him from the sparkling white lawn outside his study window.

Emma had the boys thoroughly muffled up, and he could see from her gestures and the scarf and twigs she was holding that she was encouraging them to build a snowman. The boys were half engaged in rolling an enormous ball for the snowman's body, half engaged in throwing smaller snowballs at each other.

Alex was struggling even more now to make sense of the figures in front of him.

He'd had enough. He'd done a lot of work this morning; he definitely deserved a break.

If he could get the numbers on the page at which he was currently looking to add up, he'd go outside for a few minutes to show the boys how good snowballs were *really* made.

Five minutes later, he'd come to the conclusion that

the numbers were never going to add up, and that it would be madness not to take advantage of the snow, because who knew when winter playtime conditions would be as good as this again?

Approximately sixty seconds after that he was pulling on a greatcoat and loose walking boots, winding a scarf around his neck and striding outside.

It looked as though he was the first person to emerge that day from the side door by which he'd left the castle. As his feet sank into the pristine snow and he breathed clean, frosty air into his lungs, he took in the beauty of the scene surrounding him. If he were the kind of man who painted, he'd love to attempt a landscape of this. It was...

Thump.

Something heavy and wet had hit him squarely in the face.

'Eurmph,' he spluttered, tasting snow.

'Ha-ha-ha,' shouted Freddie from the shelter of a group of trees in a copse to Alex's left, and then another snowball hit Alex on the shoulder.

'War,' Alex shouted, bending down to roll a snowball of his own.

He was bombarded by surprisingly accurate shots until he got himself hidden behind a large oak tree and poked his head round it to see Emma directing the boys in making the snowballs while she held one with her arm back, very much primed to throw, and looked around for her target, presumably *him*.

Well.

Alex bent very carefully and quietly and set about rolling the perfect snowball. Times four. They needed to be big, but not so big that they wouldn't fly perfectly through the air, and also wet, to ensure maximum dis-comfort when they landed one after the other on Emma and the boys.

Work finished, and his ammunition lined up at his feet, he stood up with a small grunt of satisfaction to check where his prey now were. As he straightened, he realised that they'd gone very silent. He couldn't hear anything at all other than a couple of cracks of twigs and...

Thump, thump, thump, thump.

When he'd cleared the snow from his face and could see again, he realised that the four of them, in addition to pelting him with one large snowball each, had jumped on his ones and destroyed them. They'd well and truly trounced him.

For the moment.

He smiled at them all lined up in front of him, laugh-ing. 'Very good. You got me there.'

'You shouted, "War," but we won,' crowed John.

'You certainly did,' Alex said.

And then he leapt forward and swept the boys into his arms and ran with them towards the snowman's body, before dumping all three of them into it.

'Outrageous,' said Emma, standing at a safe distance. 'You've ruined our morning's hard work.' She was def-initely smirking. 'And now the boys will be soaked to the skin and will need to go inside to get changed and have warm baths.'

'Have you ever heard the word "hypocrite"?' Alex asked, advancing towards her.

'No!' she said, and then picked up her skirts and ran towards the castle, shouting, 'Boys, inside now.'

Two things surprised Alex: firstly, she was fast, and

secondly, the boys actually obeyed her and sprinted inside after her.

She was an impressive woman, he reflected as he climbed the stairs in order to dry himself off.

She wasn't just an impressive woman, he thought a couple of hours later, as he looked out of the window. She was a determined one.

He wouldn't have noticed if he hadn't happened to glance out at that precise moment, but she and the boys were definitely trying to keep out of sight. They had skirted the edge of the castle, carrying what looked like some of *his* clothes, and now seemed to be occupied in rolling another big snowball. A couple more inches of snow had fallen since they'd gone out this morning, so the conditions were ideal for snowman-building again, and they were clearly planning to build a large one and dress him in Alex's clothes.

Maybe he'd wait until they'd finished and then go outside and land just one perfectly formed snowball on Emma. And then admire the snowman. And then come back inside and finish looking through these blasted books.

Twenty minutes later, he'd achieved strictly nothing further and was feeling as though he was missing out on a lot of fun with the children. He should go outside and find them. And, good Lord, how could he not have had the idea sooner? They had sledges somewhere; he should ask someone to get them out.

He asked Lancing about the sledges, shrugged himself back into his coat and boots, and went outside, following the sounds of laughter and good-natured shouting to a sheltered area.

'My word,' he said, coming to a stop in front of the snowman to which they were putting the finishing touches of what looked like one of his favourite hats, his best gloves and a scarf to which he was—had been—quite partial. They'd already finished its quite hideous-looking face. 'It looks...'

'Surprisingly lifelike?' Emma supplied. 'Like an uncannily good likeness of you, perhaps?'

'Yes, that's right.' He nodded. 'It was on the tip of my tongue to say that looking at it is like looking in a mirror.'

'Why don't you stand next to it so that we can admire our handiwork?' Emma suggested.

'Yes, Papa,' the boys clamoured.

And so he stood next to the gargoyle-like snowman, while the boys told him that it looked *exactly* like him, and Emma congratulated them on how clever they were and laughed at Alex.

He couldn't remember a time when he'd enjoyed himself so much in such a simple way.

He was going to get his revenge on Emma, though.

His opportunity came later, when they'd finished their sledging as dusk fell. The boys' nurse came to take them inside for their second warm bath of the day, leaving Alex and Emma to make their way inside after them.

'The boys have had so much fun today,' Emma said.

'I must thank you,' Alex said. 'I'm not sure how you've done it, but you've worked wonders with them. They actually seem to obey you, and they are learning from you *and* enjoying themselves.'

Emma shook her head. 'You have nothing to thank me for. Without your generosity I could very well be in dire straits now. And the boys are truly lovely. It's a pleasure spending time with them, and I love seeing them happy and enjoying themselves. And who wouldn't enjoy the feeling of victory that for the time being they seem to have called a truce on the introduction of small creatures to my chamber? In fact, I should thank *you* for the opportunity to feel victorious.'

'Very true. Perhaps we should make a mutual agreement to stop thanking each other?' Alex said.

Emma laughed. 'Perhaps.'

'I do have one last little thank-you for you, though.' Moving as fast as he could, for the element of surprise, Alex scooped a large handful of snow from the top of a wall and planted it down the back of Emma's neck.

'You *wretch*!' she shrieked. 'That's so *cold*!'

'I learned all about cold snow earlier today,' Alex said, standing a few feet away from her, ready to dart out of snowballing distance should she decide to retaliate.

She looked at him for a long moment and then smiled. 'I think we're even now.'

She held out her hand and he took it, smiling a gracious smile that said, *I think we all know that I beat you.*

She took his hand in a tighter grip than he'd been expecting, though, and suddenly pulled him very hard. She took a swift sidestep at the same time, and then let go so that he fell into a snowdrift against the wall.

'You look *hilarious*,' she said as he sat up, very much covered in snow.

Alex nodded and smiled, and then very suddenly lunged forward and pulled her down into the snowdrift too, and gave her a little roll for good measure.

'Oh, my goodness,' she gasped. 'Stop! It's so cold.'

'I'm not sure that you should mete out punishments

that you wouldn't be prepared to accept yourself for the same crime,' Alex said with a very serious air.

Emma laughed, and he did too.

And then she stopped laughing. And so did Alex.

Because it suddenly felt as though something had changed; the air between them was practically crackling with tension.

They were lying on their sides next to each other in the soft snow, their faces and bodies only inches apart. Alex still had his upper arm around Emma's waist from when he'd rolled her in the snow.

For fun. It had been for fun.

It didn't feel like fun now. It felt like… It felt like temptation.

It was snowing again, very lightly. He could see snowflakes on Emma's beautiful long, dark eyelashes. Her brown eyes looked deep and mysterious in the twilight, and her lips were slightly parted. He could see the rise and fall of her chest, her full breasts straining against the fabric of her pelisse.

He didn't have the strength to resist the temptation this time.

Very slowly and carefully, he raised himself on his elbow, and then bent his head towards hers.

They didn't sink into a deep kiss immediately. Alex brushed Emma's lips with his own with the lightest of touches, and then drew back slightly. She looked at him for a long moment, a small smile on her lips, before reaching up to him. And then they were almost dancing around the edges of the kiss, nipping at each other's lips, moving away and then back again, like opposing magnets irresistibly drawn together.

Suddenly, it was as though something just snapped

and it happened. His mouth was on hers, or maybe hers was on his, even though he was above her. Their tongues met and he felt his entire body respond to the sensation, as though he'd been waiting just for this for a very long time. He ran his hand down her side, in and out of the dip of her waist, and felt her tremble as he touched her.

'Are you all right?' he whispered.

'Yes,' she said on a sigh.

Alex moved his hand to cup her beautiful face, which he was beginning to know so well, and then slid his hand round to her neck, tugging at her hair, drawing her even closer to him.

As he held her close with one arm, he moved his other hand to cup her breast, and even through several layers of clothing he felt her respond. She arched her back so that she was pressed against him, and pushed her hands into his hair.

This felt like the natural culmination of everything that had come before, the physical temptation, the time they'd spent getting to know each other, talking, laughing together. Now his entire being, from his soul to his body, wanted to get to know more of Emma.

He was dimly aware that this was not wise, but with Emma in his arms like this, he was unable to do anything other than focus on the here and now. And, damn, she was tempting.

He kissed down her neck and undid the hook and top buttons of her pelisse with almost shaking hands, so that he could kiss and lick the hollow at the base of her neck. He undid more buttons and licked and kissed all the way down to the neckline of her dress. When he slid one hand inside and pulled the dress lower, bending his head further to take her nipple in his mouth, she moaned and arched even more. *Damn*, he wanted her, wanted her more than he could have thought possible.

He very vaguely knew that this wasn't the best idea, but he couldn't remember why. All he could think about was the taste of Emma, her seductive scent, the curve of her lips, the way her breast fitted perfectly in his hand, the smoothness of her skin, the eagerness of her kisses, the way his own body was responding to her and the promise of more.

Chapter Twelve

It was as though every nerve-ending in Emma's body was on fire. Her stomach was dipping, warmth pooling low inside her, as Alex worked magic with his mouth and his fingers on her breasts. Her hands were clutching at his hair and his upper arms—feeling the strength of his muscles there—almost scratching him with her nails in her desire to keep him there next to her.

He continued caressing, licking, sucking, and then he kissed his way back up her chest and neck and took her mouth again, his hands continuing to tease her breasts. When he moved his fingers a little away and traced around them, all she wanted was for him to move them back to her nipples. And when they were there, she could hardly bear the pleasure, and yet she knew that she wanted more, for him to touch her more, in other places.

It was mind-blowing, intoxicating. She couldn't breathe, she couldn't think, all she could do was kiss him back, mould her body to his, loving the weight of him on her and the feel of him pressing against her.

She pulled at his neckcloth and his shirt, wanting to touch his skin as he was touching hers. Wresting his shirt from his breeches, she ran her hands up his muscled torso, shivering as she did so. The hardness and latent strength in his body exactly matched his personality: he was the very embodiment of masculinity.

He pulled slightly away, smiling down at her, and his deep green eyes locked on hers for a long moment before they moved to look at her lips, and then her exposed breasts. The admiration in his eyes was so potent it was making her shiver.

He leaned down again to take her nipple in his mouth again, and then he reached beneath her dress.

'Is this all right?' he asked as he stroked her inner thigh, high up, towards the place where she felt the heaviness between her legs.

'Mmm.' She couldn't speak. All she could focus on were the sensations he was producing and where she was exploring him in her turn with her hands and lips.

And then he began to touch and caress her most intimate parts, and as sensation built she gave a deep, juddering sigh. She knew that she was moist there, and it was as though the rest of her entire body had turned to liquid too. She reached for the front opening in his breeches, fumbling, and he eased himself away to enable her to touch him better, producing a deep, 'Yes,' as she found him.

And then something large and wet landed on her face and she nearly choked.

What was that?

'Snow,' Alex said. 'The tree.'

He brushed snow away from her breasts, the touch of his fingers as they skimmed her skin making her jump.

'The branch couldn't bear the weight.' He smiled at her and leaned down towards her again, and then another large pile of snow fell on them.

He sighed and drew back. 'Maybe we should move.'

Emma nodded, hugely disappointed.

Alex sat up, and pulled her up too.

Immediately, the moment in which they'd been was entirely broken. They were now sitting next to each other in damp clothes, chests exposed, Emma's dress lifted, Alex's breeches open. And now she thought about it she was freezing cold.

Beyond their legal marriage, they weren't truly man and wife, nor in any way romantically involved with each other, so they couldn't just move to somewhere more sheltered in the garden or to a bedchamber, and continue what they'd been doing, because...

Well, they just couldn't. Because clearly neither of them had intended this to happen, and without the impetus of hot-blooded desire, or temptation, or whatever it had been, they obviously weren't going to resume.

They certainly weren't going to, anyway, if Alex didn't suggest it, because Emma was not going to lay herself open to the possibility of his refusing her.

Without looking at him she pulled her dress up and down, so that she was covered, and then drew her pelisse around herself. When she was more properly attired, she glanced at Alex and saw that he'd been busy tucking his shirt in.

The misery and disappointment that struck her in that moment showed her that she'd been hoping that he might somehow find the words—*want* to find the words—to suggest they go somewhere else together, maybe one of their bedchambers, and continue this...whatever it had been.

But of course he'd never been going to do that, and

in the interests of dignity, she certainly wasn't going to demonstrate to him that she was disappointed.

Using the tree trunk as leverage, she began to haul herself to her feet, and immediately slipped on the ground beneath. The snow there had been compressed to near-ice by the weight of their bodies a few minutes ago.

Alex shot an arm out to prevent her falling flat on her face, and had her standing solidly on her own two feet on some fresh snow within seconds, all without making any kind of eye contact.

As soon as it was clear that she wasn't going to fall over again, he let go of her as though she was scalding hot, and said, 'It's getting dark and you should get into some warmer clothes before you catch a cold.'

'You should change too,' Emma told him.

Alex nodded and they set off together in the direction of the house. They walked in complete silence, not a comfortable one, both of them looking straight ahead, and then Emma went directly upstairs while Alex made what she was sure was an excuse about needing to speak to Lancing before he changed.

Jenny was waiting for her when she got to her bedchamber. 'Oh, miss,' she said, 'you're soaked to the skin. You'll catch a chill.'

Emma felt heavy tears behind her eyelids and a very strong desire to be alone for a few minutes.

'Thank you, Jenny. I'm sure I'll be fine. I'm very healthy. And I think I'll dry myself. Thank you so much.' She took the towels from Jenny, who was frowning.

'But, miss, sorry, Your Grace, you're very, very wet.'

'And very, very capable of drying myself,' Emma said, immediately feeling guilty for her impatience. 'I'm sorry, Jenny, I'm just tired. I am so grateful for all that you do for me, but on this occasion I really can dry myself and dress myself for dinner and I will do so. Thank you.'

Jenny left the room, still protesting slightly, half under her breath. Once she'd gone, Emma sank down onto a wooden chair and put her head in her hands. She needed to be very careful. She wasn't completely sure what she was feeling now, but she did know that she had very much enjoyed Alex's company, and the way he'd made her feel just now...

Well, there were no words to describe it. It had been amazing, wonderful, glorious, and she'd wanted so much to continue, to discover how good it might have been if they'd done what she knew people did. Perhaps this was the beginning of love? Yes, she was probably falling in love with her husband. Who had made it very clear that he didn't want to love her, or perhaps just couldn't. He was almost certainly still grieving for his wife, the mother of his children, still in love with her memory.

And they wanted very different things—for example she wanted to travel and he wanted to spend his entire life here in Somerset—and she'd seen first-hand how unhappy her parents' marriage had been, despite their love for each other, because they'd been from different backgrounds and had had different wishes and needs. Indeed, it was almost as though their love had driven them apart, because they'd had such different goals that their relationship, with strong love on one side and different ambitions on the other, had become so unbalanced. She'd seen how their love had turned to near-hatred and it had been awful.

This wasn't good. Sitting alone with her depressing thoughts wasn't going to help her situation in the slightest. And she was unpleasantly damp and cold.

Shivering, she peeled her wet clothes off with difficulty, and then picked up a towel and began to rub herself dry very vigorously.

She didn't know what she ought to do next in regard to Alex, but she did know that she needed to be very conscious of her emotions and keep them under tight control.

Fortunately, it seemed that Alex felt exactly the same way and was going to take things a step further and avoid her, who knew for how long?

He made his excuses about dinner—apparently he had *huge* amounts of work to get through this evening, even though surely a duke had all manner of people to whom he might delegate—and didn't appear at all the next day, even when she sledged with the children and made another snowman with them, and allowed them to scream and shout as much as they liked, just to see if it would inspire him to come outside.

Alex had a note sent to her just as she took the children inside as dusk fell, which definitely indicated that he'd known exactly when they'd finished playing outside.

In it he 'suggested'—his word, which, despite everything she was feeling did make Emma smile, because he'd definitely noticed and responded to the fact that she did not enjoy being told what to do—that they leave at half past six for their evening with Letitia. Apparently, he'd received word that they were continuing with the dinner, as there had been no further snow during the day and the roads were all passable.

'Goodnight,' she bade the children, wondering whether she should tell Alex that she was too tired to go to the dinner this evening.

She'd woken this morning with a headache, due to her lack of sleep during a night the majority of which she'd spent turning over and over in her mind the events of the previous afternoon. Her hours outside in the cold air with the children today had cleared her head, but her headache was returning now, and the last thing she wanted was to spend an evening in Alex's company, knowing what they'd been doing yesterday, but having to behave like relative strangers.

But of course she should go. She'd very much liked Letitia when she met her at the squire's dance, and she had a life to make for herself here in Somerset. If she wasn't going to have Alex's company—which, of course, he had never promised her, so she couldn't complain— she'd be much happier if she had local friends.

She checked the clock above the boys' heads. She would need to hurry to be ready on time.

She was not ready on time.

After spending far too long choosing which dress to wear, and then having Jenny do her hair in three different hairstyles—when you'd been as intimate with a man as you'd ever been, and then he'd spent the next day doing his best to avoid you, for the sake of pride you had to look as good as you could when you next saw him— she hurried downstairs at a quarter to seven.

Alex came out of the library just as she reached the bottom of the stairs, clearly having been listening out for her.

'Good evening,' he said. 'You look lovely.'

'Thank you,' Emma said, suddenly breathless.

Just *seeing* his mouth, which looked so stern and thin in repose, but which when he smiled suddenly seemed so generous, was having a really quite unnerving effect on her. She couldn't help remembering what he'd done with it yesterday.

'Shall we go?'

'Go?' What was he talking about?

'Go outside to the chaise?'

Of course. She was losing her wits.

'Yes, wonderful,' she said.

No, not wonderful. It wasn't wonderful to go out to the carriage. It was just, well, nothing, really.

'Excellent.'

He held his arm out to her and she stared at it for a moment before recollecting where she was and what they were doing and taking it, very gingerly, because right now she felt as though touching him at all might make her feel far too much, and she really didn't want to get flustered again just before dinner. Or at all, in fact, if it wasn't going to lead to anything positive.

They walked out to the chaise, neither of them speaking, and then sat down on opposite benches. The carriage began to move, and still neither of them said anything. Emma concentrated on her gloves, and then on the blackness outside the window.

'I hear from the boys that you made another snowman and that they very much enjoyed more sledging today,' Alex said after some time.

'Yes, it was great fun,' Emma said. 'The boys are lovely. They're a credit to you.'

Alex smiled and inclined his head, and then he looked down at his knees, and then at the wall of the chaise to the right of Emma and above her head. And then in the direction of the window.

Emma, her throat holding a large lump all of a sudden, cast around for something unexceptionable to talk about that might lessen the distance between them.

No, she couldn't think of anything that wouldn't sound like an utterly pathetic and desperate attempt to create conversation out of nothing.

So there was no further conversation between them for the remainder of the journey, which in reality was perhaps half an hour but felt far longer than that.

It was a great relief when they finally arrived and could descend from the chaise.

'I'm so glad that you were able to come.' Letitia had dispensed with formality and was hugging Alex and Emma in turn. 'I hate it when we have snow and the roads are closed and we can't see anyone for ages.'

'And have to suffer only our own company and that of our neighbours to whose houses we can walk in under ten minutes, even in the deepest of snow. It's a hard life.' Arthur accompanied his words with a fond smile at his wife. Emma tried very hard not to think about the fact that Alex was never going to look at *her* like that, in either public or private.

'Honestly.' Letitia pouted at her husband, and he laughed out loud and put his arm around her waist. 'We should go inside before the newlyweds catch their deaths of cold.' She put her free arm through Emma's and said, 'I trust your husband kept you warm in the carriage?'

'Oh, yes,' murmured Emma.

Pretending really wasn't very enjoyable. If you liked the person to whom you were pretending, you felt very guilty. She almost wanted to confide in Letitia this minute the truth of her reality, so that they could begin the friendship she hoped they were going to have with honesty and openness.

'Your house looks so beautiful in the snow. Almost ethereal.'

'Your very abrupt subject-change tells me that your husband kept you *so* warm you really don't want to discuss it in polite company,' Letitia said, laughing. 'Don't worry, I'm not going to torment you any longer. Come and warm yourselves in front of the fire.'

They found four other couples in the drawing room, and were soon absorbed into the group, chatting about inconsequential matters of yet great weight, such as the ribbons newly stocked by the haberdasher in Yarford, the nearest town.

'When the snow has gone we must take a trip there together,' Letitia told Emma.

'I should very much like that.'

It was wonderful that it seemed that Letitia was as desirous as she of forming a mutual friendship. Emma did not need the companionship of Alex who, forbiddingly handsome, was currently standing talking to the other men, having positioned himself about as far from Emma as was physically possible without actually leaving the room. She was already making lovely new friends. There were plenty of women who would be ecstatic to be in her position, and she should make the most of the many positives.

She threw herself with great determination into the conversation and really did enjoy much of it, despite Alex's unnerving presence.

She was still enjoying herself when Letitia said, 'My butler has now caught my eye approximately fifty times, and is starting to look quite put out, so I must ask you all to make your way with me to the dining room, so that the food isn't quite ruined by our chattering for too long.'

She moved unceremoniously towards the door of the room, not waiting for her husband to escort her.

'I'm afraid that I'm being quite fashionable and have seated couples far apart from each other.'

Perfect. Emma's eyes flew to Alex's face in reaction to Letitia's words, and his eyes found hers at exactly the same moment. They stared at each other unsmilingly for a second or two, before both shifting their gazes away.

Emma took a deep breath. Things would settle between her and Alex; it wouldn't always be this difficult. She took another breath and fixed a smile to her face before moving into the dining room.

Emma found her name card between those of Arthur and Gideon, both of whom she liked tremendously and with whom she knew she would very much enjoy conversation. The seating plan would have been perfect for her if she hadn't been almost exactly opposite Alex across the wide table; it was going to be difficult to avoid looking at him and getting distracted by his handsome face, sombre this evening in repose, the sound of his deep voice and the way his strong hands held his cutlery.

She noticed with a flash of irritation how very much he seemed to be enjoying his animated conversation with Letitia and their friend Maria. However, both her table neighbours proved themselves to be more than adequate conversationalists, as she had known they would, and Emma found herself thoroughly enjoying herself as long as she didn't look at Alex, and focused very hard on not thinking about him either.

Some time later, they were all exclaiming at Letitia and Arthur's cook's truly wonderful swan-shaped ice cream, and Letitia was recommending that Emma request her housekeeper to purchase or have made any number of ice cream moulds in the shape of perhaps a peacock and a hare at the very least.

Emma nodded. She was definitely going to do so, although she would choose her own designs, perhaps in the shape of one of her kittens, or a pineapple from the castle garden's exotic fruit greenhouse.

Her thoughts were interrupted by Mrs Hardy, the vicar's wife, leaning across Gideon and saying, in a particularly piercing voice, into a lull in the conversation, as the company all enjoyed the creaminess of the ice cream, 'I think we still don't have the full story of how you and the duke first met, Your Grace.'

Emma tilted her head very slightly to the left and regarded Mrs Hardy and her astonishingly smug smile. Clearly, Mrs Hardy believed that she *did* have the full story, and clearly Mrs Hardy was feeling particularly malicious.

'I…' she began, not certain where she was going with her sentence, but very sure that she'd like to make Mrs Hardy feel less smug.

'Her Grace is hesitating—' Alex's voice rang out a little loudly, and every head at the table, including Emma's, shot round to face him '—because we didn't tell anyone initially. Strong, pure emotion feels like a private matter.'

'Oh, but you're amongst friends now,' cooed Mrs Hardy.

Emma found herself gripping her spoon very tightly in lieu of, frankly, *slapping* the woman, who was smiling even more smugly than before, as though she knew that she'd caught Emma and Alex out and was ecstatic to have done so.

'You're right.' Emma turned to Alex and produced a coo of her own. 'Should you tell the story or should I?'

'Why don't you?' If Alex didn't exactly coo back at her, he did manage a fond smile.

'Well. It all began one morning in Hyde Park…'

With a few embellishments on the original—including details about their clothing, their extremely heightened emotions and the weather—Emma reproduced the story they'd concocted in the inn about Alex's horseback rescue and their subsequent secret courtship.

'Even the weather was quite propitious,' she said soulfully as she drew her monologue to a close. 'The sun was warm, but not too warm, and there was exactly the right amount of breeze. It was as though the elements understood that we were at the beginning of something delicate and special and important, and that they needed to nurture it.'

'How very beautiful,' Letitia said, grinning at Emma.

From the way her eyes were dancing, it seemed clear that she'd heard something approaching the real story too, which did make it seem odd that she seemed so certain that Alex and Emma were now a real married couple.

She turned to Alex and said mischievously, 'We'd all love to hear the story from your perspective, Alex.'

Alex coughed. 'I have nothing to add. It was indeed, as Emma says, a…beautiful beginning to what I'm delighted to say is a beautiful…' He tailed off.

'Relationship,' Emma supplied. 'I feel extremely lucky.'

'I'm sure you do.' Mrs Hardy had spoken beneath her breath, but she'd definitely said it.

'The luck,' said Alex, glaring at Mrs Hardy, 'is all mine.'

'I don't know when I've more enjoyed hearing some-one's love story,' Letitia said, 'but perhaps we ladies should remove to the drawing room now, to allow the gentlemen their port. Mrs Hardy, I do wonder whether you might be wise to depart quite soon. I hear that there's been a particularly severe snowstorm, very much cen-tred on the road between here and the vicarage, and Mr Hardy would, I'm sure, be distraught not to be able to return to his parishioners. I'll ask Harris to call your carriage. It's been wonderful to see you; thank you so much for coming.'

Once Letitia had completed her skilful dispatch of the Hardys, Emma thoroughly enjoyed herself, drink-ing tea with Letitia, Maria and the fourth lady still pres-ent, Lady Clinthill.

Until Letitia leaned towards her and said, 'I wish to apologise for what Mrs Hardy said. I don't like to see people being rude under my roof. Arthur and I had barely met when we got married—our marriage was arranged very much between our parents—and we're now deeply in love. Obviously that means that I am be-holden to my mother forever, about which she reminds me far too often, but aside from that it's wonderful, and it serves as an example of how people can meet in somewhat ridiculous-sounding situations and yet de-velop very strong feelings for each other. I'm so pleased that the two of you were thrown together in the way in which you were.'

'I… Yes.' Emma just wanted to *squirm*.

'I'm so sorry. I didn't mean to make you uncomfort-able. The two of you look perfect together, and are so clearly in love, that I'm sure you'll be able to overcome any obstacles that might arise from two relative strangers marrying. I just wanted to say that others have been in the same position and overcome those issues and become stronger.'

'Thank you.' Emma could feel tears pricking at her eyelids. She wasn't sure whether it was due to the fact that she and Alex were clearly *not* in love, and were never going to be, or to how lovely it was that Letitia was being so kind, if slightly scarily outspoken on fairly regular occasion.

Their conversation was curtailed by the men coming into the room. Emma wasn't sure whether or not she was pleased; she felt that she'd have liked to have had the opportunity to glean some details about the early days of Letitia and Arthur's marriage.

Pleased with her own cunning, she had seated herself on a chair rather than a sofa, so that no comment would be occasioned if—when—Alex chose not to sit next to her. He was the second of the men to come into the room, and after hesitating for a moment, sat himself down on a chair reasonably close to Emma, but not within knee-touching distance, perfectly unexceptionable for a husband.

For no reason at all, things were feeling a lot more complicated now that Alex was here.

Maybe she should confide the truth in Letitia and begin to forge a spinster-within-a-marriage existence for herself sooner rather than later.

'You didn't take long to join us.' Letitia smiled up at her husband. 'Did you miss us?'

'Apparently so.' Arthur plonked a kiss on her cheek and sat down beside her on the loveseat upon which Letitia seemed to have chosen to sit precisely for the purpose of cosying up to her husband. Emma felt another pang that she would never share such an easy familiarity and blatant affection with Alex.

'I think we should play whist,' Letitia said, interrupting Emma's thoughts. 'Eight's the perfect number for it. We can have four sets of two and rotate. How shall we decide on partners? Having been fashionably apart at dinner, should we perhaps unfashionably partner our spouses?'

Everyone except Alex and Emma immediately exclaimed how lovely that would be. The two of them exchanged a quick glance and then both joined in with the exclamations, both perhaps a little too loudly.

Within less than five minutes, Emma was seated at a card table with Alex as her partner. He took the cards to shuffle them and suddenly Emma was fixated on his hands. They were strong, capable and lightly tanned, even though spring had barely begun, so he clearly spent a lot of time outside. And yesterday, in the late afternoon, those hands had been touching her, and just the memory of that was causing her to feel extremely hot again.

'Emma, are you all right?' Letitia asked. 'You look a little flushed. Would you like some ratafia?'

'Yes, please,' Emma said as Alex looked up from the cards.

'Are you sure you're perfectly well?' he asked her in a low voice.

The irony of him asking her if she was all right because everyone thought that she might be ill because she'd just been slightly overcome at the thought of what they'd been doing yesterday. And, oh, for goodness' sake, now she was thinking about his shoulders and his chest and how he'd touched *her* chest.

'Yes, thank you. I'm very well.' Emma buried her face in the glass of ratafia Arthur had just passed to her, took a long draught and nearly choked.

'Are you sure?' Alex asked.

'Yes, thank you, very sure. I hope you're going to prove to be a good player,' she told him, aiming for a playful just-married-and-still-coquettish-with-her-husband tone. 'We've never played cards together before,' she explained to the others.

'I will endeavour to satisfy you,' Alex replied with a little smile, which, had she not known that he was acting just as much as she was, would have caused Emma's heart to leap a little and her insides to flutter again.

He *did* satisfy her. Whist partnership-wise, anyway. He was intuitive, he was able to keep his face entirely expressionless so as not to give away any clues to the contents of his hand, and he adapted his game to hers very well. Emma liked to think that she adapted hers to his as well, and indeed that she had all the same attributes as a player.

Certainly, they beat everyone else quite resoundingly, and one of the most satisfying characteristics in Alex as a partner turned out to be that he was quite as competitive as she was.

'Perhaps just one more round?' he suggested, after the first one for a while that he and Emma hadn't won. *We can't finish on a loss*, he mouthed at her.

Emma was very tired, having slept very badly the night before, but was in complete agreement.

As soon as they'd won the next round, Alex said,

'I'm so sorry to break up the party, and indeed I'd very much like to continue showing the rest of you how it's done, but I think Emma's tired, and I see that it's very late indeed, and we don't wish to outstay our welcome.'

'I hope it hasn't snowed much more,' Emma said.

'You're always welcome here, as I hope you know,' Letitia said, 'and indeed you must also know you will be more welcome to stay here overnight with us if the snow has made the roads impassable.'

'It has indeed snowed further while you've been here,' Arthur reported from behind the room's heavy curtains. 'I think you might all be forced to stay overnight.'

'That's perfect. I couldn't have planned it better. We will absolutely love to have you,' Letitia said, beaming. 'I will ask Harris to prepare a bedchamber for each couple. An impromptu house party! I already have plans for tomorrow.'

Emma felt that she and Alex had grown adept at reading each other's glances through their card games this evening, but it didn't take a lot of skill to read the horror in Alex's eyes at this moment, mirrored, she was sure, by her own. Well, perhaps not horror in her eyes; perhaps shock. The two of them sharing a bedchamber? Good heavens.

'I feel that we should investigate further,' she said. 'I think Alex and I would both like to return home to the boys tonight if possible.'

'I agree.' He nodded. 'Especially after my recent absence in London.'

'I'm not sure you're going to be able to do so,' Arthur said, still peering out of the window. He let go of the curtains and said, 'Let me go and see.'

'I'll accompany you,' Alex said.

As they left the room, Emma couldn't work out whether she'd rather they could or couldn't get home that night. A traitorous part of her felt that it might be very nice, albeit a little embarrassing, to be forced to share a chamber with Alex.

Chapter Thirteen

How was it possible that so much snow had fallen in one evening? Ridiculous.

As he and Arthur trod a path around the house, Alex stamped his boots viciously. He was absolutely not going to share a room with Emma tonight. It had been bad enough talking to her at dinner and playing cards with her this evening. He'd enjoyed her company far too much. He hoped he had enough willpower to resist her obvious attractions if they shared a room, but based on yesterday's idiocy he wasn't so sure that he did.

He wasn't going to share a room with her. So at least one of them was going to have to go home and, looking at the depth of the snow in Letitia and Arthur's drive, they weren't going to be able to take the chaise.

Fortunately, there was a full moon, and horses dealt very well with fresh snow; they only had difficulty when there was a frozen crust on top of the snow, which could lacerate their legs. Alex would ride carefully home in the moonlight and Emma could return in the chaise when the snow would allow her. She might have to stay here for several days, which, frankly, would be ideal in terms of allowing them both to cool off after yesterday's insanity.

Back in the house, Alex told the assembled company of his plans and Letitia swept everyone except Emma into the drawing room, saying, 'We must allow the two of you a moment to bid each other adieu for however long it might be.'

'Goodbye, then,' Emma said, her hands gripping each other tightly in front of her. 'Be careful as you ride.'

'Thank you. I will.' It was ridiculous that Alex now felt a wrench at leaving her. In case someone was watching, and because it felt rude not to, he took a step towards her and kissed her cheek, her scent flooding his senses as he did so. 'Goodnight. Sleep well.'

'Goodnight.'

Alex didn't enjoy his journey home. He alternated between walking Star and riding slowly, but that wasn't the problem. The problem was his mood. He felt bereft, as though home would be odd without Emma there. And he felt guilty, as though he'd engineered leaving her behind, and worried in case she was upset.

It was going to be a good thing, though, having time apart.

It was still snowing when he awoke after a short night's sleep. The snow continued until midday, and it was clear that carriages wouldn't be able to travel that day.

By the time Alex took his luncheon with the boys, he still wasn't sure how he felt about Emma's being stranded with Letitia and Arthur.

Extremely heavy snow came with consequences for agriculture, for people living in poverty, for those who needed to travel and for many more, especially this winter after last year's lack of summer. For Alex, it had also had the unexpected consequence of giving him a reprieve from being under the same roof as Emma, having to fight the attraction he felt for her, never sure whether he ought to spend time with her out of courtesy—and enjoyment, if he was honest—or avoid her because he enjoyed her company too much.

Was he pleased to have that reprieve, though?

If he'd been asked a few days ago how he would feel about this situation, he would have stated without hesitation that it would have been very welcome. And it was still welcome, in theory, but in practice he wasn't so sure.

He hoped that she was all right.

'When will Emma be back?' asked John for about the fifth time.

'I want her,' said Harry.

Freddie looked at Alex, and then he looked at his younger brothers. 'We can manage very well without her,' he said.

Alex paused, his fork halfway to his mouth. If he wasn't mistaken, Freddie had calculated that Alex would be pleased that she wasn't there, and had decided to come down on the side of his father rather than his brothers. This was terrible; Alex was setting a very poor example.

'I very much look forward to her returning,' he said. 'And while we can indeed manage without her, I know that we all miss her. I hope that she'll be able to return tomorrow.'

And then he busied himself helping Harry with his food, until he was sure that Freddie wasn't studying his face any more and the conversation had turned to a dead squirrel that the boys had seen being eaten by crows.

The next morning was Sunday and, following no further snow and a rise in temperatures, the roads were passable, albeit somewhat slushy, and Alex attended church with the children. He always chose the village church rather than the chapel on his estate; the chapel was heavy with memories of Diana's funeral, and in addition he wanted the boys' upbringing to be as informal as possible, given that they were the sons of a duke.

'Your Grace,' trilled Mrs Hardy as they left the church. 'Is Her Grace indisposed?'

'She was detained at Letitia and Arthur's by the snow, but we look forward to her return today.' Alex carried on walking.

Mrs Hardy was not a tall woman, but such was her determination to continue the conversation that she managed to lengthen her stride to keep pace with him.

'Perhaps a welcome break from the cosh of wedlock for you?' She accompanied her words with a little titter, while Alex tightened his lips. 'But travelling on a Sunday… I don't believe I can condone Her Grace's intention.'

'My wife's regard for her husband and sons must transcend any small feeling of guilt over undertaking a short journey, which, after all, is not that much further than some people must make between home and church,' Alex said, stony faced.

Mrs Hardy made a sound a little like 'Pfft,' and flounced away, which made Alex smile. He wished Emma had been there to see the flouncing.

Emma was alighting from the chaise as they arrived back at the house.

'Emma!' Harry hurtled towards her, followed by John.

Freddie looked at Alex, who had to struggle not to shake his head at the situation. He actually *was* pleased to see Emma. He did not wish to be pleased to see her, and he did not wish to act on that feeling, but he did need to set a good example of a respectful, if not passionate, union to his boys, particularly Freddie, it seemed.

Living a lie was hard.

He smiled at the boys and then walked forward to greet Emma. He placed his hands on her upper arms and a decorous kiss on each of her cheeks.

'As you see, we're all delighted to see you returned,' he told her.

'Oh,' she squeaked, her cheeks looking a little warm, before she recovered herself and said, 'I'm delighted to see you all.'

As they all went inside the house together, Alex couldn't help thinking that from the outside they must look like the perfect family picture.

He didn't know how he felt about Emma, so it was fortunate that they had the boys to distract them over the luncheon they ate together. Afterwards, in the absence of the excuse of work on the Sabbath, he took Freddie out for a long walk during the afternoon, arriving back only at dusk.

He joined Emma for dinner that evening in the grand dining room. She was dressed in a light green dress, against which her almost black hair looked stunning. The dress was low cut, and Alex caught himself gazing at the neckline for just a little too long, and remembering their interlude in the snow the other day.

He forced his gaze upwards, but that was no better. Emma's lips were slightly parted and she was looking at him as intently as he was looking at her. It was as though there was some kind of indefinable tension between them. Indefinable, but very thick, so thick that he could almost have cut it with the knife in front of him.

'It started snowing again just as we returned to the house after our walk,' he said.

There was a good reason that English people talked about the weather so often: it was the safest of subjects and there was so much of it.

'Quite heavily, in fact,' he continued as they took their seats at the table. 'I wouldn't be surprised if we were snowed in again. Freddie had a lot to tell me about snowflakes and their different constructions, and the fact that geographers believe that no two are the same.'

Good grief, he'd resorted to reciting snowflake facts.

Emma frowned, ignoring his inanities. 'That can't be good for the crops and livestock. The drifts had only barely begun to melt.'

'Indeed.' A week ago, Alex would have been surprised that her mind had gone straight to agriculture, but now he knew her better. 'I will visit my farming tenants tomorrow to discuss what can be done to help, on foot if necessary.'

'And your other tenants? Are they able to cope in this weather?'

'I trust so. They are well-housed, and I ensure that their rent is set at very reasonable levels.'

'I would like to visit the more vulnerable amongst them, if I may. Perhaps the elderly, or any families with numerous offspring who might be struggling.'

'Of course. When the weather is improved.'

'I am also able to visit on foot.'

'It's a long way.' Alex speared some peppered broccoli.

Emma nodded and didn't say anything else, instead focusing on cutting her veal escalope into dainty pieces. Clearly, she was going to ignore him.

'If you *do* go,' he said, 'I would prefer you to take your maid, or a footman, or perhaps both.'

Emma inclined her head and placed a piece of veal in her mouth. Watching her delicate chewing, Alex completely lost his train of thought. She raised her eyebrows at him slightly as she took her next mouthful, and indeed he knew he was staring. Or gazing. Both were a little embarrassing for a grown man at his own supper table. Surely he could find some non-contentious conversation about something beyond snowflakes?

'How did you spend your second evening at Letitia and Arthur's?' he asked. He'd asked whether she'd enjoyed her stay when they sat down for luncheon, but the boys had taken over the conversation from that point on, and they hadn't had the opportunity to go back to it. 'I hope you enjoyed your stay.'

'Thank you; I did enjoy it. We played whist again yesterday evening. I was partnered with Gideon.'

'Oh, dear.' Alex had lost count of the number of times he'd trounced Gideon at the card table. Gideon was not a gifted player, and cheerfully acknowledged that fact.

Emma laughed. 'Indeed. I missed your partnership sorely.'

And then she stopped laughing, and so did he, and he realised that they were gazing at each other's mouths and eyes again. There was something about the word 'partnership'.

'I understand that it often snows very heavily in Lancashire?' Alex said, swallowing.

Snow was apparently the safest topic of conversation this evening, and they stuck to weather-related topics for the entirety of the rest of their dinner, which did less to take Alex's mind off Emma's smile and beautiful eyes than he would have liked.

* * *

They awoke in the morning to the deepest March snow in living memory, according to Lancing, who had a longer memory than most. It had already stopped snowing, though, and while travel by carriage or horse would be difficult, as any flattened snow was icing over, it was possible to walk as men had been out clearing the roads.

Alex spent an hour after breakfast discussing his farmers' needs with Parsons, and then directed footmen and grooms to divert their energies from their usual work to helping on the land where needed, and then set out on foot to check on the inhabitants of a cluster of cottages east of the castle, which were occupied by some elderly people and one couple who had three young children and were expecting a fourth imminently.

He took one of the grooms named Mikey with him. Once they'd checked on those tenants Mikey could send for any necessary assistance, and Alex would walk on to the nearest farm.

The first cottage at which he arrived was that belonging to the young couple. He knocked on the door and it was opened by…*Emma*. Holding a toddler on her hip.

'Emma?'

'Alex?' She opened the door wider to allow him entry.

'I didn't expect to see you here.'

'I thought you knew that I was planning to come?'

'I…' He looked at her. 'Your skirts, though. In the snow.'

'My pelisse is thick, and I'm wearing stout boots and where my skirts got a little wet they're now dry from the fire. The roads are entirely passable as you know.'

'Where's Jenny? Where's *everyone*?' It seemed to be

just Emma, the toddler and two slightly older children in the little cottage.

'Jenny is less hardy than I, and I knew she wouldn't want to come, so I came alone. Thomas is out checking on his livestock and Eliza is very tired, as she's eight months pregnant, so I suggested that she have a sleep while I look after the children for an hour or two.'

'Your walk here might have been dangerous, though.'

'It wasn't that far, and also…'

He looked at her. 'Don't tell me. You brought your pistol.'

Good God.

Emma laughed. 'The expression on your face is very amusing.'

'I'm glad to hear it.'

'Alex?'

'Yes?'

'I wonder whether you would look after the children while I tidy a little for Eliza?' Emma gestured around the room and Alex nodded. It could certainly do with being a little tidier.

And so the Duke of Harwell looked after three—fairly grubby—small children, while the Duchess of Harwell tidied and scrubbed.

Mikey did some outside work, directed by Emma, until Alex asked him to go and check on other tenants.

When Eliza awoke from her sleep, she almost cried in gratitude. Emma hugged her, and then the two of them hugged all the children to them, and Alex couldn't help smiling at the sight.

'We should leave,' he said eventually. 'I'm afraid I have other appointments.'

'Of course.' Emma disengaged herself and picked up

her coat from the back of a kitchen chair. 'I'll call on you again very soon, Eliza.'

'Are you going on somewhere else?' she asked Alex when they got outside.

'No, obviously not.' He gestured at the ominous clouds above them. 'I predict further snowfall today. I'm going to escort you home.'

Emma opened her mouth and Alex shook his head.

'Irrespective of your pistol, and your coat and stout boots and your desire not to be told what to do—which I do fully understand and respect—I am going to escort you home.'

'I was going to say thank you,' Emma said, raising one eyebrow.

Oh.

'Well, great,' Alex said, smiling in appreciation of her ability to take the wind out of his sails frequently. 'Let's go.'

Emma set off at a significantly brisker pace than he was expecting, which was a good thing, because it started snowing lightly within minutes of their leaving the cottage. When he worried that she was only walking at that speed because she thought she ought to keep up with him, she increased her pace even further, which made him laugh.

'This is so beautiful.' She didn't sound at all out of breath. She put her arms out and tipped her face up to the sky as she continued to walk.

'Tempted to throw any snowballs now that you're one to one with your snowball foe with no shelter nearby and might come off worse?'

Emma looked round at him, blinked snowflakes from her lashes and narrowed her eyes. 'Is that a challenge?'

'Maybe. Maybe not. Just something to think about.'

'Going by your threats, I see that your defeat still rankles.'

'Defeat is a strong word.'

Defeat was completely the wrong word for what had happened. They'd made each other soaking wet, and then they'd...

Why? Why had he brought that up now? Now all he could think about was what they'd done in the snow.

Emma was capable of thinking of other things, apparently. She'd stopped walking and put her hands on her hips.

'I see what you're doing. You're attempting to plant seeds of worry in my mind. There could be a snowball around any corner. And just as my morale is low, which might affect my strategic planning, you will attack.' She started walking again, fast, and said over her shoulder, 'Just be aware that you might have longer and better throwing arms than me, but I'm sure I'm significantly more cunning.'

Alex laughed out loud and took the three strides necessary to catch her up.

He didn't practise any snowball warfare during their walk, not keen to be tempted into any further intimacy in the snow. Instead, he showed Emma various points of interest, from a very ancient oak tree, reputed to date back to the sixteenth century and to have witnessed a visit from Good Queen Bess herself, to a copse in which he and his brother played as children.

As they reached the top of a hill, from which it was possible to see for many miles—all the way to the sea on a cloudless day—the snow suddenly changed to a heavy, driving force. Within minutes, from having been almost able to make out the horizon through light snow, they could see barely a few feet in front of them.

'Oh, my goodness,' a white-covered Emma said.

Alex took two steps towards her, reached for her hand and linked his fingers firmly through hers. 'We must hold hands so that we don't lose each other.'

The swirling snow was incredibly disorientating. Alex knew his land like the back of his hand, and still he was in great danger of losing his bearings unless he concentrated hard. The snow was very wet and very cold, and they would do well not to stay in it for too long. He was beginning to feel chilled to the bone, despite his greatcoat and winter boots, and Emma's clothing was less robust than his. She also had a much smaller frame than he, so she would be freezing very quickly.

They began to walk slowly forward, Alex feeling the way slightly ahead of Emma, using his feet. Within only a few steps Emma tripped. He caught her and pulled her to a halt next to him.

'Are you all right? You haven't twisted your ankle or anything?'

'Yes, thank you.' She was gripping his hand and arm as tightly as he was holding hers now.

'I think we need to take shelter nearby until this is over,' he said. 'I think it would be very difficult to get all the way back. I can't believe it will last more than an hour or two, and there's a barn about a hundred feet to our left.'

It was perhaps two miles to the house, and that was a very long way in a blizzard, especially for someone in female attire.

Arm in arm now, they inched towards where Alex

thought the barn was, guided only by his memory of how the hill's contours went.

'I think I might have misremembered,' he said eventually, after they'd been trudging into driving snow for what seemed like an extraordinarily long time. 'I'm so sorry. Hopefully we will at least find a wall soon, behind which we can shelter.' The snow was biting, literally painful against one's face, and he sensed Emma wince every so often. If they found a wall, he would do his best to shelter her from the storm. 'We can't walk too far, though.'

There was a river running through his land not far from here, and there were several dips in the terrain that were negligible to people who could see them, but which in this weather could cause one or both of them to break a leg or worse.

'Wall!' said Emma about ten seconds later.

'I beg your pardon?'

'Wall. I just hit a wall with my hand.'

Alex turned carefully, with his own free hand outstretched, and felt around. Yes, they'd found a wall.

'Thank God,' he said. 'I'm sure this is the wall of a building. It must be the barn.'

Emma made to let go of his hand, but he tightened his grip on hers.

'I really don't think we should let go of each other at this point,' he said. 'Let's not fail now, when we're so close to shelter.'

'Yes, you're right.' Emma moved back towards him and said, 'Let's go to our right along the wall, not letting go of it, until we come to a door or opening.'

'Good idea.'

They found the opening on the third side, and walked

through the edge of the blizzard inside, towards the back of the barn, which was fully covered and dry and half full of hay.

'That is *such* a relief.' Emma took her hand out of his. 'I can't remember ever feeling so truly ecstatic to find a pile of dead grass.' She reached up to her head and pulled at her bonnet, which had begun the day a fairly rigid, pointed shape, but which was now entirely sodden and drooping. 'My fingers are barely working from the cold.'

Eventually, she had the bonnet off and shook out her hair. 'May I sit on this hay?'

'Certainly.' Alex climbed over towards the back of the barn and held his arm out for her to take. 'If you come here you'll find that it's much warmer, or at least less freezing.'

Emma took his arm for support and climbed over, and then let go and sat down. Alex joined her, although sitting a cautious few feet away from her.

'We were lucky that we were so close to the barn when that started,' she said. 'And that you know your land so well. Or perhaps you have some kind of supernatural ability to see through incredibly heavy snow.'

Alex laughed. 'Yes, I am possessed of a special winter vision belonging only to Somerset natives. No, I've spent many, many days on this land, and I do know it well, even more so now, from a different angle, since I inherited the running and husbandry of it.'

'Well, thank goodness. I'm sure we would have been all right had we stayed out there, albeit extremely cold and wet, but I have to say I vastly prefer being inside, even in a barn. Indeed, at this moment the barn feels positively like a princess's palace.'

'It does. And I'm sure it's very good for us to be re-

minded not to take our creature comforts for granted.'
Alex paused, hearing a slightly odd sound, and studied
Emma. 'Is that sound your teeth chattering?'

'N-n-no…' It wasn't just her teeth that were chattering; her whole body was beginning to judder.

'You're freezing.'

'Please don't worry; this hay will serve very well
to warm me.' Emma pulled some hay against herself,
turning herself into a ridiculously sorry sight as some
stuck to her damp clothes while other wisps floated away
from her.

Alex stood up and took his coat off to wrap her in it.
But, no, that would be no good; it was very wet on the
outside and the damp had penetrated right through it in
parts. His jacket was also wet, and not thick enough to
provide much warmth.

Emma was shivering more and more now, her whole
body jerking. Alex knew that he needed to do something
fast, and could think of only one solution.

'I think you need to take your wet coat off, and then
I'm going to sit very close to you to warm you.'

'Really?'

'Yes.'

She pulled ineffectually at the buttons of her coat,
her fingers clearly too cold to work properly at all now.
Alex moved over to sit beside her and began to undo
the buttons, working as fast as he could, scared by how
very much she was shivering. He had the coat off very
quickly, and laid it out on the hay behind them in the
hope that it might dry a little, before wrapping both his
arms around her. Her dress was a little damp, unsur-
prisingly.

'I don't see how we can get entirely dry, short of divesting ourselves entirely of our clothes.' He wondered immediately why he'd said that, struggling to force his mind away from the thought of Emma divested of her clothes. 'But I think that if we huddle together like this our body warmth will heat the wetness, which should hopefully warm you up.'

'Thank you.' She could hardly get the words out round her chattering teeth.

Alex was getting even more scared. He could feel Emma's slender shoulders shivering in huge jerks. There was still too much of her exposed to the cold air.

'Come here.' He lifted her onto his lap and wrapped himself around her as much as he could.

'Thank you,' she said again, her voice now muffled against his chest.

They sat like that for a while—Alex couldn't tell how long—until Emma wriggled a little and said, 'I'm starting to feel a reasonably normal temperature again. Thank you so much.'

'Good,' said Alex, not releasing his grip on her. 'Let's not count our chickens too early, though. We must get you as hot as possible before I let go of you. Even when the snow's subsided enough for us to make our way back we're going to get very wet again, and you're going to have to put your wet coat back on.'

'How's it looking now?' Emma raised her head and peered over his shoulder.

'Still remarkably fierce. If we weren't wet and on foot and stranded in a barn a good couple of miles from the house, I'd be lost in happy awe of the elements.'

'It is beautiful,' agreed Emma, wriggling some more, presumably to get a better view out of the barn entrance.

Now that he was a little less worried about her, Alex

was a lot more aware of the fact that she was sitting on his lap, in his arms, and that she was wiggling her gorgeously rounded bottom against him. He really hoped she couldn't feel the effect she was having on him.

She suddenly stopped moving and… Yes, she probably had realised.

There wasn't a lot that embarrassed Alex, but this, yes, this was embarrassing. And there was nothing he could do to extricate himself from the embarrassment because he had to keep holding Emma the way he was, so that she wouldn't get cold again. So he was just going to chat to her about something mundane, and then he'd stop being so aware of her, his body would get itself under control and all would be well.

'I wonder what we'll have for luncheon when we return to the house,' he said.

Food was certainly a mundane topic.

'Something warm and hearty. Perhaps a beef stew. Followed, perhaps, by something deliciously sweet.' Emma shifted again on his lap and Alex almost groaned out loud.

'What's your favourite dessert?' he persisted.

They just needed to talk about food for longer. That way he could absolutely stop his mind and body from being so focused on what Emma was doing with her body.

'I'm not sure. I think…' Emma paused. Alex couldn't see her face, but he knew what she looked like when she was thinking. She'd have her nose ever so slightly wrinkled, and if she was about to say something sarcastic or cheeky, her eyes would be dancing.

'On a day like this, something very rich. A smooth chocolate mousse, perhaps.'

Now Alex was imagining her putting a spoon into a mousse and then into her mouth, her tongue peeking out. And now of course he was imagining kissing her again. God.

'What would you like?' she asked.

'What?'

'What would you like to eat?'

'To eat? Of course.' Alex could barely remember what food was at this point. It felt as though he had one physical need only, and it wasn't food.

Emma twisted her head to look up at him and smiled. It was the smile that undid him. If she hadn't done it maybe he could have resisted, but the smile was both sweet and slightly mocking, as though she knew what he was thinking.

He found himself adjusting her so that he could reach her face better—and, *damn*, it felt good as she moved in his lap—and then, very slowly, he lowered his head to hers. She moved to meet him and suddenly the slowness was gone and they were kissing, hard, urgently, passionately.

Far in the depths of his brain Alex knew that this was a terrible idea, but apparently he was completely powerless to resist.

Chapter Fourteen

Emma was almost panting as she kissed Alex back as hard as he was kissing her.

From the moment her teeth had stopped chattering so hard it had felt as though she might bite right through her tongue, and she'd had the ability to think about where she was, she'd loved being enveloped in Alex's arms. And from the moment she'd warmed up and moved on his lap and felt the evidence of his desire for her, she'd wanted this.

She had her hands in his thick hair, his arms were round her waist and her shoulders, and his body was still wrapped right around hers. It was truly wonderful, but she wanted *more*.

It wasn't just the physical sensation that she wanted, although she was quite desperate for that. It was also that she wanted some kind of affirmation of how their relationship had developed, in her eyes anyway. They made each other laugh, they seemed to be able to talk about all manner of topics, and Alex was a very kind, decent person whom she *liked*.

She hoped he liked her too.

She didn't just like him. She loved him.

And at this moment, she was in his arms, and she wanted to give him everything she had and receive everything he could give her.

She wriggled against him again and he groaned, deep in his throat, a sound that made her breath catch. She moved one of her hands from the back of his head and ran it up his hard chest. Then she took her other hand and pulled at the fastenings of his shirt, wanting to feel his skin as she had the other day.

She moved further against him and he groaned again, and then he plunged his hands into her hair and pulled very gently, so that her head went back a little. He kissed down her neck, licking, nibbling, nipping, caressing her shoulders with one hand and still holding her waist with the other. His kisses were moving ever lower, but slowly, and Emma felt as though her entire body was becoming taut in anticipation.

And then suddenly he lifted her, so that she was lying on her back, nestled away from any draughts, on a big bundle of hay, with him above her. With one hand he was caressing her breast and the other fumbled with ribbons and buttons, trying to remove her dress. Emma found herself pulling his shirt out of his breeches as urgently as he was trying to undress her.

Alex paused for a moment and found her eyes with his. He raised his eyebrows slightly, as though seeking her consent to continue.

'Yes, please,' she said. And if she sounded as though she was begging, she didn't care.

She smiled at him, a heartfelt invitation, and he smiled back. Then he lowered his lips to hers again, this time kissing her gently, slowly, deeply, all the while exploring with his hands.

Emma's breasts felt as though they were on fire now, and the sensation was spreading to her most intimate parts, so that she was almost *aching* for him in a way that she couldn't even describe.

He drew back for a moment, and just looked at her. 'You're beautiful,' he said.

Emma looked down at herself and gasped. Somehow she was almost entirely naked. Then she looked at him, and gasped again, because he was almost entirely naked too, and he was...magnificent.

And then she lost the ability to think because Alex began to kiss her everywhere, while his fingers touched her between her thighs gently, then more insistently, until she was arching and turning and her body was almost *singing* with sensation.

Then his body was above hers, so close, and he was looking at her again with that raised eyebrow, as though confirming again that she was happy. She nodded, realising through the haze of sensation that there was nothing with which she wouldn't trust him. Kissing her and murmuring her name the whole time, he pushed slowly inside her.

When, after the first shock, she was comfortable— comfortable to perfection—he began to thrust and thrust, and if she'd thought that her body was singing with sensation before, it was positively crying out now.

She opened her eyes for a moment and looked at his face—the face she knew now that she loved, at which she could never tire of looking—and she smiled at him and whispered, 'Alex.'

And then he began to thrust harder and harder, and she was lost, one hand in his hair, the other almost scratching his back, almost screaming with the desire for more and more of him.

Suddenly, she felt the most glorious sensation, her whole body flooded with it, and this time she really did scream, while Alex grunted, 'Yes, Emma, yes.'

And then he gathered her to him as they both lay panting.

Emma looked up at his strong jaw, his kind eyes, his mouth that could set in a forbidding line when he was angry and yet curve in such a sweet way at other times, and knew that she would never be the same again.

She didn't know how he felt about her, but she knew that she'd fallen in love with him, and that it wasn't going to be the kind of love you recovered from quickly. Or maybe ever.

She gasped again—she'd been doing a lot of gasping today—as he eased himself out of her and said, his voice hoarse, 'That was... That was not what I was expecting to do today.'

'Nor I,' Emma said after a moment, her heart cracking, because it was extremely clear that he hadn't been lying there thinking that he'd fallen in love with her.

If you'd just realised that you'd fallen in love with someone the first words that came out of your mouth would not be that you hadn't expected to do that today.

Maybe he could come to love her in time, though? Or at least enjoy her company and making love to her enough to want to live with her as man and wife, properly?

Would he want to make love to her again? Regularly? And would that be enough for her? Would she be able to hide from him how she felt?

If she couldn't hide it from him things could get very embarrassing on both sides.

She could hide it, should hide it, if it meant they could be together. Or should she? Would she in time begin to resent him? Would her love drive a wedge between them, as her parents' love had driven a wedge between them when it had become apparent that they wanted and needed different things in life?

'So.' Alex released her gently and Emma looked down at their nakedness. Alex did too. He was stirring again as they looked at each other. She felt her breath catch in her throat as she felt her own body responding to his obvious desire, and then he cleared his throat and moved a little further away from her.

'The blizzard has stopped,' he said. 'We should return while it's safe to do so, and before anyone becomes worried about us.'

Emma took a deep breath to cover her disappointment, and when she was sure that her voice would sound close to normal said, 'We should, indeed.'

She rolled to one side, away from him, looking for her clothes to cover herself. It turned out that nakedness during lovemaking was wonderful, and natural, but nakedness when the man who had just made love to you just wanted to go home felt embarrassing. And cold when you were in an open barn on a snowy day.

Alex passed her her dress and she said, 'Thank you.'

They dressed with their backs to each other. Emma couldn't remember feeling this miserable for a long time. Ironic that she'd thought—known—she could trust him with anything. She realised now that she could trust him with absolutely everything except her heart.

The good thing about getting dressed in wet clothes surrounded by hay was that it was quite difficult, and it gave Emma time to think a little more and pull herself together. The bad thing about how difficult it was was that she couldn't entirely manage by herself.

She turned to Alex. 'I'm so sorry, but I wonder if you might help with my fastenings?'

'Of course.'

As he carefully pulled her hair aside, his fingers brushed her neck, and Emma almost leapt a mile. She was really going to have to work hard to get herself under control.

'I think you should wear my coat,' Alex told her. 'It's thicker, and it didn't get so wet on the inside.' He held it up against her and said, 'Oh.'

It was many inches too long.

'It might keep me warmer, but I might fall and break a leg instead,' Emma said.

'Indeed. Each to their own coat it is, then.'

They said very little further as they made their way out of the barn, Alex helping Emma clamber over the bales of hay, and their conversation during the walk back was restricted to the most basic of issues, such as Alex's request that Emma hold his arm and hand again, in case the ground was slippery or there was a further sudden snowstorm.

Emma couldn't quite comprehend how the linking of their arms now felt so entirely functional, when their arms had been wrapped around each other so passionately so very recently.

Well, it was a strong sign of how Alex felt, and since she was going to be seeing him every day still, she would have to hide her emotions for both their sakes.

She was sure he was still grieving for his wife.

She remembered their conversation over dinner a

week or two ago, when he'd described Diana in such a tender way. Of *course* he was still grieving for her.

She felt sorry, deeply sorry, for him. She knew that if something awful happened to him now she'd be devastated, and she'd only known and loved him for a few weeks. If something bad happened to him in a few years' time she would find it horrendous.

So, having loved Diana for several years, as he obviously had, and having three children with her, he must have been utterly grief-stricken when he'd lost her. Awful. She hated to think of Alex in pain.

If she was honest, though—and this probably made her a truly terrible person—she couldn't help feeling a tiny bit (very) sorry for her own loss too, because when she thought about it like this it was quite clear that Alex was still deeply in love with the memory of his wife and that Emma would never be able to compete with that.

There was nothing she could say to him now.

They walked on in silence all the way back to the castle.

Perhaps it was a good thing that Alex was still in love with Diana and that Emma couldn't compete with that love. The two of them clearly wanted very different things, just as her parents had, and she didn't want to follow in their footsteps and have her love turn to near-hatred because they were so incompatible.

As they approached the main entrance to the castle, she took a quick glance up at his profile. He didn't twitch. She felt as though she'd lost him today, somewhere in the moments after they'd made love.

'Your Grace,' cried Jenny, hurrying out to meet them. 'Come inside directly. You'll catch your death with that wet coat on.'

Emma realised that she was indeed very cold.

'Thank you, Jenny.' She turned round to bid Alex farewell and discovered that he'd already gone.

'You need to have a bath immediately.'

Jenny and Mrs Drabble both busied themselves calling for so much hot water that the entire household could have had hot baths if the footmen had obeyed them.

'Thank you so much. But I'm very well able to bathe myself,' Emma told Jenny when the bath was ready.

She didn't want to undress in front of Jenny; what if there had been some physical change in her today that Jenny could discern?

'You're shivering. I don't want to leave you, Your Grace.'

'Thank you, Jenny, but I assure you that I will be warm again as soon as I get into the bath.'

Jenny grumbled for so long that Emma feared the bath water might already be cold. When she eventually gave in and left, Emma locked the door behind her and undressed herself before climbing into the bath. She looked down at herself. There did not, in fact, seem to be any noticeable physical change.

She had certainly changed emotionally, though; she was certain now that she'd fallen deeply and irrevocably in love with Alex.

Now she was shivering again.

She rubbed her arms hard to warm herself up. Her body, anyway. It felt as though her heart might never be warm again.

Chapter Fifteen

Alex spent only the time it took to get changed into dry clothes and visit the kitchen for a flying luncheon—to his chef's expressed horror, but not very well-hidden delight—before readying himself to set off again on foot to visit other tenants. He needed to check that the more vulnerable amongst them were all right, and he also needed not to be alone with his thoughts.

Those thoughts had intruded as he'd changed and eaten and parried comments from his chef, and they continued to intrude as he shrugged on a dry greatcoat.

This morning was the first time he'd been intimate with a woman since he'd lost Diana. He couldn't... He didn't... He wasn't sure how he felt, other than that the experience had been truly spectacular from a physical perspective and utterly terrifying from an emotional perspective.

Physically, he just wanted to do it again.

Emotionally, well, emotionally, what did he want?

He wanted to know that Emma would always be happy. He wanted—that was to say, he was *tempted*—to look after her, cosset her...

Damn it, he wanted to... He almost wanted to love her.

No. He did *not* want to love her.

The image of her smile as they'd lain together on the straw came into his head. Hell and damnation. What if she decided to go out again this afternoon and some accident befell her?

He called Lancing, and every footman he could see, as well as Mrs Drabble and Jenny, to instruct them that they must not allow Emma to leave the house in the snow by herself again.

At the last minute, just before he left, he realised his own hypocrisy. Even if he didn't have a responsibility to himself, he did to many other people, not least his motherless children. He asked his head groom, Jim, whom he knew was very fit and, crucially, also a man of few words, to walk with him.

They set off on a long and silent march into biting wind, enlivened by the occasional sideways flurry of skin-prickling frozen snow, which suited his mood very well.

Visibility this afternoon was dramatically better than it had been this morning, and he could now see the barn from some distance. Thank God they'd found it when they had. And thank God he'd been with Emma. If she'd been alone she might have been killed in that blizzard.

She was so brave. And so stupid. And so adorable. Not to mention beautiful.

He forced his mind away from the memory of her naked beneath him, and then from another, of how, in the aftermath of their lovemaking, her smile had changed from one of physical bliss to uncertainty, when she'd clearly seen that he wasn't going to repeat the experience.

That change in her smile had nearly caused him to gather her up in his arms, rain kisses on her and tell her... Tell her that he felt... Damn. He couldn't. He couldn't love her. He could not allow himself to do so. It would be very easy to do so. But difficult too. Because what if something bad happened to her?

She was extremely competent, but there were things that very few people could survive, like, for example, a fully clothed fall into a near-frozen river in a blizzard. He couldn't bear the thought that she could have died today.

He stepped up his pace and Jim grunted, 'You're in a hurry today, Your Grace.'

Alex found a small smile for him. 'You not up to it, Jim?'

'I'm up to it, Your Grace. Just a little surprised.'

Alex nodded. He was surprised too. This morning had taught him something that he hadn't known. He hadn't believed that he could ever love another woman again after Diana. Now he knew that while he would always carry his grief for Diana with him, he was capable of loving again.

What he was *not* capable of, though, was coping with being in love. Because if Emma *had* died this morning, or even just been injured, it would have devastated him, and he'd only known her for a few weeks. If he allowed himself to make their marriage real it would destroy him if anything happened to her. And the way the boys were going, loving her as they already did, it would destroy them too. He just couldn't do it.

Emma had friends now. She was established socially, he hoped. They should probably move on to the next phase of their marriage. She could move to the dower house and begin to live independently. He would make clear to his friends and acquaintances that she should be respected as a member of their circle. Perhaps he would confide in Letitia as he already had in Gideon.

'Your Grace!'

'Jim?'

'You didn't tell me we'd be running.'

'Not running, Jim, just walking fast.'

Alex increased his pace even more, so that they were working too hard for speech or, importantly, further thought. Thinking was not pleasant today.

Some time later, as they skirted the edge of a small wood at the base of a hill, a bough broke under the weight of the snow it had been holding and fell just in front of them, scattering snow as it went.

The sensation of wet snow on his skin made him think of snowballs with Emma, rolling in the snow with Emma, making love to Emma a few yards away from a blizzard. Which was ridiculous, because he was thirty-three years old and he had encountered a lot of snow with a lot of different people; but it seemed that he couldn't get Emma out of his thoughts this afternoon.

He flexed his shoulders as some of the snow went down his neck and imagined her laughing at him. Damn, he'd miss her if he didn't see her any more. Perhaps he shouldn't make too hasty a decision; perhaps he should think more about their situation first.

They arrived shortly after that at the home of Caleb Wilson, one of Alex's tenant farmers. Caleb was an elderly man who had broken his leg badly a few weeks ago, tumbling from a shire horse that a man of his age really should not have been riding.

As Alex ducked his head to go through the doorway into the cottage's main room, having asked Jim

if he would go and check on Caleb's livestock, he saw
Caleb huddled in a chair close to a dying fire. There
was a large pile of logs on the other side of the fire, but
it looked as though Caleb wasn't mobile enough to be
able to reach them.

Alex had made sure that all his less well-off tenants
had a ready supply of firewood over the winter, so it had
to be a mobility issue rather than a financial one. That
or Caleb enjoyed freezing in his own home. Other than
next to the fire, the room was barely any warmer than
the temperature outside.

His heart going out to Caleb, but knowing from experience how proud he was, Alex clapped his hands together, and said, 'It's a cold day out there, Caleb. I'm
chilled to the bone. Would you mind if I built your fire
up? I'm not sure I'll be able to get through the rest of
the day happily otherwise.'

'You're a good lad, Your Grace. Thank you.' Caleb
produced a toothless grin for him, and Alex's heart
twisted again. Sometimes his responsibility for all these
good, decent people weighed on him particularly heavily.

'I hope you don't mind if I join you by the fire?' Alex
drew up a stool and sat down next to the old man. 'How's
your leg healing?'

Caleb had a lot to say, giving the impression of a man
somewhat desperate for company. He would normally
be busy all day, and would see his neighbours regularly
too, but now with his broken leg he was at the mercy
of how much time they could spare to visit him, and in
conditions like this they wouldn't have a lot of time.

'Tess, my daughter-in-law, she's been in,' he said.
'She's a good woman, but she's busy with those bairns of
hers.' He paused and stretched out a hand to Alex, who

took it. 'You'll understand this, Your Grace. I always miss my Jeanie—' his wife had died about five years ago '—but it's at times like this, when I have thinking time, that I miss her even more.'

Alex was not in the habit of talking about his feelings but, looking at Caleb's lined face, into his faded blue eyes, he knew that at this moment he needed to make the effort for Caleb's sake. It didn't come naturally, though. And while he had experienced the terrible loss of his wife, at a horrifyingly early age, he'd never, due to his different station in life, found himself sitting all alone in the near-freezing, near-dark for hours on end.

'Yes. I was reflecting earlier today that too much thinking time is dangerous,' he said, feeling for words that would demonstrate to Caleb that he understood.

'It is. We need to move on with the future. You have your children and I have mine, and I have my grandchildren. We need to think about them, not the past. We're both lucky. Not everyone has children.'

Alex didn't want to think about the fact that he'd effectively prevented Emma from having children of her own. Unless, of course, she'd become with child as a result of their lovemaking this morning. How would he feel if she had? Pleased for her that she'd have a baby but utterly terrified that she'd die in childbirth, as Diana had.

He returned the squeeze of the hand that Caleb gave him and said, 'We might be lucky with our children, but the loss of one's life companion is very hard.'

'It is that.' They sat in silence for a moment, with Alex feeling quite useless, and then Caleb said, 'Thank you, Your Grace. Much appreciated.'

Maybe all Caleb needed from Alex was what he could

give him: his company, and the feeling that they were in the same boat.

He looked up as he heard a muffled sniff from Caleb, and reached over and squeezed his shoulder.

'Thank you again,' Caleb said after a few moments. 'I'm getting emotional in my old age. I just miss her.'

Alex clasped Caleb's hand and looked into the fire. Currently, he was dealing with life better than Caleb was. He'd reached a point where, while still grieving for Diana, he had been able to develop feelings for another woman and enjoy making love to her. He didn't want to regress, be like this again. He didn't want to be a lonely old man, missing his wife so deeply. He wanted to be happy, but not so happy that the loss of that happiness would cause a repeat of his devastation over Diana's death.

'I need to cheer myself up,' Caleb said. 'We have to let go, don't we, when we've lost someone?'

Alex nodded. 'Yes. We do.'

He wasn't talking about Diana, though. It was Emma whom he needed to let go of now. He hoped she wouldn't be hurt, but he had, after all, told her right from the beginning that he couldn't offer her anything more than his name and his protection.

If he and Jim had walked fast on the way there, now, on their way back to the castle, they'd almost give a horse a run for its money.

'May I ask if everything's all right, Your Grace?' Jim panted at one point.

'Certainly.' Alex didn't look at him; he just kept on marching, too fast for further thought.

He and Jim were very hot when they arrived back.

'Thank you for your company,' he said to Jim. 'Apologies if I walked a little fast.'

'I enjoyed it, Your Grace,' Jim said. 'Even if my feet didn't,' he added under his breath, as he headed off towards the stables with a slight limp.

Alex smiled at his departing back. Thank God he had staff who didn't stand on ceremony with him. If he didn't, he could end up as lonely as Caleb. He would make sure that he or someone else from his household visited Caleb regularly until his leg was mended.

Striding into the house, he was stopped by Lancing, who told him that Mrs Hardy had called for tea and had expressed a particular desire to see Alex, should he return before she left. She was currently in the green saloon with the duchess.

'Of course.' Alex could barely imagine a person to whom he'd less like to speak today, and was strongly tempted to turn tail, but he couldn't leave Emma to Mrs Hardy's mercies.

He entered the saloon just in time to hear Mrs Hardy, seated with her back to him, say to a rigid-looking Emma, 'And I must repeat: if you would like any advice on comportment, you know you only have to ask and I shall be very happy to guide you. I am, of course, the granddaughter of an earl. In my capacity as vicar's wife I am here to assist those less fortunate than myself, such as you with your background.'

Emma's eyes had widened as Mrs Hardy spoke. Now she said, one eye on Alex, 'I count myself incredibly fortunate to have you available to assist me should I require such help. Thank you.'

Alex knew that she was being sarcastic, and he knew that she would be able to laugh about Mrs Hardy's ridiculous rudeness, but he was nonetheless filled with real rage at how the woman had spoken to Emma, not least because he was scared that others would hear her express such thoughts and imitate her.

'You are indeed kind to make such an offer, Mrs Hardy,' he said, injecting ice into his voice.

Mrs Hardy turned her head very fast and then rose to her feet, wreathed in smiles, before curtseying. 'Your Grace,' she said, holding her hands out to him.

Alex ignored the hands. 'While you are kind, Emma has no need of your advice. Firstly, she is herself the granddaughter of an earl, through her mother, and also of a princess, through her father. I am certain that she is too well-bred to have discussed her breeding with you, so you were perhaps not aware of that.'

He could see Mrs Hardy's smile fall at his implied criticism and Emma, beyond her, smiling at him, her eyes beginning to dance.

'Secondly, of course, true breeding comes from within, and certainly from my perspective I have nothing but admiration for Emma's character and comportment, and I am sure that the vast majority of her acquaintance feel the same way. Good afternoon.' He moved back to the door and held it wide open and bowed to Mrs Hardy.

'I see that you are in a bad humour this afternoon, Your Grace,' she said, glaring. 'No doubt it is the weather. Much can be excused of a duke, fortunately.'

When she'd huffed herself out of the room, Alex closed the door behind her very firmly and sat down on a sofa opposite Emma.

'Thank you,' she said. 'That was spectacular.'

'I cannot regret my rudeness. The way she spoke to you was completely unacceptable.'

'She was so rude that I just wanted to laugh. But I was very glad that you were there to witness it, to share in my enjoyment.'

Alex laughed. '"Enjoyment" is a charitable word.'

There was a short silence between them.

They needed to talk.

He put his hands on his knees, and then lifted them to adjust his jacket. Perhaps he should have changed before they started this conversation. No, formal clothing would not have helped. He placed his hands back on his knees and crossed his legs, and then uncrossed them.

How to begin?

'How has your afternoon been?' Emma asked into the uncomfortable silence. 'I believe you went to visit other tenants?'

'Yes.'

Describing to Emma his visit to Caleb was a relief: it felt like a partial unburdening, or at least a sharing, of the responsibility Alex felt.

'So he's going to feel his loneliness greatly while he remains incapacitated with his broken leg?' Emma said when Alex had concluded the story of his visit.

He nodded.

'We should arrange for him to have regular visitors. Certainly, I shall visit him, perhaps with one or more of the children, by carriage if you think it appropriate?'

'Yes, I do, and indeed I trust you quite implicitly in your judgement in regard to the children.'

Emma's cheeks flushed. 'Thank you. That's quite the most lovely compliment anyone has paid me for a long time.'

This wasn't really how Alex had envisaged his conversation with Emma going, although he was very grateful to know that she would visit Caleb.

'We need to talk,' he said, more shortly than he'd intended.

'I am at your disposal,' Emma said, her smile gone.

Alex took a deep breath. And then said nothing for a while.

Emma straightened her shoulders and took a deep breath of her own.

'I feel,' Alex began eventually, 'that perhaps now might be a good time for you to move to the dower house.' He looked at her. 'If you would like to.'

No. He couldn't. He could not actually ask her to move out of his—now their—house. How could he have said that? Appalling.

'I'm sorry; that was unconscionable. Please don't move there, unless you'd like to. You might wish to do so. You might not. I'd like to make it very clear that I am, in fact, in no way asking you to move there. I thought that perhaps you would be more comfortable there. But of course you might feel that you would be more comfortable here.'

He stopped talking, aware that he was sounding like the imbecile he apparently was.

For a long moment, Emma just looked at him. Then she leaned forward a little, and said, 'I feel that now is a time for honesty.'

Oh, God.

'And, honestly, you were babbling.'

Alex pressed his lips together and nodded. After Mrs Hardy's departure, he'd sat down, planning to tell Emma that what had happened between them earlier today couldn't be repeated, and that he thought it would be best if she moved to the dower house. Or he thought that was what he'd been planning to say. Now he could barely even recollect what his thoughts had been.

Whatever the case, something had happened in the space of perhaps a minute, and now he didn't know what he wanted. He did know that he'd made an incredible mull of attempting to explain in a dignified fashion that he could offer Emma no further intimacy. All the dignity was on Emma's side.

'My observation,' she continued, 'is that you wanted to tell me that you regret what happened between us today and would prefer not to repeat it. You therefore thought that you wanted me to remove immediately to the dower house, but, on saying the words aloud, you realised that you were telling me that I had to leave your house, and since you are a kind person, you don't feel that you can, in fact, do that.'

'I…' Alex shook his head. And then nodded. Yes. She was probably right. She *was* right. But…

'I have something to say.' Emma was sitting very upright now. She looked very stern and very beautiful, and if he were a different man with a different life he would want nothing more than to take her in his arms and make slow, reverent love to her for the rest of the day. For the rest of time.

But there was no such thing as the rest of time, as both he and Caleb knew.

'Go ahead,' he said.

'It seems to me that you are still grieving the loss of your wife and still in love with her. I cannot compete with that, and I do not wish to compete with that. I agree that what happened this morning was a mistake. I am happy to remove to the dower house if that is what you deem best for both of us, and of course for the boys, but I am also perfectly content to remain in the main house, to live amicable but separate lives. Like you, I would not like to repeat this morning's mistake.'

Alex thought he saw her eyes glistening before she lowered her lids and studied her hands with seeming great interest. He wanted so much to correct her misapprehension that he couldn't love again. But if he told her he loved her he would be doing both himself and her a great disservice.

'Perfect,' he said.

He didn't even know what he was agreeing to.

Chapter Sixteen

The snow disappeared almost overnight. The temperature rose too, and when Emma and the boys went outside in the late morning to begin a walk, Emma realised immediately that they would need to change their thick coats for lighter ones or be uncomfortably warm in the bright sunshine.

'It feels as though we dreamt the snow,' Freddie observed as they sat down on sun-dried grass, next to the lake at the far end of the lawns directly in front of the castle. 'It's so hot. But there was a blizzard this time yesterday.'

'I agree,' Emma said.

She did agree. At approximately this time yesterday, she and Alex had taken refuge in the barn and made love. Today, only four-and-twenty hours later, it was as though their lovemaking had never occurred. Well, not entirely; it wasn't something she would ever forget. But their relationship had in no way developed as a result of it. Well, it *had* developed, but backwards rather than forwards.

As Freddie had said, it now felt almost as though the whole thing had been a dream.

'Emma!' Harry had his face very close to hers and she jumped as he shouted. 'You weren't listening.'

'I'm so sorry,' she said. 'I was a little distracted thinking about the snow.'

And your father. And the miracles he was working this time yesterday on my body.

She shivered. No. She should try hard not to think about that again, and she should try *really* hard not to think about it in front of the boys.

She forced her mind away from Alex and said to Harry, 'Tell me again what you said and I promise you that I will listen very carefully.'

And she did concentrate very well on his surprisingly detailed monologue about dragonflies. She simply needed to apply herself carefully and she would soon be able to stop thinking about Alex in a romantic way. Hopefully.

By the afternoon, the last vestiges of the snow had melted away under a March sun as unseasonably strong as the snow had been, in direct contrast to the frost that seemed to be settling more and more around Emma's heart as the day wore on. An entire day spent with three lively young boys left little time for reflection, and yet, bit by bit, the full reality of what had happened yesterday, and her own and Alex's reactions to it, were permeating her brain.

Later, she couldn't help revisiting in her mind yet again the situation between her and Alex as she finished reading an excerpt from *Gulliver's Travels* to the boys in the nursery.

It had been as though an invisible force had drawn the two of them together. From her side at least it had been based on both a strong physical attraction and a thorough enjoyment—even love—of his company. Their lovemaking had been wonderful and, while Emma had no previous experience to draw on, she was certain that Alex had simulated nothing and had been equally as passionate as she in that moment.

However, where she had then known for certain that she was in love with him—a feeling that was increasingly settling inside her—he had clearly realised that she could never compare to his Diana. He had therefore done his best to inform her that they should henceforth lead separate lives. It was the only time she'd experienced him being inarticulate.

She sniffed.

'Emma, are you crying?' Harry pointed his chubby finger at her face.

Emma shook her head, wiped her fingers under both her eyes and said, 'I think the wind must have blown down the chimney and sent a little smoke from the fire in my direction.'

'Oh.' Harry climbed onto her lap and hugged her. Emma wrapped her arms around him and buried her face in his hair for a moment. Children's affection was so much more straightforward than that between adults.

Alex came in shortly afterwards to see the boys.

'Excuse me,' Emma said, directing a bland smile at them all. 'I must go and change before dinner.'

'And get the smoke out of your eyes where it made you cry,' Harry shouted.

'I think we might all be able to hear you without you shouting so loudly,' Alex admonished gently, avoiding looking directly at Emma.

Did she want to move to the dower house, she wondered as she closed the nursery door behind her.

She didn't want to live by herself. After her father had died, an elderly aunt had come to join her for her mourning period, and the two of them had lived together with her father's servants in splendid and very lonely isolation. Emma had no desire to live like that ever again.

She would also miss the boys, and she hoped she wasn't flattering herself in believing that they would miss her too; and they certainly should not be made to suffer. But she was sure they could be very happy with a new governess, and Alex clearly wanted her to go. And of course she didn't want to make him miserable by inflicting her presence on him.

Dinner was a miserable affair, involving many plates of delectable food for which Emma had absolutely no appetite, and stilted conversation with Alex. The highlight of their interaction was when a conversation about the next day's weather involved a small, unintentional pun involving crows on Alex's part, which they both realised at the same time and which caused them both to smile a little.

Other than that, Alex was very much living up to his Ice Duke sobriquet. Emma didn't feel as though she had the energy to coax him out of it, and she had far too much pride to try. If making love to her once had caused him to be like this, then that was the way it was. She could only be grateful that she'd had the strength to tell him that their lovemaking had been a mistake from her perspective too. If she was going to have to carry on seeing him regularly—and while that would be difficult, it wouldn't be as bad as not seeing him at all—she needed to keep her pride and dignity intact.

* * *

After a miserable night, Emma was delighted at breakfast the next morning to receive a note from Letitia, asking her if she would like to visit the shops in Yarford with her that afternoon. She had her response written and dispatched within minutes of receiving the note.

A few hours later, she and Letitia met outside the draper's on Yarford's high street.

'I hear that they've just taken delivery of the most divine silks, medium-weight, from India, perfect for spring robes.'

Letitia pulled her into the shop.

'Where precisely in India do these come from?' asked Emma as the shopkeeper showed them different fabrics.

'I believe them to be from the Bengal and Gujarat regions,' he said.

After some detailed discussion on the different fabrics, Emma directed Letitia to some plain silks from Bengal and some more elaborate ones with flower designs from Gujarat, which she thought would be ideal for the dresses Letitia had in mind.

'I'm impressed. You're very knowledgeable about both silks and India,' Letitia told her.

'My grandmother was an Indian princess, and my grandfather met her travelling in India to buy silks and calicos for his textiles business, which my father inherited from him.'

'I see, and that's where your famous wealth came from? That's fascinating. Would you care to walk through the town with me for a while? I have so many questions to ask you.'

Emma hadn't realised until now quite how restricted she'd felt in polite company, having had it drummed into her by her aunt that she must not under any circumstances discuss *trade*. She'd spoken to Alex about her background, but very quickly after their marriage he had ceased to feel like *company* and had felt more like, well, family, she supposed.

'I do declare that I'd like to set up a factory myself,' Letitia enthused. 'Think how much pin money we could claim for ourselves. And, on a serious note, it's wonderful that you ensure such good working conditions and pay for the factory workers. It's so interesting to learn all these facts. There's so much wonderful history involved.'

Emma smiled at Letitia. Their conversation reminded her of ones she'd had with Alex, which just showed that she could be perfectly happy spending time with her friends rather than with him. Really, she could be perfectly happy maintaining only a distant relationship with him. She did not need him.

'The weather is so beautifully clement that I wonder whether we should continue our promenade for longer?' Letitia suggested.

'Certainly. I would like that.'

As they strolled, Emma asked Letitia to tell her more about the plans for her husband's land. She'd already learned that the fashionable, frivolous exterior Letitia presented to the world hid a shrewd brain and a strong interest in agricultural advances.

Letitia's shrewdness wasn't confined to agriculture.

'I do enjoy discussing all these things with Arthur,' she said as she concluded her thoughts on field enclosures and the introduction of different crops such as clover to increase soil productivity. 'Of course, whenever we disagree, we discover subsequently that he was wrong and I right. How are you and Alex settling down into married life?'

Emma blinked. Letitia was clever. Emma had not expected her to manoeuvre the conversation so easily in this direction.

'We...' She really wasn't sure what she wanted to say.

'It must be difficult, being married to a widower?' Letitia asked, considerably more tentatively than usual. Emma nodded. Suddenly, she wanted to hear anything that Letitia might know that she didn't. 'I know that he loved Diana very much. Still loves her very much. It must have been incredibly hard for him when she died.'

'Yes, he did and yes, it was.' Letitia paused, and Emma waited. 'Rumour did reach us, even here in the depths of Somerset, that you and Alex didn't have an entirely conventional beginning to your marriage. Although, what is convention in the ridiculous circles in which we move?'

'Indeed,' said Emma. She wanted to say, *Tell me everything you know about Alex and Diana, now.*

'We, Alex's friends here, all care very much about him. Well, not everyone cares about him. Mrs Hardy, for example, before her marriage cared a great deal about his title and wealth and nothing for his happiness, and is quite green with envy that you have succeeded where she did not. However, those of us who are his true friends do wish him every happiness, so we were, of course, a little concerned for him at first, on hearing about his very sudden wedding. But when we met you we were just delighted. I am selfishly delighted, because I like you so much as a friend for myself, and I'm also delighted for Alex, because the two of you seem so, well, so in love. Which is, of course, deeply unfashionable amongst the *ton*, but I'm unfashionable like that and so is Arthur, and so were Alex and Diana. And you and Alex seem so particularly well-suited.'

'Thank you,' said Emma faintly.

'The way he looks at you when you aren't looking at him is too adorable. And you do it to him too. The clearest sign that two people love each other.'

'Oh.' Emma would love to think that Letitia was right. And perhaps Alex *would* have loved her if he hadn't met Diana first. But he *had* met Diana first and that was that, and of course Emma couldn't begrudge him his marriage to her. He had the boys as a result of it, and they were wonderful.

'It is difficult, though—' Letitia flicked an imaginary something off her shoulder, as though she was trying to appear nonchalant, which gave Emma the very strong impression that she'd been planning whatever she was about to say for a while '—in the early days of a marriage, when you are not particularly well acquainted with each other, however easily you have tumbled into love. There must of necessity be a period of adjustment on both sides, which might feel quite difficult at times.'

'You're a wonderful friend to Alex,' Emma said, suddenly wanting to confide in Letitia. 'I do love him, and I do think that he might have loved me if he hadn't met Diana first. But he did. I'd like to tell you something in confidence.'

'Of course.' Letitia took Emma's hand.

'Alex and I do not have a real marriage.'

An image of Alex kissing her on the hay pushed its way to the front of Emma's mind, and she pushed it away again, hard.

'We made a bargain. He is wonderful, and kind, and

did not wish to see me ruined, so he offered me his name when someone else tried to compromise me, as perhaps you heard, but he made it very clear that he was unable to offer more than that. He suggested that if I would like to I could act as informal governess to his boys, and that is working very well. But we do not have a real marriage.'

'And yet,' murmured Letitia, 'when he looks at you he really does look like a man in love.'

Emma shook her head. 'He is a very good actor. As indeed am I. I am feeling a little despondent about our situation, but I think I've hidden my despondency very well from him. From everyone except you now.'

'Oh, Emma. It has been very little time. Love can grow. Perhaps he does not yet realise that he loves you.'

Emma shook her head. 'We have…explored our situation very thoroughly, and we have established together that we will not have an intimate marriage.'

'I'm so sorry.' Letitia squeezed her hand hard.

'Thank you, but I must not be an object of compassion. But for an accident of fate, Alex might not have been there that evening, and then we would never have met, and I would instead be either married to someone quite dreadful or working as a governess or indeed much worse. I count myself fortunate indeed and must never complain.'

'Emma, you have every right to complain, at least to yourself and to your closest friends, if the man you love does not love you. Although I believe that he does.'

Emma shook her head. 'All I need is some time to recover myself.'

An idea was dawning. She couldn't pretend to herself any more that it was going to be easy to see Alex every day in the near future.

'I think that I should perhaps make the journey to Lancashire to visit my family's factories and my cousins. And then perhaps I will journey to France.'

It would be practice for the much longer journey to India that she hoped to undertake in due course. She could visit Paris and the half-siblings she had never met, her mother's younger children. But even Letitia might not be open-minded enough not to be shocked if she described *that* scandal to her, so she wouldn't elaborate on that for now.

'Not alone, I trust?'

'Not alone, no. I will be accompanied by my maid, and perhaps two or three male servants for safety. And I will visit relatives, so that no scandal can possibly attach to my travels.'

'Or you could stay here a little longer first, so that you and Alex can get to know each other better?' Letitia suggested.

Emma shook her head. 'I don't think so.'

She and Alex had already got to know each other quite a lot better than she was going to admit to anyone. She needed some time away from him, to come to terms with her love for him coupled with his inability to love her. Travel would be the ideal distraction, and until then she would make herself very busy in preparing for her journey, together with visiting Alex's more vulnerable tenants and caring for the children.

The next few days passed in a blur for Emma.

During the daytimes she was very busy with the children, and with setting in train preparations for her journey. She also visited tenants, including Caleb Wilson and Eliza and her new baby.

Holding the baby caused Emma's stomach to twist horribly. She would have loved so much to have had the opportunity to bear and hold a baby of her own one day, but unless she was very lucky and last week's lovemaking led to pregnancy, she would never be in that position.

On the first two evenings, she and Alex dined together and made horribly desultory conversation, so on the third evening Emma sent word to him that she had the headache and thought it better to dine alone in her sitting room, and she did the same the next day.

And each night she struggled to sleep, due to the thoughts going round and round in her head, so before long she had extreme tiredness to add to her general misery.

Her misery increased when her monthly courses came and she had to accept that she wouldn't be having a baby.

She knew now, she thought one afternoon, as she walked back from visiting Caleb, that of course a journey to Lancashire wouldn't cure her of her love for Alex.

Somewhere along the way, she'd realised that the fact that her parents' love story had ended badly wasn't relevant to her own love story, or lack thereof. If Alex could love her, she knew that she would abandon her travel plans and stay in Somerset for ever with him rather than lose him.

She couldn't continue like this, and she would find it very difficult to be happy living in loneliness in the dower house, catching sight of him every so often.

What she should do was return to Lancashire and set up home there with Jenny, and make herself busy with local matters and visiting and hosting her friends.

Decision made, she felt her shoulders already less rigid and her step lighter. Perhaps she would allow herself one final dinner with Alex tonight. Not just dinner, if she was honest with herself. It would be one final attempt at trying to tempt him into falling in love with her.

If she didn't succeed tonight, well, she would have lost nothing, and tomorrow evening she would retire very early in preparation for leaving at dawn the morning after. She would tell no one in advance other than Jenny, so that Alex wouldn't make any kind of quixotic attempt at preventing her from going or accompanying her.

She dressed for dinner with care, choosing a new gown of lilac silk overlaid with delicately embroidered net. The dress suited her, she thought, regarding herself critically in the mirror, and, if there was a hint of grey shadow under her eyes from tiredness, Alex would, she hoped, be distracted by the very flattering neckline of the dress.

It was perfect: it looked nice without being too overtly dressy, the ideal dress for a duchess trying for one final time to...yes, seduce her own husband.

At the very least, she decided, as Jenny brushed her hair into an elaborate chignon, she would tell him tonight that she cared greatly about him, so that, even if her seduction of him didn't work, he would have that memory of her. Even if he couldn't love her, she didn't want him to think that she couldn't love him.

Her heart was thudding in her throat as she descended the grand staircase for dinner.

'His Grace is still above stairs,' Lancing informed her as she waited nervously by the great fireplace in the drawing room opposite the dining room.

'I will await him in the dining room,' she said.

It was irregular, but surely she could do as she wished

in what was—for now—her home, and standing there alone was not enjoyable.

Shortly after she sat down, Lancing brought her a note, her name written on the envelope in Alex's distinctive hand.

Emma stared at it for a moment, before opening it slowly, quite sure that she wasn't going to want to read the contents.

Alex had written that he expected she would be eating in her own sitting room again this evening, but just in case, he wanted to let her know that he had supped early, in his study, and was now setting off to visit Gideon for a quiet evening of cards.

'Thank you, Lancing,' Emma managed to say around the enormous lump that had appeared in her throat.

And then, for Alex's sake more than her own, to avoid more gossip amongst the servants than there had to be, she sat in solitary state and ate her dinner. Which she supposed, thinking about it—and there wasn't a lot else to do than think while she ploughed miserably through several dishes—was exactly fitting for her last full evening under the same roof as Alex.

Chapter Seventeen

The next morning, back from a furiously fast crack-of-dawn gallop across his land, which had afforded him only short-lived respite from thinking about Emma, Alex shoved open a side door to the castle and crashed straight into Emma and Harry.

His superior size and speed knocked them both off balance, and he shot his arms out to hold on to them both, so that for a moment the three of them were effectively locked in a three-way hug, tangled up with his riding crop.

'Papa, you were *running*,' Harry said, throwing his arms round Alex's legs to join in with the hug.

'I imagine that he was in a hurry.' Emma was very much *not* joining in with the hug. Her arms and hands were very firmly clamped to her sides and from where he still had an arm around her shoulders, Alex could feel that her entire upper body had tensed.

'Yes, I was. Very silly of me. I apologise.' Alex let go of Emma fast and swooped Harry up into his arms. 'Where are you off to?'

'Emma has been telling us about Maggan and sailing. We're going to the lake to imagine it's the ocean and think about sailing round it.'

'Maggan?' Alex queried.

'Magellan. I'm killing two birds with one stone—history and geography—and talking about his circumnavigation of the globe.'

'The first ever circumnavigation?' Alex thought he remembered learning about Magellan.

'Yes, we believe so, although of course we don't *know* that the Vikings did not sail all the way around the world.'

'I want to be a Viking,' Harry shouted.

Emma laughed, not catching Alex's eye, and said, 'We should go and find your brothers.' As Alex put Harry down, she glanced at him. 'Their nurse is with the boys. I did not send them to the lake alone.'

Alex shook his head. 'I had not even questioned it in my mind. I have full confidence in your care of them.'

Emma's eyes met his for a long moment and then she said, 'Thank you.'

Alex couldn't take his eyes from hers. One would never tire of looking into their rich brown depths. 'No. Thank *you*. The peace of mind is wonderful.'

It was the only thing that made up for the torture of her still being here in the castle. To be fair, it was a big thing. And the fact that she was so good with the boys did make it very difficult to countenance the idea of her entire removal from their lives. They would still be able to see her every day if she were living in the dower house, but he would not be so conscious of her presence.

'We must go and join the others,' Emma said again, pulling her eyes from his.

'Yes. Of course.' Alex put his son down and Harry immediately put his hand into Emma's.

Alex couldn't help remaining in the doorway for a few moments to watch the two of them as they walked across the lawn. He was indeed lucky that Emma was educating his boys, and with such enthusiasm. He wouldn't mind listening to her lesson on Magellan himself.

After a good hour of dull correspondence at his desk in the library, during which Emma intruded into his thoughts more than he would have liked, he stood up and walked over to where his father—a keen historian— had kept his world history books. Sure enough, after a few minutes of searching, he found an entire book that seemed to be devoted to the life and travels of Magellan.

The book was written in Spanish. Or maybe Portuguese; Alex was not particularly familiar with any of the Iberian languages. It might still be of interest to Emma and the boys, though. It included a number of interesting maps and, knowing Emma, she might well turn out to be proficient in whichever language this was.

It wouldn't be hugely respectful to the memory of his father, or indeed to anyone who might aspire to own such a fine volume, to take it outside on what was now a drizzly morning and possibly ruin it, so he would wait until Emma and the boys came inside before either taking it up to the nursery to show it to them or inviting them into the library to look at it.

Just before luncheon, his correspondence completed for the time being—praise be—he decided to go up to the nursery to show the boys the book.

When he got there the door was slightly ajar and Emma was sitting in an armchair, in full flow, still on the subject of Magellan. The boys were rapt in front of her. Even Freddie's habitual air of nine-year-old cynicism had disappeared.

'Yes, we do remember him today as a very brave man and a hero,' she said, apparently in response to a question from one of the boys. 'While he did die during the voyage—which was very sad—he died doing something he loved, and I'm sure that he would never have regretted his choice to make the journey. It's important to stay as safe as one can, of course, but if one doesn't take any risks at all, one risks never being truly happy.'

Alex stilled. She might have been talking about him. Perhaps she *was* talking about him. No, of course she wasn't; he was being vain. Perhaps she was talking about herself. Or perhaps, and more likely, she was answering a final question about Magellan and attempting to instil some wisdom into the boys.

Her words had resonated strongly with him, though, as she spoke. Would he be better off taking the risk of allowing himself to love again, or just not loving again? With greater risk came the possibility of greater reward, as well as greater misery. How brave was he? Brave enough to allow himself to love Emma and live a rich life full of joy—for now, anyway—or not? Was it better to live a duller, less happy life, but one which would not then be marred by loss?

He was beginning to think that Emma was right, that one should be brave.

He stepped into the room and cleared his throat. 'I found a book in the library that might be of interest to all of you,' he told them, holding it out.

'This is beautiful,' breathed Emma.

'Do you know what language it's written in?' Alex asked.

'Catalan,' she said, not looking up from the book. 'It's surprisingly easy to read if you speak French, much easier than Castilian Spanish, in fact.'

Alex nodded, pleased that he'd been right. Of course she knew.

He continued to be preoccupied with his thoughts as he ate a solitary luncheon. When he had finished, he stood up, knowing what he wanted to do this afternoon.

He sent word to the stables to ask for Star to be saddled for him, and then made his way there. He felt as though he was in too much of a rush to walk.

Twenty minutes later, he dismounted outside Caleb Wilson's cottage.

Caleb was limping around the corner of the building with the aid of a stick. 'Good afternoon, Your Grace. Good of you to come to visit.'

'My pleasure, and I'm delighted to see you on your feet again.'

'It certainly makes life more interesting.' Caleb nodded his head in the direction of his chicken house. 'I'm about to collect some eggs. Just trying to work out how to do it with my stick.'

'Perhaps you'd like some help?' Alex looped Star's reins around a tree.

'I would that.'

'You know,' said Alex a few minutes later, 'I haven't collected eggs since I was very young. There's something very enjoyable about it. I think my boys would very much like to visit you and meet your chickens.'

'They came yesterday, Your Grace. Did Her Grace

not tell you? We had a marvellous time. We agreed to the visit in advance, just to make sure that I wouldn't be out gallivanting when they arrived.'

Caleb roared with laughter at his own joke and Alex smiled, enjoying Caleb's humour and completely unsurprised that Emma had been to visit without trumpeting it, and that she'd brought the boys too.

Eggs—including some beautiful pale blue ones—collected, Alex accompanied Caleb inside his cottage, warm from the now very well-made fire in the corner.

'I have a question for you, Caleb,' he said, accepting a glass of ale. 'I want advice, I suppose.'

'Go on, Your Grace.'

'I wanted to ask…' He stopped and shook his head. 'No, I realise now that it's a stupid question, and one to which I already know the answer.'

Caleb looked at him steadily, but didn't speak.

'I was going to ask whether you had any regrets about marrying Jeanie because you've been so sad since you lost her. But of course you don't.'

'No, I don't. Do you regret loving and marrying Diana, Your Grace?'

'No. I don't.'

'But you're scared of loving again and losing again.' Caleb's words were a statement, not a question.

Alex nodded. 'I think I'm beginning to be less scared, though. Who knows what the future holds?'

'I count myself fortunate, young man, that I've had the happiness I have. I wouldn't have had that happiness without Jeanie, so I could never regret anything. I do miss her, as you know, and I always will, but she lives on in my memories of all our wonderful years together and in the lives of her children and grandchildren.'

'You're very wise, Caleb.'

'Of course I am, Your Grace. I learnt most of what I know about life from Jeanie, and she was a very wise woman. Your new duchess is another wise woman.'

Alex nodded again. 'She is indeed.'

'Seems to me that you might have something to tell her?'

'Yes, I think I do.' He was going to need to be careful with his words, though, not rush straight into conversation and say something stupid. He would spend the evening planning what to say and then he'd ask Emma tomorrow if they could talk.

He'd allowed her to believe that he was unable to love her because he was still grieving for Diana. He needed to explain how wrong he'd been and hope that she felt the same way about him as he felt about her, and that she would believe that he wouldn't be so stupid again.

Alex slept better than he had for a long time that night and woke later than usual. He partook of a leisurely breakfast before going in search of Emma and the boys, none of whom he had seen yet today.

He found the boys in the nursery with their nurse, but there was no sign of Emma.

'I wonder if you know where Emma is?' he said.

'She's going on a journey,' Harry told him very seriously.

'A journey?' Alex replied, not really paying a lot of attention.

He'd spend a few minutes with the boys now, and then ask Lancing if he knew where Emma was. He realised that he didn't know her daily routine; he'd been too busy recently trying to distance himself from her.

'She's gone to see the factories,' John said.

'In Lancashire,' Freddie clarified. 'She said we can visit her there one day when we're old enough, but she needs to discuss it with you first.'

'I'm afraid I don't understand,' Alex said, frowning.

'Emma has gone on a journey to visit the factories in Lancashire,' Freddie repeated slowly, as though to a person with limited comprehension. 'She's gone for a very long time, but we will see her again, because we can visit her there and she can come and visit us here too.'

Damn. *Damn.*

Alex stood up. 'I have to go.'

He went straight to the library for some solitude in which to think. Why had she not told him she was going? She'd told the boys. She'd said they could visit her. But she couldn't have left for good? No, surely not. They must have misunderstood what she'd said. They'd definitely misunderstood; they were only young. She wouldn't have just gone. He was quite certain of that.

A trickle of fear was making its way down his spine, though.

He found himself pacing back and forth beneath the long shelves, his mind going in circles. The library was on two floors, the upper floor accessed by narrow wooden staircases at each end of the room. He walked up one flight of stairs and along the gallery, not pausing to look at any of the books, and then down the flight at the other end.

This was silly, he realised on his second turn past the long windows in the middle of the room. He should ask Lancing now what he knew of Emma's plans. He would word his question so that he didn't sound as though he had absolutely no idea whether or not his own wife had left for Lancashire.

He turned towards his desk to ring for Lancing and saw an envelope propped up against the inkwell, with the word 'Alex' written on it. He recognised the script as Emma's, from letters she had left out to be franked.

The trickle of fear that he'd been feeling turned into a veritable deluge of panic as he pulled a single sheet of paper out of the envelope.

Dear Alex,

I had planned to tell you this in person, but in the end did not find an opportunity to do so.

I wanted to let you know that I have decided to travel back to Lancashire and make my home there.

I have made arrangements with Nurse to continue the boys' studies according to the notes that I have left, and hope that you will soon find a replacement governess.

I have come to love the boys very much and did not wish to leave them. I hope that they will not miss me—but am not sure that growing up with the example of our distant marriage will be good for them.

I—like you, I imagine—would hope that they will grow up to marry for companionship and intimacy, or not at all, should that be their choice.

I have told them that I am leaving, and that I hope you will allow them to visit me in Lancashire, where the landscapes are quite different from those in Somerset but equally beautiful.

I have left the kittens in the stables so that the

*boys are able to continue to play with them. They
have grown quite attached to them, and I did not
want to add to any loss they might feel on my departure.*

　*I must thank you again for your great kind-
ness in marrying me and saving me from what
would, as you rightly said, have certainly been
an unpalatable alternative. I will remain forever
in your debt.*
Yours,
Emma

Momentarily stunned, Alex re-read the letter.

She'd left. Left *him*.

Or had she in fact been driven away by his effective
rejection of her after they'd made love? Would he ever
know now?

What if something bad happened to her on the journey? What if she was set upon by highwaymen? A
duchess travelling with only a small entourage must inevitably attract a great deal of attention. She would no
doubt have her pistol, which he was sure wouldn't help
her in the slightest in such an eventuality.

What if the carriage developed a fault, or one of the
horses were injured, or startled, or any one of a number
of things, and Emma were injured herself?

What if something truly terrible happened to her and
she never knew that he loved her?

He put the letter back in the envelope and then took
it out again.

What if, in fact, she didn't love him?

He read the letter for a third time. What would she
have written if she *did* love him? If she *didn't*? And what

if there was nothing that he would be able to say to convince her to return?

He needed to stop imagining catastrophes and he needed to know.

He stood up, almost knocking his heavy oak chair over in his haste. He was at the library door in a few strides and at the stables only a couple of minutes after that, instructing Jim to prepare Star.

He needed to leave immediately.

The hard ride helped calm the very worst of his fears. By the time he was passing by Bristol he was able to believe it was highly unlikely that any accident would befall Emma. It was also unlikely that he would fail to catch her up or indeed ride straight past her while she stopped for a rest, because, even journeying with just one carriage, a travelling duchess would always occasion comment.

Alex stopped regularly to ask if she had been seen, and ascertained that she was heading directly north. She'd set off very early this morning, and had two or three hours' advantage over him, but the chaise had been built for Alex's mother in her later years and had been designed for luxurious comfort rather than speed.

Perhaps Alex would ask Emma if she would like a new travelling carriage, one designed to her own specification and needs. One built for more regular travel, if that was what she'd like.

When he thought about it, she'd fitted herself into the extremely small space he'd made for her in his life and tried very hard to make the best of it, while he had made little effort to accommodate her.

He spurred Star to go faster, desperate to catch Emma.

As the morning ended, he began to wonder where she would take her luncheon. There was no sign of her at the first two staging inns at which he enquired, and as he left the second one he wondered whether somehow he'd missed her. It was busy and the people at this inn hadn't been able to say either way whether she'd passed by on the road outside.

And then, at the third inn, he found her. Accompanied by Jenny, she was leaving the inn as he arrived in a flurry of dust in the courtyard.

He dismounted, handed Star's reins to an ostler, and strode forward.

'Emma.'

'Oh!' She hadn't been looking in his direction when he arrived and clearly hadn't realised that it was him.

'Alex. Is something wrong? Has something happened to one of the boys? No, you'd be with them if something had.'

'Nothing has happened.' Other than that he'd come to his senses. Hopefully not too late. 'I came to speak to you.' He looked around. 'I wondered if we could talk somewhere, alone.'

Chapter Eighteen

Emma stared at Alex, standing in front of her, sternly handsome in his riding garb. What was he doing here? Was it a coincidence that he was here? Had he been planning to journey north anyway? Surely not. It seemed a lot more likely that he'd actually ridden all the way here to speak to her. About what, though? Did he think that she ought not to move to Lancashire? Was he worried about the scandal that might ensue?

He was looking at her, bright-eyed, his eyebrows slightly raised, as though he was waiting for the answer to a question.

'Would you be happy for us to talk in private?' he said.

Oh, yes, he *had* been waiting for the answer to a question.

Emma didn't want to speak to him. Even just seeing him here in front of her hurt. But she'd left him with no notice and she owed him a lot.

She drew a deep breath and said, 'Yes.'

'Thank you,' he said, smiling faintly.

He held out his arm to her and after a moment's hesitation she took it, trying not to react to the feel of the corded muscle in his forearm.

'Perhaps inside? In a private room.'

'Of course.'

Her voice sounded a lot steadier than she felt on the inside. She had no idea how she was going to respond to whatever he had to say. If he wanted her to return and live in the dower house, she didn't know whether she could bear to go. He must have something of note to say, though; it was hard to believe that he would have ridden *ventre à terre* such a long way just to say good-bye in person.

The landlord, who'd been very kind to Emma and Jenny, was now bowing deeply in front of the two of them.

'We'd like to be shown to a private parlour, please,' Alex said.

'Of course, Your Grace. Allow me just a few moments to make one ready.'

Shortly afterwards, there was a small commotion. It seemed that several young men dressed in aspiring Corinthian style had been asked to leave the room they were in.

'Alex, we can't—' Emma began.

'We can,' he said. 'Good afternoon, Giles.' He nodded at one of the men. 'Younger brother of a friend of mine,' he told Emma. 'They're young and fit and can very happily go somewhere else. It cannot be possible that what they have to say is as important as what I have to say.'

'Oh.' Emma was beginning to feel so overcome that it was a good job that she had Alex's strong arm for support.

'The room is ready, Your Grace,' the landlord announced a very short time later, having had what must have been almost every member of staff in the entire inn flying around with cloths and brooms, while Alex and Emma stood in uncomfortable silence in the inn's entrance hall.

'Thank you.' Alex pressed several coins into his hand and held the door wide for Emma to enter the room.

She walked in ahead of him and over to the window, which looked out onto an inner courtyard, which was populated by chickens and goats. She clutched the windowsill for support for a moment, feeling momentarily lightheaded.

She heard the door click closed and felt goosebumps from head to toe. This was it. The moment. Alex was about to say whatever it was he wanted to say to her. This could be the last conversation they ever had.

Would she have the strength to tell him now in person that she loved him? Just so that he knew? She'd wanted to tell him before she left, but hadn't found the words to include the sentiment in her letter.

He joined her at the window, standing at her side, perhaps two feet away from her, and then...said nothing.

Emma waited.

Alex cleared his throat twice, but still...nothing.

'This is a very pretty view, isn't it?' Emma said eventually, unable to take any more of the silence, but not wanting to say anything that would precipitate the conversation she knew she didn't want to have. She pointed out of the window. 'I particularly like those black chickens.'

'Delightful,' Alex said. 'Emma...'

She sensed him turn to face her.

'Emma,' he repeated.

'Yes?' She turned her head in his direction, but couldn't bear to look at him properly.

'Emma.'

She looked at his face and her breath caught in her throat. He was gazing at her with a very tender look in his eyes and smiling a crooked little half-smile that caused her...

That caused her to *hope*.

And that hope made her stomach clench uncomfortably and her heart beat faster.

'Thank you for agreeing to speak to me,' he said. 'I followed you here because I want to tell you something.'

'Yes?' Emma found herself clutching the window-sill again.

'What I want to say is...'

What was *wrong* with him? Whatever it was, she just wanted him to get on with it now.

'Yes?'

'Um.' And he stopped again.

For goodness' sake.

Emma was on the brink of screaming, *Tell me*, when Alex very suddenly went down on one knee in front of her. She gasped and put her hands to her mouth.

Alex reached up and took her hands while Emma tried to squash the enormous hope now blossoming inside her, just in case, somehow, she was misreading the signs.

Alex cleared his throat. 'This is the way it should have been,' he said, holding her hands tightly. 'What you deserve, and what I would have done if I had already known you and learned not to be scared.'

'Scared?' Emma was so stunned by seeing Alex on his knee before her that she felt as though she'd entirely lost her wits.

'When I met you, I was scared of grieving again the way I grieved after Diana died. I didn't know whether or not I could ever fall in love again, but I did know that I was determined not to, because I didn't want to lay myself open to the pain of loss again, and love does often give rise to grief.'

Emma nodded, unable to speak but still hoping.

'Since we stumbled into each other's lives I've learned two big things.' He drew her towards him. 'Firstly, I learnt that I was able to fall in love again, because I fell in love with you. I know that I allowed you to believe that I was still in love with Diana, and I suppose I am, or at least with her memory, but I'm also deeply in love with you. I was scared to allow myself to become close to you. But I'd already fallen in love with you, and I realised that without you in my life I wouldn't be happy. I overheard you talking to the boys about Magellan and bravery. *I* need to be brave. I want a full, happy life, with you, not an emotionally safe but empty one without you.'

Emma was beginning to smile.

'What I'm trying to say, in a very verbose way, is that I love you. I love you so much, Emma. I love your smile. I love your passion for knowledge. I love the way you tilt your head to one side when you're considering how to reply to me when I've annoyed you. I love your kindness. And in addition to that, I would like to be married to you, properly. If we weren't already married, I would be proposing to you now.'

'Oh,' said Emma.

She could hardly breathe and she could barely process Alex's words. This was everything she could have hoped for and indeed so much more. She sniffed, but a tear still plopped out and landed on their hands. She sniffed again and more tears fell.

Alex folded his lips together and swallowed, and then said, 'Emma?'

'Tears of happiness,' she said.

'Are you sure?'

'Yes.' She sniffed again, in probably a very unalluring way, but Alex just smiled lovingly at her.

Goodness. She hadn't actually replied to him. 'I love you too,' she said, rushing the words out.

'Oh, thank God.' Alex was beginning to beam. 'I was starting to worry that you were crying tears of pity and that you just wanted to get away from me.'

'I *did* want to get away from you, but only because I found it too difficult being near you and yet so far from you.'

'I'm sorry. That was my fault. I was stupid.'

Emma shook her head. 'You weren't stupid. You're a widower. That's difficult.'

'I *was* stupid. But fortunately I came to my senses. I had actually worked out yesterday—before you left— that I wanted to tell you I love you and ask you to live properly with me as my wife. But in a further act of stupidity, to compound all the rest of it, I decided to wait until today to tell you. And then I discovered that you'd gone.' Alex stood up and shook his legs. 'Deeply unromantic, I know, but that floor is both hard and uneven.'

Emma laughed and sniffed again, and then Alex drew her into his arms. He held her against his beautifully solid chest for a long time, with his cheek resting against the top of her head. And then he moved a little, tipped her chin up with his finger and leaned his head down to hers.

Their kiss was different this time. There was the knowledge that it would be good, the knowledge that they both wanted it and that they loved each other. And there was also the knowledge that they could take things to their natural conclusion, and that that would be good too—truly wonderful, in fact.

It was gentle at first, their lips just brushing. Emma almost sighed into the kiss. She wrapped her arms round Alex's neck and he held her very tightly. And then their kiss deepened, their tongues exploring, their hands moving too. There was physical urgency, but it was also as though they both knew that they had time now, and that they should enjoy fully every stage of their lovemaking.

The kiss went on for a long time, the two of them moulded together in front of the window. And then Alex ran a hand up from Emma's waist until it came to rest on the underside of her breast. Even through her dress his touch caused her to shiver, both from what he was doing with his thumb, causing her nipple to tighten, and from the promise of more to come.

And then with both his hands he took her round the waist and lifted her. She found herself with her legs wrapped around his waist, pressed against the wall, with Alex lifting her skirts with one hand to reach between her legs.

'What would you like to do now?' he murmured into her neck.

'I don't have the words,' she gasped as he bit her very gently, while plunging a finger somewhere very moist deep inside her.

'Come home with me.'

'Yes,' she said, beginning to pant.

'But first—' he kissed her mouth again and deepened his touch, and Emma moaned against him '—I think we should take a room here, now, for the night. Just one room.'

'Anything,' Emma managed to say, judders running through her as he touched her deeper and deeper.

'I love you, my duchess.'

'I love you too.'

Epilogue

Venice, February 1821

'This is wonderful,' Emma breathed, peeking out of the window of their *palazzo* bedchamber at the carnival in St Mark's Square beneath them.

'You're wonderful,' Alex said, coming to stand behind her and putting his arms round her waist, and looking over her shoulder.

The square was full of puppet theatres and all sorts of performers, including acrobats, tightrope walkers and clowns.

She turned to face him and slid her arms around his neck. 'Thank you so much for arranging this tour.'

They had held a ceremony to repeat their wedding vows on the first anniversary of their London wedding, and Alex had wished to mark their anniversary every year from then on.

On the third anniversary of their wedding, he'd presented Emma with an intricately embroidered mask like those worn at the many masquerades held at the carnival in Venice, knowing that it was an aspect of the Grand Tour that she'd particularly wanted to see, and wanting to give her a clue to the fact that he was planning that they would go on a Grand Tour of their own. And now this year, on their fourth anniversary, here they were in Venice.

He knew that Emma also harboured a strong desire to travel to India, and he did wish to gratify that desire in due course, but it had seemed wise to venture 'only' to Europe for their first foray into travel abroad with, as it turned out, an extremely large entourage.

They were accompanied by their children—they now had twin daughters as well as the boys—and attendant nurses, footmen, grooms, chefs, and others, as well as the stray dog, the abandoned bear cub and the indigent juggler that they—Emma—had collected along the way. For someone who was normally so pragmatic and unfussy, Emma did not travel particularly lightly.

'There's no need to thank me. Thank *you* for being my wife. I'm enjoying our tour.'

Suddenly looking serious, Emma said, 'I really hope you *are* enjoying it. I mean, you seem to be, but I know that you love our corner of Somerset and would happily stay there for evermore without venturing further afield.'

'No.' Alex shook his head. 'I do, of course, love Somerset, and, yes, I am of course a reluctant traveller in anticipation of any journey.'

Reluctant was an understatement when it came to his crossing the English Channel. The only person on their boat who was a worse traveller than him in a storm at sea had been Emma. While the rest of their party had been perfectly happy on the boat, the two of them had spent the entire crossing green at best and hideously ill at worst, and had been united in an immediate decision to make the rest of their trip over land only.

'But from the moment the ground stopped rocking beneath us after we disembarked the boat—' it had taken until some time after they'd arrived at Emma's mother's very bohemian but quite delightful villa in Paris for them both to lose the sensation that they were on a rocking boat '—I've loved our journey. My first Grand Tour was good; this is wonderful.'

'What's different about it?' asked Emma, twinkling at him and pressing her body to his, then kissing along his jawline while she ran one hand down his back before bringing it to rest on his backside. 'And, yes, I am indeed fishing for compliments.'

Alex smiled at the promise in her actions and reached down and kissed her full on the mouth, and slid one hand into her hair and cupped her breast with the other. 'I think we could spare a few moments before we go to the masquerade.'

He picked her up and crossed the room with her to land her right in the middle of their canopied bed. He lowered himself over her and began to rain kisses on her eyelids, her nose, her mouth, and down her neck, while she smiled and wriggled and pulled his shirt out of his pantaloons, and he applied four years' worth of expertise to undoing her stays as quickly as he could.

And then, as he traced his fingers around the underside of her breasts, smiling at the way she responded and then groaning as she reached for him inside his open breeches, he remembered that he had a serious point to make.

'What's different about this tour?' he said, still caressing her and smiling as he saw her eyes glaze a little. 'The opportunity to make love very regularly to my beautiful wife is, of course, one difference, but the greatest difference is the chance to share all the different spectacles and experiences with you and witness your enjoyment of them. With you as my companion, every journey that I take will always be better.'

Emma focused her eyes on him and smiled her beautiful smile. 'Thank you,' she said. 'And I, in my turn, know that I couldn't ask for a better companion to share this or any tour with. Nor a better husband to share my life with. I love you, Alex.'

'I love you too.'

He kissed her on the lips again. And then she gasped as, very deliberately, he began a slow but very enthusiastic demonstration of his physical love for her.

* * * * *

How the Duke Met His Match
is Sophia Williams's debut.

*Be sure to look out for her next book,
coming soon!*

HARLEQUIN
PLUS

Try the best multimedia subscription service for romance readers like you!

Read, Watch and Play.

Experience the easiest way to get the romance content you crave.

Start your **FREE TRIAL** at
www.harlequinplus.com/freetrial.